WITHDRAWN

WITHDRAWN

PRINCESS

25/84/75

55/1

101 N. Main
501

PRINCESS

by Alan Brown

M
B877
C.1
WITHDRAWN

A Birch Lane Press Book
Published by Carol Publishing Group

92F18C52

1795

923081

A Birch Lane Press Book
Published 1990 by Carol Publishing Group

Editorial Offices
600 Madison Avenue
New York, NY 10022

Sales & Distribution Offices
120 Enterprise Avenue
Secaucus, NJ 10022

In Canada: Musson Book Company
A division of General Publishing Co. Limited
Don Mills, Ontario

Copyright © 1989 by Tim Brown and Alan Rustage

All rights reserved. No part of this book
may be reproduced in any form, except by
a newspaper or magazine reviewer who wishes
to quote brief passages in connection
with a review.

Queries regarding rights and permissions
should be addressed to: Carol Publishing Group,
600 Madison Avenue, New York, NY 10022

Manufactured in the United States of America

Library of Congress Cataloging-in-Publication Data

Brown, Alan.
    Princess / by Alan Brown.
        p.   cm.
    "A Birch Lane Press book."
    ISBN 1-55972-017-4 : $16.95
    I. Title
PR6052.R5865P7   1989   89-29499
823'.914–dc20   CIP

Authors' Note

The authors most certainly had no intention of shocking or upsetting anyone, least of all the British or Spanish royal families, when devising and writing *Princess*. The Basque terrorist separatist organization ETA has been the greatest single threat to Spain's democratic process. It is second only to the IRA in Europe in the campaign of violence it uses to achieve its ends. There was a serious attempt in the '70s against the Spanish monarch which was foiled by Intelligence. In later years, police in both France and Spain have seized documents concerning the King and his movements, some of which give details of the royal family's Zarzuela Palace just north of Madrid. Those of us who have reported on visits by heads of state and government are only too aware of the impressive security arrangements that provide blanket safety precautions.

The list of terrorist actions and acts of violence perpetrated in the world today against both prominent and ordinary people is truly horrific. Who can but shudder at the outrage of Pan Am flight 103 which exploded over Scotland, killing all passengers and crew. Despite greater cooperation among nations and ever increasing security measures, the kidnappings, the murders and the bombings continue.

The greatest fear of security men is an operation directed at their charges. *Princess* is intended to spotlight that threat, a threat which is always there—whether politically motivated or the product of a single deranged brain. There is a real Decker, although of course that is not his real name. There is a Martinez. There is also a look-alike Princess. Other characters are drawn from a potpourri of our knowledge and experience.

Therefore I should say that any resemblance to real characters, living or dead, is totally intentional.

Tim Brown, a former Fleet Street sports reporter, went to Spain to freelance in the early '60s. He was captured by the ambience of Spain, which was emerging from some three decades of international isolation. Brown is now a correspondent for the *Daily Telegraph* and several other national British newspapers. For many years he has been aware of the ETA terrorist movement and the impressive security that protects the country's leaders and visiting dignitaries.

Alan Rustage has studied at the universities of Wales, Manchester and Oxford. He taught for a number of years, including a period in Iran during the fall of the Shah. His last teaching post was as Deputy Head of the British Council School in Madrid. He now writes full-time and, like Tim Brown, lives in Madrid. He has been married for the last seventeen years to a computer-software specialist.

Alan Brown is a pseudonym for Tom Brown and Alan Rustage.

'If a terrorist bullet has your name on it,
there's not much you can do about it.'

—Prince Charles, the Prince of Wales, as
reported by Europa Press, the Spanish news agency,
Madrid, April 21, 1987

SUNDAY

Chapter One

The man on the BMW 900 cruised down the fast lane of Madrid-Coruña highway. His blue crash helmet was not only protection, it was also an escape from the spotlight. Just the act of putting it on gave him a sense of freedom—and scared the hell out of the men whose job it was to guard him.

These infrequent escapes were precious to him. A short time alone at 100 kilometers an hour brought the pressure down and gave him the sense that he really was a man of the people. And that was part of the image that had made him so popular, as his nation evolved from dictatorship to democracy.

These early evening excursions were not state secrets. Spaniards loved such informality. Everyone had chuckled at the story of him stopping to help a fellow-biker who had run out of petrol. The man had refused to believe his rescuer's identity until King Juan Carlos removed his crash helmet at the gas station.

On his spontaneous jaunts like this, his security men's main worry was not an attack, but an accident. The sportsman King had once fractured his hip when skiing and had gone through a glass partition during a game of squash.

Besides, they could always track him by the transmitter attached to his bike, and an unmarked security car was never far behind. And as he went through the gates after the long drive down through the palace park, it was routine for the duty office to radio a warning to *Guardia Civil* traffic units in the area that a certain motorcycle was on the move again.

That night, they knew the spin would be a short one. He was just paying an informal visit to his royal guests—and distant cousins—the Prince and Princess of Wales.

The biker was duly logged by the parked Civil Guards, as he sped through the underpass to complete the U-turn and head towards the Pardo Palace—a residence reserved for visiting VIPs.

Fat José, the driver, shifted his gut so that it nestled more comfortably against the wheel, and turned to his partner.

"Ten kilometers over the speed limit," he said. "Let's give him a ticket, Paco."

His partner grinned.

"The chief would love that, José. 5000 pesetas speeding fine. Received with thanks—from Don Juan Carlos. Jesus!"

José picked up the mike and radioed the standard code of a Bluehelmet sighting.

The main gates were closed. The King could have had them opened but chose, as most visitors did, to pass through the village and enter the high-walled complex by the side road.

At Manolo's Bar, across the road from the palace, the warm early evening had brought out customers in droves. White-coated waiters rushed between the pavement tables and the bar, carrying trays of drinks and light snacks. But one didn't seem to have his mind on the job. Every few seconds, for the last hour and a half, he had glanced at the palace's side-gate, and now, as he saw the barrier lift, he put down his tray on an empty table and headed back towards the bar.

"Can you cover for me a couple of minutes?" he asked a passing colleague. "I've just got to phone the wife."

The pay-phone was located near the bar, where Manolo, the owner, could keep an eye on it. He scowled as he saw the young waiter insert the coins. He did not approve of employees making calls in working hours. This new boy had better watch himself, or he'd be back on the unemployment line.

The waiter had dialed the seven digit Madrid number. He would deliver his message, work for another half-hour, make an excuse, and leave. By the time the police got round to checking up on him, he should be back in the north.

"Maria?" he said loudly, "I might be working late tonight, darling."

"Check," said the man on the other end, and put the phone down.

The Prince and Princess were strolling through an avenue of magnolia trees. In the background, the sound of gushing fountains blended with evening birdsong from the high chestnut trees. The Princess sighed contentedly. For a brief moment, she thought of the children at home and wished they were there to make the family complete. But even if they had come, she would not have been able to spend much time with them—the State visit was so hectic and this was the only real evening off, away from the public gaze.

"How beautiful this is," the Prince said, "wonderfully peaceful. Lovely to be able to relax at last."

Slipping an arm around her waist, he drew his wife close and brushed her neck with his lips. She nestled her head on his shoulder, but did not speak.

It seemed to her to have been such a long time since they had been so close. She relished the moment. The coming night sky was soft and soothing.

What with the affairs of state, the pressures never seemed to go away. And those awful newspapers! Every day there was something about them, most of it nonsense. Oh, to be a normal couple—but there again, normal couples, she was certain, had their problems too.

The tranquility was disturbed by a deep gurgling sound. They looked up to see the motorcycle cruising down the driveway.

"Here comes the speed ace," the Prince said affectionately.

It was too much to hope that they would be left alone for long!

The Prince had come to know the King well during a series of private visits the latter had made to England in his ten year reign. He admired, and was slightly envious of, the way the King had led his nation almost single-handed through a series of coup plots: there was little scope for the British monarchy to play such a significant role.

It had become a close family friendship too, and the previous summer the Prince and Princess had been guests at the Spanish royals' seaside home.

The King cut the engine and coasted the bike to a stop. He lifted off his crash helmet, ran a hand through his hair, grinned and then held up a second crash helmet for the Princess to see.

"Buenas noches, señores. I've come to collect a pretty Princess and whisk her into the beautiful Spanish countryside," he said in heavily accented English. Then, changing to an English public school accent, added, "You don't mind, do you, old boy?"

It was totally unexpected—but typical of the King. On this visit, there had already been an unscheduled, late-night excursion to a flamenco club, and the tourist walk-about around Toledo. And memories were still vivid of summer nights in Majorca when they had seemed to be part of a holiday island, like ordinary tourists—just having fun.

No, the Prince corrected himself, it was not *totally* unexpected—he had merely forgotten about it. After the last run, up the high island mountains, Juan had promised that when they visited Madrid he would take Diana for a ride over a flatter Spain—the rolling plains of Castilla. And given their busy schedule, that evening was the only one on which the King could fulfill his promise.

The Prince didn't like motorcycles, or the thought of his wife riding on the back of one. And somehow, the mood was not the same as it had been the previous summer. The small holiday island was a very different place from the area around the busy capital city. He could even hear the steady hum of motorway traffic from the Palace gardens.

"I'm not sure that. . ." the Prince began cautiously, but the Princess clapped her hands with excitement and the invitation was accepted.

The crash helmet—the same color as the King's—fitted quite well, causing the Princess to wonder whether the Queen had snuggled up on such excursions.

"Hold on tight." The Princess placed her arms around his waist, he slid the bike into gear.

"We won't be long," he said. "Don't worry, I will return your Princess safely to you."

Charles watched the motorcycle disappear down the drive. He sometimes thought his wife considered him a little stuffy. Well, maybe he was. He had been brought up to be a king one day, and he took his responsibilities very seriously.

From the entrance to the cobbled courtyard, Inspector Woods, the Prince's bodyguard, had been watching discreetly and wondering whether to step forward and advise against the trip. But he liked to interfere as little as possible in the Prince's life—and this seemed safe enough.

As the King drove slowly from the pebbled path to the palace forecourt, a radio message that Bluehelmet was on the move again was already being transmitted.

Iñaki Irribar, one of the high command of ETA,* sat alone in an old stone farmhouse on the French side of the Western Pyrénées. He was always alone when operations were underway—it was safer.

He had opposed the plan at the start. There were too many risks, too many imponderables. A few years earlier, he would

---

*ETA is the Basque Marxist-Leninist seperatist movement, founded in 1959. The initials ETA stand for Basque Homeland and Liberty. Its members are called Eterras.

never have been talked around. But things had changed. The French had at last agreed to extradite members of ETA, and much of the leadership had been dispersed to Central America or Africa. The Spanish authorities had smashed ETA's elite group, Commando Madrid. Funds were low.

And on top of that there was GAL—the shadowy, right-wing Anti-Terrorist Liberation Group—which had assassinated several important Etarra commando leaders inside France. Some people claimed that GAL was financed by powerful Basque businessmen, tired of paying ETA's revolutionary tax. But he knew that however it had started, there was not a direct—but hidden—link with the Spanish anti-terrorist police. It was a dirty war, like the ones being waged against the IRA in Ireland, the Red Brigade in Italy—the one that wiped out the Baader-Meinhof Gang in Germany, the same strategy employed against every minority fighting for justice.

It was desperation rather than hope which had pushed Irribar into sanctioning this mission. Even the codename he had chosen—Operation Serpent—reflected this seriousness. He had taken the name from ETA's symbol, a snake curled around an axe hasp, because the mission was vital to ETA's future.

He looked at his watch. Fifty-five minutes left.

It would be another hour before there was any point in placing a call to Bilbao. Irribar took a sip of wine and tried to calm down.

The commando cell had been in place for over a month. The team was the best available. The plan had been sharpened to a razor edge of timing and coordination. All they needed was ninety seconds, a splinter of time, to get to the target. But they had no control over the bloody traffic!

The two motorcyclists on the gas station forecourt had been pretending to fiddle with the tuning of one of the bikes. Now, as they saw the two blue-helmeted figures shoot past, they mounted their own machines and eased out into the traffic. The green Ford Transit van was moving in the inside lane, but picked up speed as the motorbikes overtook it.

The beaten-up Seat 1500 station wagon was already in a rest area just before the first turn-off, waiting to pull in behind.

Guadaña leaned forward, putting his head between the girl at the wheel and the man in the passenger seat. He had noticed the man run his tongue over his lips.

"No one's nervous, eh?" he asked.

The girl snorted.

"Of course not."

"There's nothing wrong with nerves," Xabier said quietly. "They can help to prevent mistakes."

Guadaña ignored the comment. He had never experienced fear, not even when under sentence of death in Generalisimo Franco's time.

"Just keep in tight behind the van," he said, settling back and putting one hand on the sports holdall which contained his Uzi submachine gun, four magazines of ammunition and and a couple of grenades.

The girl, Idoia, was all right, but he had his doubts about the younger man. Had he been on active service before? Was he hard enough? He didn't know. He had been told nothing about his companions, except for their *noms de guerre*. That was High Command policy. The less you knew, the less you would reveal under interrogation.

He put his hand in the holdall and felt the comforting touch of the weapon. It might not be necessary to kill on this operation . . .

The Guardia Civil traffic car was still parked on the hard shoulder near the gas station.

"You should have given him that ticket after all," Paco said to his partner gloomily, as he put down the radio mike. "I promised Reyes and the kids I'd take them out tonight. Now it looks like there's no chance."

"Damn it! Where's he going now?" José asked, clipping in his seat belt. "And who's he got on the back?"

"Don't know. Looks like a woman to me. I just hope he's

not going to go too bloody far."

José laughed at the double entendre and put the car into gear.

The King was in his element—the open road. He overtook a large rig and pulled back into the slow lane. The diesel fumes left a sour taste in his throat and nostrils.

"We'll be better off in the open countryside," he thought.

He passed the sign to Pozuelo village, flicked on his indicator for a right-hand turn and moved into the turn-off.

The Princess was singing quietly to herself . . .

The whispers in the morning
Of lovers sleeping tight

Somehow that tune invariably came to her mind whenever she was happy, whenever she was at peace. The whole world seemed to be singing *The Power of Love* a few years ago. For her, it was sheer romance and the song had stayed as a firm favorite, the sort that most couples keep at the back of their minds.

Her hands were tight around the King's waist, her knees firm against the seat. She smiled to herself. She hoped that if the King heard the song, he wouldn't think she was flirting. She felt perfectly at ease. She wished her husband would do things like this. Just occasionally.

"It's Route A," Guadaña said. "We hit him in five kilometers."

Idoia moved smoothly into the exit lane. She had no worries about the car. Its ten year old body hid a new and souped up engine.

She looked across at Xabier and smiled.

"Things are going well," she said.

She could have been a very pretty girl, he thought, irrelevantly. Her black hair was thick and silky. The green of her eyes reminded him of the grass on the lush hillsides of home. And her smile was nice too. If only she hadn't had the purplish burn that disfigured part of her face, which even the clever hairstyle could not hide.

"Start practicing your English," Idoia said. "You're soon going to need it."

"I know my part," he said harshly. Then felt guilty. It was Guadaña he was angry with, not the girl. He touched Idoia's shoulder lightly. "We all know our parts. We're going to pull this off."

The villagers had learned to live with the constant flow of traffic, and neither the families relaxing in the gardens nor those taking an early evening walk paid any attention to the passing of the three motorcycles, the green van and Seat 1500 that were spaced within a few hundred meters of each other. Two kilometers behind, the Guardia Civil patrol car also turned off the highway, much to the relief of motorists who had been on their best behavior.

The two unmarked cars from the King's Security were even further behind. Knowing that the King usually did a circle of only a few kilometers, the officers were content to leave it to the patrol car to stick close to him.

The King drove slowly through the center of the village. At the red stop light, he turned to speak to the Princess.

"Having fun, Diana?"

"Oh, yes!"

"Brunete's only a few more kilometers. It's a village I'm very fond of, full of lovely old houses. We'll stop for a drink there, and then head back."

It was the sort of thing that he liked to do—make an unexpected call at a bar, order a coffee and a bun while other customers looked on in amazement.

"That sounds lovely," the Princess said enthusiastically.

The light changed, the King pulled back on the throttle and the motorbike shot forward towards the narrow country lane that led to Brunete.

11

The two machines following closed the gap between themselves and their target.

Chapter Two

The motorcyclists were about to make their move when they saw the oncoming headlights.

"Shit!" one of them murmured to himself, pulling back. It was the second time, and there were only a few kilometers left before the outskirts of Brunete.

The family car, back seat crammed with fidgeting kids, two bikes strapped to the roof-rack, slowed to pass them. The terrorist scanned the distance. No more lights! They had the road to themselves for at least a minute. He raised his gloved right hand in a slow forward gesture, which was visible both to his companion and the van behind. The bikes speeded up.

The Princess leaned slightly back, took her hands from the King's leather-jacketed waist and raised her visor.

"Mmm," she whispered, as the evening breeze flapped the strands of hair which had escaped from the crash helmet. In front of her, tinges of red from the setting sun reflected on the last of the winter snow on the distant mountains. "This is quite heavenly."

The King noticed the relaxed movement of his pillion passenger and half-turned. He saw a bike moving up fast and, checking his mirror, spotted the second. He eased his hand on the accelerator to give them a free run past. One bike drew level, and then dropped its speed to match his. The other tucked in close behind and to the right.

Idiots! he thought.

He signalled for the rider on the outside to overtake. The man maintained his position, but the biker on the inside seemed to be nosing forward. Annoyance gave way to concern. He could normally deal with *chulos* like these, but not with the Princess on the back.

The bike on the inside moved up, almost touching, forcing the King to veer towards the crown of the road. He was sandwiched now between the two machines. Speed was no answer. If he accelerated, there could be a nasty spill. He turned his head slightly.

"Grab my waist and hang on!" he shouted, and as the Princess did so, he slammed on the brakes.

His bike skidded to the right. He shifted his weight and placed one booted foot on the ground. The bikers ahead seemed to have been expecting this. They slowed, turned slightly, and then stopped, their front wheels meeting at an acute angle in the crown of the road, effectively blocking the way.

This was not irresponsible riding, he thought. This was an attack. And even as the idea flashed through his mind, he saw the men reach into their jackets.

He engaged gear, and pulled violently on the handlebars, the heel of his boot digging into the tarmac. And then he saw the green van, slewing across the road behind him—cutting off his escape.

Idoia saw the cluster of lights two hundred meters ahead, pulled into the middle of the road, and stopped. The rearview mirror showed a clear road behind.

"It's working!" she thought.

Guadaña already had his Uzi on his lap. He half-opened the

passenger door and turned to watch through the back window.

The Guardia Civil traffic unit eased over the slight rise. Its headlights picked out the Seat 1500 blocking the road.

José turned to Paco.

"What the fuck's he doing?" he asked.

As the gap between the vehicles closed, José turned on the flashing police warning light, and braked. The Seat didn't move.

"Is it abandoned?" he asked.

"No, I can see someone in the back. Maybe it's broken down."

"Then where's the red warning triangle? Why haven't they pushed the car out of the way? I'm going to sort these guys out."

José wrenched open the door and strode towards the offending vehicle.

"I'll stall him," Xabier said. "Tell him I've broken down."

There was a click of a safety catch being released on the back seat.

"No need," Guadaña said. "I'll take care of this bastard. You get the other one, Idoia—and fast."

He kicked open the door, and was out in the road, weapon in firing position. José didn't even have time to free his .38 before the bullets hit him. Half a magazine, ripping into his neck and chest, hurled him on to his back.

The awesome sound of automatic fire and the sight of José's jerky dance of death momentarily froze Paco in horror. Then, his hand clawed for the radio mike and his thumb pressed down on the button.

The girl appeared from nowhere, half-crouched, her gun thrust forward, pointing at him. It was the last thing he ever saw. The windshield disintegrated. Brain tissue and blood spattered the interior of the car, his lifeless finger fell away from

15

the mike.

The killers moved quickly. Guadaña gestured to Xabier to join him and together they lifted the murdered policeman from the road and bundled him into the back seat of the patrol car.

Idoia climbed into the front and, using her weapon, knocked out the few shards of glass which were all that remained of the windshield.

If she was aware of the policeman in the passenger seat, his head nothing more than a bloody pulp, she did not show it, Xabier thought.

When the windshield was cleared, Idoia started up the engine.

"Get it off the road as quickly as you can," Guadaña shouted over his shoulder.

Terrorists! Total fear gripped the Princess. Her stomach turned to water, her toes seemed to be electrified. Ever since her marriage, when she had exchanged her safe and almost anonymous life for that of a Royal always in the public spotlight, she had known that this was a possibility. But she had never really, deep down, thought it would happen to her. Her arms closed tightly around the King's waist, seeking reassurance.

From the back of the green van, two men emerged. They were armed. The first leveled a pistol at the Princess.

"Off bike!"

"Do as he says," the King said calmly.

The Princess climbed shakily off the machine. She stumbled before finding her balance, then stood trembling. The King dropped the bike to the ground, put an arm around her shoulder and pulled her to him.

"Don't speak, don't move!" the terrorist snarled. "Just listen. We're taking the woman. She will not be harmed as long as you don't do anything stupid."

The King removed his crash helmet—slowly, to show he was trying no tricks.

16

"I am the King. Let her go. Take me instead . . ."

"Shut up! We know who you are. And who *she* is, too. This is an ETA operation. We are only letting you go so that you can persuade your government that our demands must be met."

From behind, gloved hands wrenched the Princess away from him. The King spun round instinctively to protect her, and the second motorcyclist struck him on the back of the head with the butt of his pistol.

The King crumpled and fell to the ground, his crash helmet bouncing in front of him. The Princess screamed.

"Shut up!" the man from the green van said and grabbed her shoulders.

Struggling, the Princess was dragged to the van, followed by the two gunmen. The motorcyclists moved rapidly. They righted the King's BMW, pushed it into the ditch, then mounted their own machines. As they gunned the engines, the green van started to move. The whole operation had taken a little over sixty seconds.

Idoia saw the lights disappearing into the distance.

"They're on the move," she said.

The Seat roared into life as Guadaña slammed the rear door. The car's headlights picked out the figure of the King, on his knees, making a weak attempt to flag them down. Idoia turned the wheel and swerved round him.

"Pathetic," spat Guadaña.

But he relished the image of the King of Spain, wounded and alone, appealing to ETA for help.

The operator in the radio room at the Civil Guard Command Headquarters was trying to raise Unit 54. As each request to come in brought only silence, his concern mounted.

"Don't like it," he said, turning to his colleague.

"Radio on the blink?" suggested the other man.

"Possibly. But I thought I heard shooting. Bluehelmet's in that area." He sat in silence for a moment, ignoring two

17

routine calls, then reached for the phone. "Fuck it! I'm not taking any chances."

He summoned the duty Captain. Seconds later, the operator switched over to the special band connected to palace security.

"Falcon? Possible alert. Code Green. Over."

There were three people with her in the back of the van. Only one had spoken to her.

"Keep quiet—no speak," he ordered, and then he tied her hands behind her back with cord and plastered a large strip of surgical tape across her mouth.

The Princess's shoulders still ached from being wrenched backwards. Her hands and arms were beginning to go numb, so tight were her wrists tied together. She lay on her stomach, her head to one side, a rough blanket covering her. The bounce of the van jarred her body.

She occasionally heard rapid, meaningless exchanges. Apart from that, there was only the noise of the engine and the sound of wheels on tarmac.

The sheer panic that had almost paralyzed her when they pulled her off the motorbike was slowly ebbing away. She clenched her teeth tightly and ordered herself into calmness. They had said that they wouldn't hurt her—but they had hurt Juan. She prayed to God the King would be all right.

Who were these people? What on earth was going on?

Light from an oncoming car flooded the back of the van. It seemed to help, reminding her that the nightmare in which she was trapped was confined to this van, that she was separated from the real world, from ordinary people, only by a few thin centimeters of metal. There had to be a way out! But perhaps that was what the fly said to itself as it looked out on its familiar world and struggled ineffectively against the sticky web which had entangled it.

Her mind wandered. The walk in the gardens had been real enough, she was sure of that, so was Juan's arrival. Had they gone back to the palace after that? Had the motorcycle ride happened? The van bounced again and her bonds cut deep into her wrists. It was no dream.

Her eyes met the gaze of the man sitting on the wheel-rim, a gun cradled in his lap. There was neither hatred nor compassion in the terrorist's eyes.

"He's looking at me as if I was just an object," she thought, and the terror returned, snaking its way from her stomach to her heart. If the gag had not been there, she knew she would have screamed.

There was another gutteral command from the front. The van swung sharply, jolting her onto her right shoulder. Then it started to slow down.

The team in the Falcon mobile unit, a Renault 25, was already moving towards the stationary bleep. Although not thinking that anything was wrong, it was routine to close the gap on these jaunts whenever the king stopped for any length of time.

"Knowing him," said Inspector Montero, a long-time royal bodyguard, "he's probably called for a drink."

The Green Code announcement soon destroyed that theory. One step down from a full Red Alert, it was used sparingly, only when something could no longer be explained away.

"Estimated distance from Bluehelmet—three kilometers," Montero said. "Moving now. Maintaining open radio channel. Over."

He reached out of the window and placed the blue light on the roof. The wail of the siren and the flashing light carved a path through the evening traffic and they were doing well over 120 kilometers an hour as they swung over to the village turn-off.

The wound on the back of the King's head was still throbbing, but the bleeding had stopped and his mind was clear. His only thought was to raise the alarm. There were no houses nearby but he could see the lights of the village in the distance and he started to run towards them. Each step sent shooting pains through his head, but he did not slow down. As he began to sweat, he slipped off his heavy leather jacket and let it fall into the road.

"Keep going," he said to himself as he gasped for air.

A car came up behind him. He turned and flung up his arms. The driver had no intention of stopping for a disheveled man on a lonely country road. He accelerated away.

The King cursed. Then he heard the siren of the approaching Falcon Unit. He stood in the middle of the road and waited. Already he was organizing the details of the snatch in his mind. He didn't have the van's registration number but he could describe it.

Montero's first thought was that there'd been an accident. There was the King, but where was the Princess?

The Inspector had the door open and had leaped from the vehicle even before it stopped moving.

"Ramon," the King gasped, "they've got her! ETA! Green delivery van, a Ford Transit, no side windows, fairly new. At least three terrorists in it. And two motorcyclists on black Kawasaki 750s."

"Are *you* OK, sir?"

"I'm fine. For God's sake, get the alert out. They can't be more than five minutes away—less even."

The King's body was overcharged with emotion. He felt an overwhelming shame that he had allowed the Princess to be kidnapped; anguish that a woman he was fond of was in danger. As Montero reached into the car to pick up the mike, the King grabbed his wrist.

"That van must be intercepted at all cost. But it must be done with care. No chases, no shootouts. Make sure they understand."

But even in his personal suffering, he was still a monarch who had learned to put the reputation of his country above all else.

20

"Wait," he said. "No mention of the Princess, Ramon, not to anyone."

As the message went through, the King leaned heavily on the side of the car. Only now did he feel able to give in a little to his own pain. He took a deep breath.

The driver carefully examined the scalp wound.

"It's not deep, sir," he said.

"It doesn't matter," the King said impatiently.

He placed his hand on the roof of the car, then bent over to talk to Montero. It made his head swim.

"Any developments yet, Ramon?"

"Nothing, sir."

The inspector looked at the King anxiously. He was very pale.

"What do we do now, sir?" he asked.

The King climbed gingerly into the back of the car.

"Now, we sit and wait."

The Green Alert had become a top Red Emergency. Falcon Control, still on the special wavelength, was in contact simultaneously with Civil Guard and National Police headquarters. Units moved in to form a tight cordon. Within minutes, all roads within fifty kilometers of the snatch were sealed.

The Civil Guard barracks at Navas del Rey on the road to the mountains set up its roadblock just outside the village. A Landrover and a patrol car formed a V, leaving only the center of the road free. Four officers checked the light traffic flow.

They could see the headlights cutting through the rapidly falling dusk, and knew, from the angle, that it was probably a van. But it was not until it got quite close that they could tell that it was pale, possibly green. There was still no real cause for alarm. There were hundreds of such vehicles in the areas, and this one could be perfectly innocent. The difference was that this van braked and stopped abruptly before it had even reached the roadblock.

21

"That's got to be the one," the sergeant said quietly.

A waiting car was waved through.

"Get a move on," one guardia told the driver. "There could be trouble." He walked rapidly to another vehicle on the other side of the barrier. "Turn round. Get out of here as quickly as you can."

The van suddenly lurched sideways across the road, its gears grating, half a U-turn completed. The four guardias hiding behind the trees a hundred meters from the roadblock, stepped out and leveled their automatic weapons at it.

"I'll take the tires out," shouted the corporal in charge. "You do nothing. If they shoot, take cover. Do not, repeat, *not*, fire into the van. That's the order. Direct from the colonel."

The van began moving towards them, picking up speed. The corporal opened fire, squeezing off two carefully aimed rounds. The front tires exploded, the van swerved to the side. The engine screamed in protest, then stalled. The front end of the vehicle, its air cushion gone, sank down a little.

The van was close enough for them to see the driver as a black shape. The guardias watched as he slowly wound down his window, then changed his mind and opened the door. He stepped out, his hands raised above his head and stood still. The officers on both sides trained their weapons on his trunk. They did not move. There might be other terrorists in the van. And no one spoke.

It was the terrorist who broke the tense silence.

"This is ETA!" His voice carried clearly across the fifty meter gap. "Stay where you are. One suspicious move and the woman dies."

"Woman? What woman?" the sergeant asked the man next to him. "Get on the radio and tell them we've got the bastards trapped."

Chapter Three

The powerful spotlight picked out the scene below as the helicopter began to circle and descend. The road was a long black snake, cutting its way through the seemingly endless fields of ripening corn. Yet in contrast to this vastness, the drama itself was being played out in one tiny area.

Colonel Valdés of the Guardia Civil, ex-Franco loyalist, now confirmed monarchist—but above all, a policeman—took in the whole scene. There was the van in the middle of the road. Fifty meters away from it were the police vehicles, their headlights pointing directly at the Etarras. The other three sides of the vehicle were surrounded by men, some up to their waists in corn. The terrorists were completely encircled.

"Land in that field," Valdés ordered. "Put it down next to the other helicopter."

On the ground, awaiting his arrival, was a team of men in paramilitary combat dress, their faces blackened. Heckler and Koch MP5 submachine guns were slung over their shoulders. GEO—the Special Operations Group. It was the toughest section of the anti-terrorist organization, at the peak of fitness and rigorously trained in techniques developed by the British SAS.

The team was ready to move in. But Valdés could give no instructions yet. The order, from the very top, was to await developments. The colonel wondered why. At first glance, it looked like a simple operation.

He needed to familiarize himself with the situation before the arrival of the man who had issued the order—the Minister of the Interior, Miguel Santana.

"Get me the sergeant in charge of the roadblock," he ordered.

The two cars pulled off the road and into the corn field almost simultaneously. Out of one stepped the Minister, but Valdés gasped when he saw who emerged from the other. What the fuck was the King doing here?

He walked towards the two men, who were now in conference. Santana looked up when he heard his approach.

"I believe you already know Colonel Valdés," Your Majesty.

As Valdés came to attention and saluted, he noticed that the King seemed to be a little unsteady on his feet, and was holding his head at an unnatural angle.

Was the King injured? And if he was, why wasn't he getting treated, instead of standing in this field in the middle of nowhere? Whatever was happening, it had to be something big.

"Brief us on what has happened so far," the King said. "Has any contact been made?"

"Only when the van was intercepted, Your Majesty. Then the terrorists said something about killing a woman if we tried to storm the van." He turned to the Minister. "*Is* there a woman in the van, sir?"

It was the King who answered.

"This is in the strictest confidence, Colonel Valdés. There is indeed a woman in the van—the Princess of Wales."

"How the hell did that happen?" Valdés demanded. Then he remembered who he was speaking to and added, "Excuse me, Sir."

The king did not respond but merely looked at the ground.

"It doesn't matter how it happened," Santana said, breaking the awkward silence. "What do we do next, colonel? Attack the vehicle?"

"Only a last resort, sir. First, I would like your permission to talk to the terrorists."

"Agreed. But before that happens, all non-essential personnel must leave the area. What is going on here must be kept as secret as possible."

The sergeant from Navas del Rey was leaning against his Landrover, but snapped to attention when he saw Valdés approaching.

"You and your men have done a magnificent job," the colonel said. "Return to barracks, but remain on full alert. Instruct your men not to talk to anyone about the woman in the van. Not to their colleagues, their wives, girlfriends, not to anyone. As far as they are concerned, it's simple ETA terrorists—nothing more."

"At your orders, my colonel," the sergeant said in the best Civil Guard tradition.

He saluted and turned to go, the slight droop of his shoulders hinting at disappointment at being relieved. He became ramrod stiff again when he heard the colonel add, "What you did tonight, sergeant, will not be forgotten."

Such praise could only mean that promotion was on the way. The sergeant would make damn sure that his men remained silent.

Valdés had seen American movies in which policemen dropped their weapons before negotiating with terrorists. That was not the Spanish way. He would not unstrap his gun to appease an *Etarra*. But some compromise was in order, and as he walked slowly down the road he held a megaphone in one hand and kept the other firmly in his pocket.

He could see one man, sitting in the driver's seat. There must be others crouched in the back of the van—no chance of snipers with night-sights taking them out.

He stopped a short distance from the vehicle, raised the

bullhorn to his lips and said, "It's time to talk."

The driver's door opened, and the terrorist who had issued the initial threat swung his legs clear of the seat and on to the road. He was stocky, in his late twenties, and his black hair was cut short.

"You can put that thing away," he said pointing to the megaphone. "If you're here to talk, let's do it!"

The colonel stepped up to the van. The eyes of the terrorist and the officer met and locked together. Valdés was disturbed by what he sensed. This man was too much at ease.

"You can forget the preliminary crap about giving up and nobody getting hurt. This is our demand. We want a helicopter with one pilot, tanked up with fuel, with room for four. We're taking the woman with us. Only when we're safe, will we let her go. If you accept the terms, no harm will come to her. If not, she dies."

The terrorist had made his first mistake, Valdés thought. He had revealed how many there were in the team. Not only was he overconfident, but he was careless and inexperienced. Why had ETA put him in charge of such an important operation?

"You could all be killed, you know," he said. "We could finish you in a second."

"You know ETA. We are willing to die if necessary. Our lives are unimportant. It is the cause that matters. So you needn't bother with the threats. We've got the woman and we have you bastards by the balls."

He was right.

Valdés tried another tack.

"What guarantee do we have that the lady will be released?"

"You don't. Just our word," the terrorist said laconically, "but you have no other option."

"How do I know she's all right now?"

The ETA man moved his feet slowly to the ground. He turned and opened the door fully, beckoning the colonel. Valdés could smell the sweat as he glanced under the raised arm and into the vehicle. In the shadow at the back of the van

26

he saw the blonde-haired woman lying under a blanket. Another terrorist sat beside her, a gun pointing at her head. A torch was flashed briefly on her face. The colonel saw that she was gagged and her eyes were wide with fear.

Half closing the door, the terrorist said, "She's fine . . . for the moment. Now get back there and start organizing the helicopter."

Valdés tried again.

"You've made your point. You'll get all the publicity you want, and it will be far more favorable if you let her go now. I can arrange for you to be given the helicopter, but only after the hostage is freed. You can take me as insurance."

"I've told you what I want. Now go back and fucking do it!"

The terrorist got back into the van and slammed the door. The negotiations were over. For the moment.

Santana was amazed that the King, who had shown such political acumen in leading his country successfully out of dictatorship and into Europe, could have made such a suggestion.

"I believe, with the greatest respect, Sir, that such an exchange is entirely out of the question," Santana said firmly. "I understand your feelings but you are the Head of State.

"Look sir, you *are* the new Spain, at least as far as much of the world is concerned. Nothing can be allowed to prejudice your safety. I cannot allow you to offer yourself in the place of the Princess. You know that the Prime Minister's answer would be exactly the same."

The King knew the Minister was right. He was a constitutional monarch. He had deliberately stripped himself of the absolute power he had been bequeathed, and given it back to the people. However much personal guilt he might wish to assuage by changing places with the Princess, Spain must come first. But he was bitterly disappointed.

"What a bloody mess, Miguel," he said to the Minister.

He looked hopefully at Valdés, who was just returning from the van. The colonel explained the terrorist's demands quietly

27

and precisely.

"In all situations like this, sir," he explained, "the important thing is to keep the terrorists talking. The more time that passes, the more vulnerable they become. They feel isolated, they come to need contact with us. In an hour, they will ask for the helicopter again, and I will stall them. Gradually, talking to me will become as important to them as any of their demands."

The black car cut deep swathes through the corn field as it bounced over the uneven ground. The back-up car followed its tracks. The two stopped beside the waiting King. The Prince got out of one door, his Scotland Yard bodyguard out of the other. The Prince was pale; concern was etched deep into his face. The King clasped his arms around the Prince's shoulders, and embraced him. The retinue of security withdrew to a tactful distance.

"Where is she?"

The King turned and indicated the van now fiercely illuminated by two mobile spotlights.

"In there," he said.

The Prince turned to walk to the terrorist vehicle. The King put a restraining hand on his shoulder.

"I know how you feel. But they wouldn't let me do that, and they won't let you either. And they're right. I'm so deeply sorry. Somehow we'll get her out. It's my fault she's in there. It was a bloody stupid thing to do."

"I'm not blaming you. She wanted to go with you, and let's face it, I consented. What are they doing to get her out? What's happening?"

As the King explained in full, the Prince kept his eyes unwaveringly on the vehicle. He had seen his wife change from a fun-loving, almost irresponsible girl into a mature woman and wife. He had never really understood until now quite how much he had come to rely on her, how he needed her, and above all how much he loved her. They *must* get her

28

back! The thought of life without her was unbearable.

"Colonel Valdés saw her a few minutes ago. He's with the Minister now. Let's go and talk to them," the King said.

The Prince nodded anxiously as he zipped up his windbreaker. He was shivering, but he didn't put it down to the chill of the early summer night.

Only a few hours earlier, they had been so close. . . just for a few moments in the gardens of the palace. If only he could turn the clock back.

He felt it was his fault that the occasions when they laughed, relaxed and forgot the outside world had become far too rare. That was probably the reason why she had seized the chance to jump on the back of a motorcycle and go for a spin. The chance to do something normal.

Had he taken that spark out of their relationship, the fun that they had both shared? Why hadn't he suggested more often that they go out to a discothéque where they could listen to the music that she so enjoyed, and sit, unrecognized, close together in a quiet corner? They had done that in the past. Now he made excuses; they would be spotted, there would be no peace. She had, he was sure, come to think that she was trapped, a victim of royal routine—of royal protocol. He had become too selfish, failing to take into account that his lovely wife was above all a young woman for whom romance was an important element of living.

He looked up again at the terrorist van.

"Dear God," he prayed, "let her walk out of there alive."

"I want to pilot the helicopter myself," the Prince told Santana.

There was silence, then the Minister said, "Sir, I am afraid there can be no helicopter. I have already explained to His Majesty the King that there can be no deals with terrorists. You know that is the policy of your own government as well."

"For God's sake, man," the Prince exploded, "that's my *wife* they've got in there!"

"I know that, sir, and if it were my wife I would feel exactly the same. But I hope I would behave as I am doing now. We'll do all we can to get her out, but not by giving in. Those men have already killed two of my officers tonight."

There was always a conflict between private life and public role. The Prince had accepted his responsibility to put matters of state before personal considerations. It was a choice he had made gladly. And in marrying, he now realized, he had laid the same burden on his wife.

"You're right, Minister, I'm sorry," he said. "I'll try not to get in the way."

With that the King and the Prince returned to the Falcon Control Center.

"I've got to tell the Queen what's happening and the Prime Minister must be informed. Can we get a secure direct line to Buckingham Palace from here?"

"Your Ambassador is on his way," the King replied. "He doesn't know yet. I think we should seek his advice first."

"But when the Ambassador *does* find out," Colonel Valdés thought as he caught the last remark, "the shit will really hit the fan."

The wind had dropped and the young moon cast a little light on the seemingly endless Castillian Plain. The scene was static, almost like a picture. Only the drone of an incoming jet bound for Barajas Airport disturbed the silence. Everyone was watching the van—and waiting.

"Something stinks about all this," Valdés said to the Minister. "They're far too cool. Their only chance of getting clear away by helicopter is in the dark, yet they seem in no hurry. It's been over an hour since I talked to them. They should be screaming for an answer by now."

"Is there any chance of storming the van without the victim getting hurt?"

The Colonel studied the target again, the ditch and the

30

hedgerows on either side, and the concealed marksmen.

"The GEO could be on top of them in seconds. A stun grenade through the rear window, another through the front. They might damage her eardrums but my men should be inside before the terrorists could react. I would put the chances of getting her out in one piece as high as 90 percent. But, Minister, would *you* regard such odds as acceptable?"

Santana turned and looked at the King and Prince standing quietly together by the Falcon Control Center. Which would be worse for Spain? he wondered. To have the victim murdered by a terrorist during and assault on the van or to have them kill her out of frustration when their demands were not met?

"There's a very good chance that if we do nothing, ETA won't kill her," he said.

They had often released hostages before. But Santana also remembered the trussed-up nuclear power engineer, dumped under a tree, his blood seeping into the ground—executed after the government had refused to dismantle an atomic plant. And ETA hadn't even been under pressure then—not like they were now.

The car bombs in Madrid the previous year had killed seventeen police officers. One bomb had even been planted outside a maternity home and had blown a large hole in the wall. No one was safe. There was that American executive out on an early morning jog—he died, caught in a blast which had ripped through a police bus. ETA was like a cornered, wounded animal, its claws out, willing to strike at anything and everything.

Yes, they might very well kill her.

"They know if they shoot her, they'll never get out alive themselves," Valdés said. "And the one I talked to didn't act like a man about to die."

They weren't suicidal, and yet they must know they had no chance of escape. What on earth were they playing at?

More time passed. Valdés could feel the tension crackling in

31

the air around him. But he got no such vibrations from the van. Maybe he had been wrong about the Etarra. Perhaps his casualness came from an acceptance of imminent death, the total liberation of having nothing more to lose. Could it be that they were just waiting for the press to pick up the story before they executed the Princess?

He dared wait no longer. He would ask the Minister's permission to contact them again. And if they failed to respond, he would have to order the GEO into action—whatever the risk to the hostage.

He was just about to address his chief when the door of the van swung open and the terrorist leader got slowly out, one hand held in front of his face to protect his eyes from the glare of the searchlights. At first he stood and appeared to stretch. To Valdés, the terrorist seemed like a man getting out of his camper early in the morning and enjoying his first breath of fresh air. Then the man took two steps forward and stopped.

"He's not armed," Valdés said to the Minister. "He wants to talk again."

The colonel moved forward a few steps. There were twelve paces between the two when the Etarra spoke.

"You can dim those fucking lights. We're coming out and we don't want any trouble."

The colonel was confused and groped for the right words.

"We haven't got permission for your helicopter," he said. "It could be hours yet. These things take time. Authorization's got to come from the top."

The terrorist gestured into the darkness, beyond the scope of the powerful arc lights.

"I can imagine "the top" is all out there now—Santana and the rest of the jackals. You just can't stop bullshitting, can you, colonel?" He looked at his watch although Valdés was sure that he knew exactly what the time was. "I make it 23:15. Do you agree with that?"

"Yes."

The Etarra grinned.

"That's fine. You needn't play games any longer. We don't want a helicopter. We're giving up. The operation's over, colonel."

The Prince felt his throat constrict as he saw the four figures slowly clamber from the driver's door and begin to walk up the road in single file. The lights reflected on the blonde hair of the third person. Her hands were free but the plaster strip covering the lower half of her face was still in place. A blanket was draped over her shoulders, covering her almost to her feet. Instinctively, the Prince began to move forward, only to find his way blocked by Inspector Woods.

"Be patient, sir," he said. "Give the security forces time to do their job."

Charles strained to look at the developing scene. Beside him, he heard the King say, "Thank God. She looks all right."

Valdés still suspected a trick. These were desperate men who had just killed two police officers. They would not give up without a fight. Yet here they were, walking as if they were out on an evening stroll. They had no weapons in their hands, and they were covered by the guns of thirty expert marksmen. It just had to be a genuine surrender.

He waited until all were well clear of the van, then signaled his men to move in to separate the terrorists from the hostage. Not a word was exchanged. Finally the victim stood alone, facing Valdés. She seemed to be in good physical shape, but made no effort to move. As he went to escort her away, she shook her head.

"She's waiting for her husband," he thought.

He gestured, and fifty meters away, the Prince's detective stood aside. Forgetting all protocol and dignity, the Prince ran forward, shouting her name.

The victim reached to her face and in one movement stripped away her gag. She smiled at the Prince.

He stopped in his tracks, stunned. His arms, stretched out

33

ready to sweep her up, froze in mid-air and then collapsed weakly at his side.

"Who the hell are you?" he asked, in a choked voice. "Where's my wife?"

Chapter Four

"Why are you so sure that the Princess is somewhere in the city, colonel?" the King asked.

Valdés pointed to the map, perched on a temporary easel next to a Velasquez hunting scene.

"The kidnapping took place here, sir, outside Brunete. The switch must have taken place somewhere between there and Navas del Rey. By the time they could have got to any of these points," he drew a large circle with his finger, "the roadblocks were in place. They could be holed up in a small town or village within this area, but I doubt it. They'd stick out too much. What is more likely is that they took this minor road, through Villamanta, and then joined the main highway to Madrid—it's only fourteen kilometers—and are now in a safe house."

The King looked anxiously across the Prince, sitting on the sofa. He was a tall man, but he seemed almost swallowed up by the cushions. He had taken off his windbreaker and was now in a short-sleeved blue shirt. The chalky soil from the corn field clung to his shoes. His eyes still showed the shock they had registered when the woman decoy had revealed herself, smiling broadly at the successful deception.

The King walked over to him and clamped a hand on his shoulder. Reacting to the reassuring pressure, the Prince braced himself and squared his shoulders. He smashed his right fist into the palm of his other hand.

"What have the terrorists told you, Colonel?" he asked. "I mean the people in the van."

"It's very early in the interrogation, sir, but I don't expect them to reveal much. They won't *know* anything beyond their part of the operation. Not even the code names of the people who are actually holding Her Highness. That's how ETA works."

Since the terrorist surrender, it had been obvious to everyone in the room that the King intended to play a major role in the crises.

The Minister recalled the long night that followed the storming of the Congress, the lower half of the Spanish Parliament, by extreme right-wing Civil Guards on the 23rd of February 1981. The entire government, along with every member of the assembly, was being held hostage at gunpoint. Armored divisions were poised to move out of barracks. Tanks were actually on the streets of Valencia.

The fascist military plotters backed by still-powerful civilian members of the old Franco regime had not taken into account King Juan Carlos I.

Wearing the uniform of Commander-in-Chief of the Armed Services, the King had gone on national television and radio to command his generals to obey his orders to defend democracy and the constitution. Then he spent the rest of the night on the telephone to make sure his orders were followed. The coup attempt crumbled. The King had averted a bloodbath with his shrewd leadership.

Now he had taken command again. He turned to the Minister.

"I want the best team we have on this job. If they're in the Basque country, pull them out. Now!"

"Sir, the most experienced officers we have will be in Madrid within a few hours. I have been in contact with the Premier. He was in Seville but he should be on his way back by now. He has asked me to stress that every resource will be made available." He turned to Valdés. "How do you intend to handle it, colonel?"

How indeed? It had taken years of concentrated effort to discover the hideouts of ETA's Commando Madrid. And they had been active, carrying out machine gun ambushes, hand grenade attacks and bombings, and even launching rockets at the Defence Ministry in broad daylight across the city's main avenue. This group would lie low—do nothing. They were somewhere out there, hidden in a city of over four million people. And how much time did he have to find them?

"I already have men out on the street, sir," Valdés said, "checking on new arrivals, looking for the unusual. As soon as I leave here, I intend to set up a small team, two or three men with solid anti-terrorist experience, to coordinate them."

The British Ambassador, Sir Hugh Henderson, spoke for the first time.

"I have been in consultation with my Prime Minister on this matter. She accepts that the incident occurred on Spanish soil, and must be handled by the Spanish authorities. Nevertheless, since we are dealing with the fate of a member of the British royal family, she feels it would be proper for us to send one of our own men over."

"As an observer?" Santana asked.

"Oh, a little more than that," Henderson replied, the firmness in his voice belying the informality of his words. "I would think more in terms of a member of the coordinating team to which Colonel Valdés just referred. And, of course, I would expect him to keep me appraised of all developments."

Santana didn't like it, but he saw no course open to him but to agree. He nodded his assent then turned back to Valdés.

"What will ETA do next, colonel?"

"I believe they will not make any announcement until they have their kidnapping operation working smoothly. That could be at least two days. If we can maintain secrecy ourselves, it will be of immense value to the undercover work which has

37

already begun."

Keeping it secret for as long as possible would not just benefit the police work, Santana thought. It would also be vital for Spain—and for Anglo-Spanish relations.

"The only people besides ourselves who know what has happened are those closely connected with the operation. The press does not even suspect that it was anything beyond a normal ETA outrage." A look of sudden concern crossed his face, and he spoke to the Prince. "When is your next public appearance, sir?"

"Just the farewell at the airport."

"Could you not, sir, have Her Highness postpone the return because of an indisposition?"

The King looked questioningly at the Prince.

"We could do," the Prince said finally, "but the press would go to town on it. Everything my wife does interests them. There'd be all kinds of speculation. They might even work out the ETA angle for themselves."

A gloomy silence descended over the room as each man visualized the newspaper headlines. Then another image flashed across the King's mind, the face of a girl smiling down from the billboards. He had even met her once, at a charity gala. He had been struck then by the resemblance.

"Suppose we could find a substitute for the Princess?" the King said, "Someone who could be at the airport tomorrow? Someone to act her role? That would give us time."

"Of course, sir! The hair-bleach girl!" Santana exclaimed.

Hair-bleach girl? The Prince looked at them as if they both insane, but for the first time since the start of this ordeal, the King was almost smiling.

"Your Princess is so popular in Spain," he explained, "that there is a model who makes a very good living just out of looking like her."

"The similarity is quite uncanny," Santana said.

Good God, it's not just a question of looks," the Prince exclaimed. "My wife was brought up as an English aristocrat, and even she had trouble adjusting to her new role for the first few months. Do you really think that a fashion model could learn enough by tomorrow to carry it off?"

If we keep the press and the cameras far enough away," the King said, "and speed everything up, we could just get away with it. We could dress her in a wide-brimmed hat, even sunglasses. It's like a conjuring trick—people will see what they expect to see."

He had spoken confidently because, if it was to have any chance of working, the Prince had to believe in the scheme. Yet even as he spoke, he could see his own grave doubts mirrored in his friend's face.

Valdés was very pleased with the idea. ETA High Command would be working on the assumption that the world would know about the kidnapping long before they claimed responsibility. They would be shocked when they saw the scene at the airport. Then they would realize that they would have to rethink their carefully worked-out plans—improvise. And where there was improvisation, there was scope for mistakes.

The enormity of what he had agreed to, suddenly struck the Prince. He was going back to England, leaving his wife in Spain—in the hands of fanatics. If it would help in any way to get her back, then he would go. But he wanted a man on the scene whom he could personally trust to help handle the situation. Friends were no good, they would be as lost as he was himself. It had to be an expert.

When the others had left, he took Henderson quietly into a corner.

"Hugh," he said, "our man on the coordinating team—I'd like to have a say in who he is."

The Ambassador's eyes hardened.

"It is a specialist job, sir, and . . ."

"I know that. The man I have in mind is a specialist."

"I really think it's a matter for the government to decide, sir."

The Prince felt his anger rising.

"You and I both know that I will be leaving Spain at least partly in the furtherance of government policy. I have always accepted my responsibilities, put my duties above my personal concern. Very well then—now I want something back."

The Ambassador was forced to admit to himself that there was considerable justice in what the Prince had said.

"What I can do, sir," he began cautiously, "is to pass on your request and make a personal recommendation that if the man you have in mind has the necessary qualities, he should be selected."

"That is all I ask."

"Who is he? And how do we contact him?"

"His name is James Decker. He's a captain in the SAS, on special detachment in Northern Ireland."

They had met, if that was the right word for it—at one of those informal, off-the-record gatherings for brave men whose exploits could not be publically recognized with decorations because they were still active in the field.

The officers had lined up to meet him in the Mess, looking splendid in their dress uniforms. The Prince had been amused to note that these men, who risked their lives daily, were a little nervous in the royal presence. He passed down the line, shaking hands, making jokes, putting them at their ease. Decker was near the end, a broad man with sandy hair and deep green eyes. He didn't seem nervous—just angry.

"Something the matter?" the Prince asked.

"No, sir."

Clipped, emotionless, neutral, but the Prince felt he was holding something back. Perhaps he would have passed on but for a hint of a transatlantic accent beneath the Sandhurst tones.

"I say, are you American?"

"My mother was, sir."

Again, minimum information. Why the reticence?

"Were you brought up there?"

"No sir, South America. My father was a mining engineer."

He was controlling it well, the Prince suspected that he controlled everything well, but there was still a note of resentment in the man's voice. Not against the visitor so much as the whole situation. The Prince was used to stock responses to his questions. Sometimes he yearned for the unusual, the unexpected, and this man fascinated him. And the fact that the colonel was getting edgy and wishing to move him along only added to that fascination.

"Do you object to being here?"

"I obey orders, sir. Without question."

It was enough. In fact, it was almost impertinence. The Prince turned to the next man.

But later, after the meal, after the coffee and liqueurs, when the atmosphere had relaxed, the Prince noticed Decker again. He was standing next to the regimental trophy case, looking thoughtful and, unlike most of his brother officers, completely sober. His seriousness made him seem much older than the others, although physically he looked to the Prince about 28 or 29. He excused himself from the men he had been talking to, and went over to Decker.

"Captain Decker," he said, *"what's the matter with you?"*

For a second, he thought he would receive the same blank response as he had been subjected to earlier. Then Decker's freckled forehead creased as he reached a decision.

"This . . . show. It should never have happened."

"Don't you think it's good for morale?"

"Theirs maybe," he swept his hand across the room, indicating the other officers, *"but not mine. I maintain morale by staying alive, and this isn't helping."*

"Why not?"

Decker spoke slowly and clearly as if explaining to a child.

"I'm working undercover, mixing with some very nasty people. I never touch base—never. And now I've been called in because you. . . because Your Royal Highness wants to meet

41

some of the men in the front line. What if I've been spotted by the IRA? What if one of the orderlies here sees me outside, throwing a brick, marching to a funeral, and his expression gives me away? Months of work wasted!"

The two men looked at each other.

"Esto es jodido!" *Decker said.*

The Prince looked puzzled.

"Sorry," the captain continued. The thought of what could happen if his cover was blown had made Decker revert to his second language—which had once almost been his first—to express himself. But he couldn't tell the Prince that he thought the command to be present was a fuck-up. "Spanish, sir. It means that it would be no tea-party if the Provos got on to me because of this gathering."

"And you'd probably be dead," the Prince added quietly.

The colonel appeared from nowhere.

"You mustn't monopolize His Royal Highness, Captain Decker," he said, and smoothly steered the Prince back into the center of the room. "Decker's a bit offhand, sir, but that's just his way. He's bloody good in the field. He understands the terrorist mentality, knows what they're going to do before they've even decided themselves. He's the best man we've got."

The colonel's words echoed through his mind. The Prince appreciated as well as Valdés the enormous problems of finding the Princess in a large city like Madrid. He *needed* the best man they'd got.

Diana lay on her back on an iron bed in a space no wider than her outstretched arms. She looked up at the ceiling just five feet above her head. They had told her it was a People's Prison, but it felt more like a coffin. A cheap bedside lamp with a low voltage bulb stood on a cardboard box on the floor.

The wall on one side was thin—she could hear a tap dripping; the others were old and solid. There was nothing else in

42

the cell.

She had wept for a good hour, but now there were no more tears left in her. She felt desperately alone. Turning on the thin mattress, she looked at the concealed door through which the young man who spoke English had guided her, assuring her that everything would be all right if she caused no trouble.

She could imagine what was happening outside. The King must have raised the alarm by now.

The image of her husband flashed across her mind. He must be frantic with worry. How she needed his arms around her now. She knew that he hadn't been keen on the motorcycle excursion. He had been right, he so often was, so often more sensible than she.

Sensible! There was one consolation in that. Charles would know what to do about the babies. God, they must have been so excited that Mummy and Daddy were coming home . . . when was it? Today? Tomorrow? There was already confusion in her mind.

"Where am I? Is it daylight?"

The police would be searching for her everywhere, but how would they ever find her here, in this secret room, in an old house, somewhere in Madrid?

She had seen narrow streets as she sat in the back of the Seat 1500. The man with the white face and the cold eyes had sat in the front, but had kept turning round and staring at her as if to make sure she was really there. The young man who'd been next to her had a pleasant voice—but he'd kept his gun jammed in her side.

The girl driver, with the defacing burn on her left cheek, had said nothing, just nodded her head when Pale Face had spoken. But she still frightened the Princess. At the transfer point, as the girl was cramming the long black wig over her fair hair, she had seen a look of pure hatred on her face.

She heard the sound of footsteps and the door swung silently open. The young man stepped into the room, squeezing the wall and the bed. The Princess sat up. The room was so small

43

that without any intention on either of their parts, they were almost touching. The young man was wearing thin kitchen gloves and carrying a plastic tray. On it was a bowl of beans, a small plate of cheese and ham, a glass of water and a bread roll. A paper tissue gave the suggestion of a touch of service.

"This is your evening meal. It's a little late tonight. In the future, I'll bring it in about nine o'clock."

In the future?

"How long are you going to keep me here?"

Xabier balanced the tray on one hand, removed the lamp from the cardboard box, and put the supper down in its place.

"That depends on how long it takes the capitalist oppressors of my homeland to meet our demands," he said aggressively. Then, noticing the look of puzzlement and fear on her face, his voice softened, and he added, "It shouldn't be too long."

She didn't understand what he was talking about. She hadn't understood anything that had happened to her in the last few hours. The food lay untouched as she looked at him.

"Eat your beans while they're still warm," Xabier said.

The Princess had no appetite.

"Who are you? What is it you want?"

Xabier returned the gaze and realized that this woman had no idea of the struggles and suffering of the Basques. He would educate her, but now was not the time.

"Try to eat a little, and get some rest."

He knew that she was beginning the most uncomfortable night she had ever spent. She had been cushioned from the rough side of life till now. But it rankled that she appeared to know nothing about his nation's cause. He wondered if she even knew where the Basque country was.

"What we want is justice," he said, as he turned to leave.

The door clicked shut and the Princess was left alone.

Chapter Five

Xabier stood in his back against the People's Cell. As he left the prisoner, it occurred to him that this was possibly only the second contact between the Basque nationalists and the British royal family in the hundred year struggle with Madrid. The first was when the father of Basque nationalism had written a letter to Queen Victoria requesting that she make the region a protectorate of the British Empire. The Basque flag was actually copied exactly from the Union flag of Britain, with green replacing the blue.

"But this time, we are not asking for British help," Xabier thought, "we are demanding it. And we have the future Queen of England as a prisoner of the People."

"Thinking about that pampered royal?"

Idoia was standing at the bathroom door. He wondered if she'd been eavesdropping, even though she didn't understand the language.

"No, I was thinking about the ironies of history."

She waited for a explanation, but he didn't bother to give one. He had recognized her fanaticism from the start, weeks earlier, and had admired it. But since they had snatched the Princess he had noticed a cold hatred, an open hostility to the hostage, as if she were a personal enemy. And some of that hostility seemed to aimed at him too, as the Princess's keeper.

"It doesn't do us any good to frighten her too much," he said. "You look after your gun, don't you?"

"Yes," Idoia answered, puzzled.

"Then don't misuse the best weapon we've got. Her!"

It had come out more sharply than he had intended—because he didn't like her attitude. Personalities must never come into it. Nothing could be allowed to endanger the Cause. He was being as guilty of bourgeois individual preference as Idoia.

"Come on," he said, injecting friendliness, or at least comradeship, into his tone, "let's go and get some food ourselves."

They found Guadaña sitting at the round table looking at the late-night news.

"There hasn't been a mention. They're going to keep it quiet as long as they can. But we knew they would."

Guadaña picked up a bottle of wine and filled three glasses. They drank in silence. There was no toast to the so-far successful operation. They all knew they had been working against the odds and that wasn't ETA's way.

The whole operation had been based on hope rather than certainty. That evening had been the only one free in the visiting royals' agenda, the only possible one for the jaunt. If there had been spring rain, if the King had had indigestion—if for any reason he had decided not to take the Princess out—the mission would have failed. And only Xabier knew how flimsy was the evidence on which the hoped for bike ride was built.

It had all come from a casual conversation overheard in San Sebastian in August the year before.

It had been well past one a.m. and the clients in the Bar Concha were in that animated condition created by a combination of a summer night, holidays and a fair amount to drink. Not one of the plush leather seats at the copper-topped tables was free; the bar stools were all occupied and groups of people stood amid a hubbub of conversation. The wealthy Basques living in other parts of Spain had returned home for the vacation.

46

"Got the new machine outside," one young man said—loudly, even by Spanish standards. There was a slight slur to his words. He was drinking his third whisky in an hour. "Did the motorway from Bilbao in forty-five minutes. A hundred and two kilometers. Would have done it faster if it hadn't have been for the lines at the toll booths. Bloody tourist traffic."

"What is it?" his friend asked.

"BMW 900. Handles like a dream, goes like a bat out of hell. Got the idea from the King. He showed me his—and I was sold."

"Your father's still working at the palace, then?"

"Not for much longer. He's fed up with planning official visits. He's asked for a transfer back to the diplomatic service."

The man in the smart lightweight blue suit, who was drinking alone at the bar, did a casual half-turn on his stool. This might just be interesting, he thought, as he pretended to take a general interest in the lively, noise scene around him.

"Anyway, what's the King want a big bike for?" the friend asked. "To drive round the palace grounds? What a waste!"

"Hell no! He's a real biker. He loves it. He's always driving off into the Sierra. It was the same in Majorca. He even took Princess Di out with him there. And her bodyguard was bloody terrified."

"I should think she was bloody terrified herself."

"No! It was her first run on a bike but dad said she loved it and wanted to do it again. The King had to promise her he'd take her for another spin when they came to Madrid. And you know, they are coming—next year sometime. I wouldn't mind having her up on the back myself. She's gorgeous."

He lit a American cigarette. "After the summer, I'm going to strip the bike down and make some modifications. For a start, I'm putting in a racing carburettor because you really need that extra..."

The man swiveled back to the bar and drank from his glass slowly. That snippet of information, whatever its worth would

*be passed on, simply because the King had been mentioned.
What a way to help the cause—sitting in a capitalist watering-
hole.*

*The report had landed up on Xabier's desk. Xabier, who,
since he had been recruited as a student at Pamplona University, had worked in ETA Intelligence, analyzing countless documents like this one. He had almost discarded it as useless,
either idle speculation or drunken boasting. But if it was true!
The King was known as a man of his word. If he promised to
take the English Princess for a ride, he would do it. And surely
the opportunities for such an excursion should be so few that
ETA could cover them all. He saw how the information could
be transformed into an operation which, if it worked, would
strike a decisive blow for ETA. It would be the most spectacu-
lar operation ever undertaken by the organization. It would
rock two capitals and stun the whole world.*

They did not speak much over the meal, they were all still
tense, still wound up. Besides, Guadaña thought, something
had happened between the other two. He noticed the abrasive-
ness and would have to put a stop to it if it became worse. But
at the moment it was keeping them both alert.

He could understand Idoia's point. Out there in the countryside, Xabier had wanted to stall the policemen, while Idoia had
seen the need for action. He was convinced now that Xabier
was a college boy, a theoretican, and the young man annoyed
him. But he was too much a professional to let the irritation
show and he realistically accepted the fact that Xabier was
doing a job that he would have neither the ability nor the pati-
ence for.

"How is the woman?" he asked Xabier.

"Pretty frightened, almost in shock. She'll be better when
she's got through the night."

"Why waste time talking about *her* state? She's well-fed. A
bit of a rough ride might show her what life's all about." Idoia

48

caught the expression on Xabier's face. "Listen. You think I'm tough on her don't you? When my unit was smashed, I had to spend five days hiding in the crypt of a church. There was nothing to eat—nothing at all. In the end, I was chewing at my belt. I had to drink the condensation off the walls! And God, it was cold at night. Do you think she's ever suffered like that?"

She stopped, realizing she had spoken too freely. All talk of background, friends, previous operations, was strictly forbidden. What Idoia had told them was not much, but if they were captured and revealed it under interrogation, it just might fit in with other small pieces of information and lead to the arrest of a fellow Etarra.

Idoia flushed bright red, heightening the rawness of her scar.

"Next week she'll be free," she said, angry and defensive, "and we could be in a police cell. That won't be like a hotel either."

"If we're in a police cell," Guadaña thought, "the woman won't be free—she'll be dead."

A soft rain had started to fall. The duty policeman stepped back as far as he could into the doorway of No. 10 Downing Street, the Prime Minister's official London residence, only to have to emerge again as the first car arrived. When the third vehicle pulled up, he began to wonder what the hell had happened to cause so much activity at such a late hour. He saluted the Foreign Secretary who was the last to reach Downing Street, and received a preoccupied nod in return.

It was too small a gathering to bother with the Cabinet Room; the Prime Minister used her office instead. She made no apology for the late hour; she expected her Ministers to be on call twenty-four hours a day. The Home Secretary stifled a yawn and tried to give the impression of being fully alert. His dinner still lay heavy on his stomach, he wished he'd not ordered that last drink.

The Prime Minister briefly outlined the events in Spain.

"It's quite unbelievable—astonishing," the Foreign Secretary

49

exploded. "What on earth is happening over there? A motorbike ride—and no security, it's . . ."

"No one is immune from terrorism," the Prime Minister cut in sharply. "We must accept what's happened as a fact, and deal with it. I have already made it clear to the Spanish government that we insist on having a man on the spot—at the nerve center of the operation, as it were. His Royal Highness has made a personal request on this matter, and the suitability of his candidate is currently being checked on . . ."

The Private Secretary knocked and entered, carrying a tray of tea. He laid it on the desk and then discreetly withdrew. The Prime Minister poured a cup for each of her advisors. It was little touches of domesticity like this that sometimes led those she had to deal with to assume that beneath the hard exterior was a soft, vulnerable woman. It did not usually take them long to realize their mistake.

She did not ask the Ministers whether they took milk or sugar, these were the sort of details she always remembered. She could also have told them their grandchildren's names and the dates of their wives' birthdays.

"This must be a short meeting, gentleman," the Prime Minister said. "I am due at the Palace in an hour."

Of all her official meetings with Her Majesty, this was the one she least relished. There were deep personal implications, and yet the interests of the nation must come first. She would have to make that clear. Despite her many years in office she had never felt quite so unprepared to cope with a crisis. But she knew that by the time her car turned into the side entrance of the Palace, she would be in command of the situation.

"The Princess is arguably the most popular figure in the country," the Prime Minister went on. "If she is killed, there will be a massive public outcry. I need not tell you what the papers will make of it, particularly the tabloids. There will not have been such anti-Spanish feeling since the Armada." She turned to the portly man on her left. "Do you have any comment to make at this point?"

50

The Home Secretary removed his glasses.

"Well," he said, "It's quite likely that gangs of British hooligans would go on the rampage, attacking Spaniards and Spanish property."

"Which in turn would lead to retaliation against Britons living in Spain," the Prime Minister continued. "And there are tens of thousands of them. British companies would suffer too."

The Party Chairman crossed his legs, and then uncrossed them again.

"We would, as a government, be in a disagreeable situation," he said, "caught between the people on the one hand and the needs of international diplomacy and economics on the other. Very difficult!"

The Ministers had at first seen only the implications for their own areas of responsibility. Now they were beginning to get the total picture—and it appalled them.

"It may be necessary, politically, to respond to public pressure and take some action against Madrid," said the Prime Minister, agreeing with the Party Chairman. "It would be easy enough to take economic sanctions, we are one of Spain's biggest customers. But the EEC would bail them out—and that means us. In other words, though we might have no choice but to punish Spain, *we would really be punishing ourselves!*"

The Chairman could see the logic behind the argument. Any government which did nothing, however futile, to revenge the Princess's death, would never see office again.

"Well, let face facts, If we did not impose an official boycott, sanctions of some kind, I'm certain the public would," the Foreign Secretary said. "Can you imagine the effect on the Spanish Treasury if the best part of six million customers cancelled their Spanish holidays? It would severely dent their economy."

He saw that the Prime Minister was looking directly at him and realized that she had not finished the catalogue of possible disasters.

51

"As you well know," she said, "I have been using my influence as Spain's Common Market partner, to pressure Madrid to keep the American bases in Spain. But if there is a breakdown in relations, I can no longer negotiate. And that would *not* please the White House."

She got out of her seat and began to pace the room. None of those present had ever seen her as agitated as this.

"There is one more vital point. Spain's democracy seems solid enough now, but there are still plenty of extremists who are constantly working to undermine it. I need not remind you of the attempted coup in 1981. But for the King's cool-headedness and prompt action, the country might now be a military dictatorship."

She stopped walking, and rested her arm on the marble mantelpiece. It was cool to the touch.

"National pride is a major element in the Spanish character. If the Princess is harmed, it will suffer a great blow. There will be calls for more power for the military. This will, of course, be strongly resisted by the left-wing elements. Add to that the weakened economy of Spain—and there would be a climate that all extremists could exploit to the full. I am not being melodramatic, gentlemen, when I say that we could face the prospect of mass civil unrest in Spain."

The Prime Minister paused and looked at each of her male colleagues before adding with emphasis, "And gentlemen, wouldn't that be relished by some quarters in Moscow?"

The Foreign Secretary shifted uneasily in his seat. The Prime Minister was correct in her analysis, as usual.

The death of the Princess could spark off the biggest international crisis of the '80s, certainly in Europe. With Spain so unsettled, NATO and the Western Alliance would be affected, even more so if the Soviet Union used the opportunity for political agitation on the Iberian Peninsula. Yes indeed, a potential crisis of major proportions.

"I am not heartless, gentlemen," the Prime Minister continued. "The safe return of the Princess is my deepest concern.

But you have to understand, you must understand, that being who she is has taken the issue beyond the realm of one kidnapping—one life."

MONDAY

Chapter Six

The girl was dressed in a pair of jeans and a light sweater. She looked pale and nervous, and despite the fact that she was the same height as the Princess, she seemed much shorter.

Of course, there were reasons for her state. Being pulled out of bed in the early hours of the morning by Colonel Valdés, and told that she was wanted at the palace—but that she mustn't tell anyone—was enough to disorientate anyone. But even allowing for that. . .

The King's head throbbed—his wound was giving him trouble—but he knew that he had to see this through. He forced himself to smile, and when he spoke his voice was full of a confidence that he did not feel.

"The job we want you to do is very important, both for the Prince and for Spain. It will be very difficult, but I am sure that you can carry it off. Do you understand, my dear?"

Isabel Ruiz nodded dumbly, but the King was pleased to see that she had relaxed a little.

There was a knock on the door and the Prince entered with a tall aristocratic looking woman in her thirties.

Isabel tensed again.

"This is the Princess lady-in-waiting, Lady Margaret Wainwright," the King said. "She's going to be with you all the time, to help. And the gentleman, you must know from photographs."

The Prince, realizing hc was being introduced, favored Isabel with a wan smile. The lady-in-waiting walked up to her and curtsied. Isabel stood open-mouthed at such a gesture.

"Hopeless," the King thought, "absolutely hopeless."

The Prince had been right all along. It took years of training to develop the right attitude, the poise to be a princess. They had a matter of hours. And the girl didn't speak a single word of English.

Lady Margaret looked the young Spaniard up and down, making a critical appraisal. The hair style was exactly right, a perfect copy of the Princess's. The figure wasn't quite the same, but that could be disguised by altering the clothes.

She cast her mind over what the Princess had brought with her. The turquoise dress with the white border would do. And she could wear a hat with it—that would help.

But her stance, her movements, were all wrong. Lady Margaret turned to the King.

"I wonder, Your Majesty, if you could ask Isabel to walk up and down."

"I'll accompany her," the Prince said, moving across to the girl. "It might make her feel more comfortable."

Isabel and the Prince crossed the room two or three times. Her gait was still-limbed and clumsy.

The King held back his exasperation.

"Isabel," he said gently, "pretend you're in a fashion show. Just walk as if you were modeling clothes."

She tried again, and this time it was a little better.

Captain Decker was sitting in Paddy Flynn's late-night drinking club, just off the Falls Road. It wasn't much of a place, more like a converted front room than a bar. The wallpaper was brown from the smoke of countless cigarettes, the windows were dirty, the beer was warm.

But the atmosphere was friendly and close, as it can be when all those present have a common bond, a shared understanding. Every man in the bar was an IRA supporter, if not an active helper—and they thought that Decker was one of them.

Military Intelligence had never succeeded in establishing such deep cover before. If any of the men around him had been told that Decker was a British officer, they would have laughed. He had proven his loyalty to the cause, and the fact that half the operations he had been involved in had resulted in disaster could be written off as bad luck. He had not been asked to kill anyone—yet. He would handle that problem when it arose.

But even with as good a cover as his, he was in constant danger. The drink, which he had to consume as one of the boys, might one day make his tongue slip momentarily out of his painstakingly acquired Ulster accent. Or he might say something that a country boy from Derry should have no knowledge of. Or perhaps he might be involved in one operation too many that backfired, and someone, somewhere, would stop seeing it as a coincidence.

Then, one morning he would awake to find hard-faced men standing around his bed. He would be interrogated and tortured, perhaps for days. When they finally decided that he could tell them no more, and were tired of punishing him, they would place a black hood over his head, and shoot him.

Time was not on his side. The longer he stayed in Northern Ireland, the greater the risk. He only hoped that, if the moment did come, he would have a chance of fighting back, of taking some of the bastards with him.

There was a frantic hammering on the door. Paddy Flynn walked over, looked through the peep-hole and then drew back the bolt. A small thin man with slicked-down hair and nervous eyes entered. He glanced around the bar, then made a beeline for Decker.

"Soldiers!" he gasped. "About ten of the fuckers. They've just taken your place apart."

Before Decker had time to respond, there was a loud crash

59

and the door splintered and burst open. Framed against the street light were three large paratroopers armed with submachine guns. They moved their weapons in an arc, sweeping the bar.

"Nobody move," the sergeant barked.

The order was unnecessary. The drinkers had been through all this before.

Decker glanced out of the window. He saw more dim shapes standing in the street. There would be at least six other men out there, covering the neighboring buildings against sniper attacks.

One of the soldiers stayed where he was, his gun covering the bar. The sergeant and the other man moved down the line, scrutinizing faces. The room was completely silent.

The sergeant stopped in front of Decker.

"Michael Patrick Boyle?"

Decker said nothing.

"I said, are you bloody-well Boyle?"

"Yeah, I'm Boyle. What about it?"

The sergeant gestured towards the door with his head.

"Out!"

Decker looked round the bar at the other customers. Their features were emotionless, only their eyes burned with hatred. He picked up his glass, drained it, and then placed it back on the bar.

The second para was now standing on the other side of him. They didn't want trouble in this bar, but they could only let defiance go so far.

"Out, I said," the sergeant repeated.

Decker sauntered to the door, the two soldiers following. Then he stopped and turned.

"See you later, lads,"

"See you, Mick," several men called back.

They were out in the street before there were cries of, "Fuck the British!"

Two soldiers grabbed an arm each, while the rest, moving

60

rapidly and nervously, provided cover.

The Saracen was parked about fifty yards down the street. The sergeant opened the door.

"Get in there, you heap of shit!" he ordered, assisting Decker with a blow from his machine gun butt to the base of the spine.

Colonel Valdés climbed the stairs from his own office in the Ministry of the Interior, up to his boss's, two floors above. His back ached, his eyes were bleary, but he knew he still had several more hours work ahead of him.

Santana was conferring with two of his officials. When he saw Valdés, he dismissed them.

"Who have you come up with?" he asked, looking at the file under the colonel's arm.

"Inspector Julio Martínez," Valdés said.

"Martínez, Martínez," the Minister mused, wondering why he recognized the name. "Wasn't there some trouble with him a couple of years ago. Something about a general's daughter?"

"General Pelayo," Valdés supplied. "Martínez had just split up with his wife. Or rather she'd just split up with him. Couldn't stand the strain of being a police widow. He went on a spree. The general's daughter was just one of his conquests. But the general didn't like it."

Santana raised a quizzical eyebrow.

"Martínez's not divorced. Just separated. His wife's a good Catholic."

"So what happened?"

"The general had a lot of pull, and he used it. The girl was infatuated with Martínez, apparently, and Pelayo wanted him out of the way. That was just about the time that ETA was threatening to bomb the beach resorts, to disrupt the tourist trade. We didn't know at the time they would be more like fireworks than bombs, and we used it as an excuse to shift Martínez out of the way. He's been there ever since."

"This is a serious matter," Santana said sternly. "I want the

61

best talent available—not some policeman-playboy."

Valdés bristled, as he always did when one of his valued men was attacked.

"I suggest you read the report sir. Martínez might be a bit of a womanizer in private, but he's a first-rate officer. He's intelligent and he's an expert on urban terrorism. His arrest record is excellent.

"And he's dedicated. He was in a shoot-out with ETA three years ago and caught a bullet in the shoulder. Virtually any other man on the force would have taken sick leave—but not him. He wouldn't rest until he closed the case and that's the kind of man I want on this job."

The Minister considered it.

"All right," he said finally. "If you want him, you've got him.

The colonel saluted and marched smartly out of the room, showing no signs of the tiredness he was feeling.

The Minister sat back and congratulated himself on what he thought was political astuteness. Valdés was bloody good at his job. He knew the terrorist mentality. Yet despite what he had said, Santana was not that convinced that Martínez was the right man. But if they failed to get the Princess back—and the Minister thought that was likely *whoever* was in charge—heads would roll, scapegoats would be found. Santana would do his best to see that *he* wasn't one of those who would be clearing his Ministry desk. And by laying the blame on Valdés' poor judgment in selecting his team, Santana thought he could probably survive himself.

They were still working when the first shafts of dawn light came in through the Palace window. Isabel had walked miles up and down the carpet, while Lady Margaret criticized and the King translated. It was better, infinitely better, than it had been, but was it good enough?

"She'll have to rest soon," Lady Margaret said. "It's only eight hours to her flight."

The King nodded in agreement.

The knock on the door startled them all. Palace servants had been instructed to keep well away from this room.

The King opened the door himself, cautiously at first, just wide enough for him to see who was outside. When he saw the tall, thin, slightly gray-haired man, he threw the door open.

"Paco! Thank you for coming!"

The man bowed stiffly.

"Your Majesty."

Then he and the King embraced each other. They had been friends for a long time, since they were cadets at the Zaragoza Military Academy.

The King led the other man into the room and introduced him in English to the Prince and Lady Margaret.

Then he turned to Isabel.

"This is a good friend of mine, the Duke of Casla," he said. "He will accompany you to England and help you with this little deception."

The Duke stepped forward to shake Isabel's hand, then froze in his tracks. She had held out her own hand, but palm downwards. Her eyes were angry, as if she had been insulted. Her bearing had become imperious.

The Duke of Casla held the preferred hand in his, and bowed.

"Your Royal Highness," he said.

In the Saracen, the soldiers were openly hostile to Decker.

"Just make one wrong move, you bastard," the corporal threatened. "Just one—and I'll have your guts splattered all over the wall."

Back at the barracks, he was taken to a detention cell and left, but only for five minutes until the soldiers who had arrested him were well clear of the area. Then a very polite captain opened the door and told him that the C.O. would very much like to see him.

"Sorry about picking you up like that, old chap," The

Brigadier said as Decker was ushered into the room, "but London wants you in a hurry. Don't ask me why, they didn't bother to tell me. But there must be one hell a flap on. The RAF have sent transportation for you."

The Brigadier wasn't telling Decker anything he hadn't already worked out for himself on the ride in.

"It took a great deal of pressure to get Intelligence to tell us where we might find you," the Brigadier continued. "That's the trouble with you deep cover operators. We never know where you are when we want you." He held out of his hand. "Well, you'd better get going. Good luck with it, Decker—whatever *it* is."

Once on the aircraft, Decker lay back in his seat and let his nerves unknot. It was always like this when he came out of the field. After weeks, sometimes months, of playing a part, both his body and mind screamed for relief. . . a period of normalcy. Usually, he would go to his small flat just off Shepherd's Bush Green, and lie on his bed, sometimes sleeping, mostly gazing blankly at the ceiling, for anything up to two days.

Not until the image of the gray Belfast streets, the air polluted with grime and hatred, finally shifted from the forefront of his mind, would the desires and appetites of life begin to seep back into him.

But there wouldn't be even that luxury this time; no healing period, no opportunity to unwind. He wasn't on leave. He didn't know what was happening or where he was going, but he knew he would be out on a mission soon. His trained mind tried to fight the automatic reaction that always set in as soon as he left Northern Ireland.

Chapter Seven

Calle Hortaleza is one of the many narrow streets radiating out from Madrid's old center. By day the street bustles with activity, small shops and cafes cater for the non-stop stream of citizens scouting the area for cheaper goods than are available on the fashionable Gran Via. At night, it fills up with bar-hoppers, and occasionally a gay or transvestite who has strayed from nearby Chueca Square, the self-imposed homosexual ghetto.

Six-thirty in the morning is the changeover period of any working day. The red-light clubs on the side streets are locking up, the ordinary cafes and bars are swabbing down and laying out the saucers for the early morning breakfasts of coffee and buns.

Ignacio, the barman in the *Cabo de Trafalgar*, had seen his first customer of the day several times before, but the young man seemed very quiet, and they had never exchanged more than the most casual of greetings. As usual, his customer ordered only coffee. Today he looked tired, as if he'd been out on the town. Ignacio knew he was the new tenant on the third floor above the bar. He had moved in just after the workmen, who had been there for weeks, had finished their renovations. It had been a big job, but the place needed it—it had been empty for years.

Xabier paid and walked down the road to the Gran Via. He bought cigarettes and three daily newspapers, then retraced his steps.

He'd only dozed fitfully during the night. When next would he be able to get a full eight hours sleep? He wondered how the other two had slept. They seemed so much more on top of the situation than he was. Idoia had been sound asleep when he had shaken her for the start of her shift at four A.M. He had heard the sound of a radio coming from the room that Guadaña had chosen as his headquarters.

"He probably never needs rest when he's on a operation," he thought. "He's that sort of man. Cold. He seems almost inhuman at times, but maybe that's the kind we need in charge."

He realized he hadn't even thought about the woman in the cell since he left the apartment. He had heard her tossing and turning during the night and once or twice he heard her mutter aloud, but it hadn't made any sense to him. The orders were to gag her again if she started screaming, even though the outer walls on the apartment were thick. But she hadn't made enough noise to justify that. Besides, he hadn't wanted to disturb whatever sleep she was getting.

"Because," he told himself, "awake, she would be more difficult to handle."

He stopped at the bakery to buy fresh bread and then returned to the apartment.

"The Princess—the woman—will probably be hungry."

He was angry with himself for giving her a title. No one deserved privilege!

Conchita Marques, Colonel Valdés' secretary, was so absorbed in her work that she did not hear the office door open, and only became aware that someone was there when a bunch of flowers magically appeared under her nose.

She looked up to meet the gaze of a man in his early thirties, of slightly more than average height. He smiled.

"How's the most beautiful girl in the Ministry—if not in all of Spain?"

She smiled back.

"Lovely to see you returned from exile, Julio."

He was a rogue, she knew he was, with his good looks and his smooth line in patter. But he was still hard to resist. Only Martínez, awakened at three in the morning and ordered back to the capital immediately, would have found the time to stop and buy her a bouquet.

"The colonel's not here," Conchita said, "but you're to go and wait in his office. I don't suppose there's any harm in you knowing, since you're involved in this," she lowered her voice, even though there was no one else around, "but he's at the Palace."

Martínez had known his new assignment must be important if they'd called him back so suddenly—and if they were prepared to tolerate him in the vicinity of the general's daughter. But he had never thought it would be this big. Still, he was slightly annoyed at being pulled off the coast. Because after two years of fruitless investigation into the beach bombings, posing as a low-level playboy, a "remittance" man living off a monthly check from home, he had finally got a lead.

It had come about because of a combination of instinct and training. He had spotted the man first in the company of a girl, walking along the promenade at Benidorm. Two uniformed municipal police crossed from the sea front as if to approach them. He saw the man's hand grip the girl and they made to turn, then hesitated. As the officers carried on by, he noticed an exchange, a look of relief. They could be dope dealers or some other kind of petty criminals. He had registered the face, but thought nothing more about it until the next day when two small bombs left craters in the beach, giving ETA wide publicity in the European press, even though the blasts hurt no one.

It was a week later when he spotted the couple again. He

was playing a game of beach soccer on the long, broad sands of the Levant beach.

To the kids he was playing with, a hodgepodge of nationalities, he was always "Mr. Pirri," the name of a previous Captain of Real Madrid and the Spanish National Team. The games were impromptu—he would stroll across and start kicking the beach ball with them. He gave the English lads names, such as "Bobby Charlton" or "Georgie Best." It soon caught on until all of the lads had chosen the names of stars. There was always some little fair- or dark-haired youngster named Maradona or Platini. All seemed to like the Spaniard with the warm and friendly smile who kept the score and welcomed any child into the game.

Martínez loved the kids. The shouts, the laughs, of the soccer games were very much a break from duty. The almost daily relaxation was also an escape from the image of the remittance man, the playboy, the woman hunter.

The kids reminded him of something, too. The fact that there had been no children from his own marriage. The doctors had talked about ovaries and said that a baby was most unlikely. A family might have healed the rift that had developed between him and Ana.

"Oh, to have a lad like these here," he often thought as he kicked the beach ball with his young friends.

"See you later, boys," he said, the moment he saw the couple. Grabbing his sandals, he made for the promenade, blending himself in with the passersby.

He followed the couple for most of the morning, and sat near them while they sunbathed. No alarm bells rang. When he finally gave up and went back to the pickup football game, the holiday kids had gone. The couple had messed up his game, apparently for nothing.

But had it been for nothing? Three days after the second sighting, a package was found hidden outside a hotel just a few miles up the coast. Experts discovered that it contained 150 grams of plastic explosive, packed into a corned been tin.

Again he thought of the couple and was puzzled.

Martínez had spent weeks hanging around the student bars of Valencia before he saw the man again, and this time he trailed him back to the university campus.

There, checks had shown that Emilio García was a second year engineering student, with a poor record both in attendance and achievement. Martínez had put in a request to the Burgos police—where García's identity card had been issued—for more details. And García had suddenly dropped out of sight.

Martínez had searched his room the previous morning. There was no stamp of the man's personality on it; no letters, no communication with anyone. And *that* wasn't normal.

Martínez didn't like leaving the investigation at this crucial point.

"And I'm going to miss the girls!"

With his charm and Latin looks, he had certainly been successful with the foreign girls on holiday. They had found his Spanish accent attractive, his English soft, his manners impeccable. The combination had rarely failed. There had been many brief and passionate romances with promises made but never kept.

But it was good to be back in Madrid, at the center of things, where real police work was done. And he might even see Ana, his estranged wife.

If Martínez had had any doubts about the seriousness and importance of his new task, one look at Valdés' face would have vanquished them. It took the colonel fifteen minutes to explain the situation. At the end, he invited questions.

"What's all this about an Englishman working with me?" Martínez asked. "Surely this is our affair."

"It's their Princess," Valdés said. "Besides, we've no choice. It's a political decision. And Julio, you're going to have to learn to get on with him. And whoever we have to work with, we've got to crack this case."

Diana reached out with her right hand to touch her husband.

69

It was the reassurance she automatically sought when beginning to stir from her sleep. Instead of the warm, comforting firmness of her man's shoulder, her knuckles grazed against a cold hard wall. She was instantly awake.

The low ceiling, the narrow cot, the cheap bedside light, the congealed supper on the cardboard box, all brought back the terror of what had happened to her. She stifled a scream, then dug her fingernails into the mattress.

"Think! For God's sake, think! Don't panic. If I'm ever going to get out of here, I've got to keep calm."

It was almost a prayer.

"Are there three of them? Or more?"

Her eyes searched the cell. There were no windows. The only way out was the door which, she remembered, opened on to a bathroom. There was utter silence. Even the tap which had been dripping as she tried to get to sleep, had been turned off.

Charles would be getting things organized. Her parents must know by now. Poor Daddy and Mummy. The children. . . they would be up and about already. Oh, to hug them. And what on earth must they be thinking at the Palace?

"It's all my fault. Such a silly thing to do. Stop blaming yourself. Stop feeling like a poor, frightened woman."

She was a Princess. The Spanish government would have launched a massive operation to find her. Was there anything she could do to help them, to speed up her release from this frightful place? She lay still and started to nibble one of her painted nails. Suddenly, she knew what she must do.

She heard the door click. The woman terrorist was looking down at her, her face expressionless.

"Good morning," the Princess smiled. "er. . . *buenos dias*."

That was almost the full extent of her Spanish vocabulary.

The woman ignored the greeting. The Princess realized that she couldn't be the one, it would have to be the younger man, the one who spoke English.

The terrorist had kept the door open with one hand. With the other, she gestured towards the bathroom. It was an order, not a suggestion.

Diana got to her feet, and slipped into the flat-heeled shoes she had been wearing the night before. She spotted the gun, a small automatic, sticking out from the belt, just as the woman turned and went into the bathroom.

The woman pointed to the washbasin, the toilet, the towel and soap, then leaned against the door that led into the main part of the flat. The Princess felt a mixture of indignation and embarrassment.

"Could you leave, please?"

The woman shrugged to show that she didn't understand and was not even interested. Then when the hostage defiantly turned her back to the basin and folded her arms, she opened the door and shouted. Seconds later, Xabier entered the bathroom and exchanged a few rapid words with the woman.

"You must understand," he said to the Princess, "that when you are given an instruction, you follow it. This is your only opportunity of the day to make yourself clean and comfortable."

"I'm not washing while she's here, and I'm certainly not going to use the lavatory."

"You either do it while she is here, or not at all. It's your choice. What do you think she is—a voyeur? She has not the slightest interest in *you*. You will feel better for a wash, and after a while you won't even be bothered that she's here."

There was a hint of kindness, of some understanding, in that last comment. He was her only chance and she could not afford to antagonize him.

"I suppose you're right. I haven't any option, have I? Not if I'm going to keep myself clean. But please could you tell her to look the other way? I can't run off, can I?"

Their eyes met and she could see that her surrender on the issue had pleased him.

Step One.

The man spoke quietly to the woman, his hands moving as

he made his point. As she turned on the wash basin tap, she heard the door close. Looking in the mirror, she could see that although the woman was in the same position, her gaze was directed to one side. It was only a minor triumph over the woman, but it was little victories like this that would give her the strength to see it through.

Captain Decker sat aboard the Learjet on his way to Madrid, asleep. He had been briefed on his mission by the Prime Minister, and knew that until it was over, rest would be a luxury to be grabbed while it was available.

He was dreaming. It wasn't an Ulster dream—Orangemen fleeing and leaving their banners in the dirt, British soldiers being ambushed, Ireland united—his Mick Boyle dreams. This dream belonged to the subconscious mind of James Decker.

He and his father in the Andes, rucksacks on their backs, stout sticks in their hands. The older Decker in his early forties, Jimmy perhaps nine or ten.

"I'm tired, Daddy."

"Keep going, Jimmy."

"Daddy, I can't. I've got a blister on my foot."

His father bending over him, his breath sour with a taste that, in those days, Jimmy did not recognize as whisky.

"What kind of son are you? It's a hard world out there. You've got to be the best. Where's your backbone, boy?"

He had looked on his father as a god, a superman, so he *had* kept on despite the pain—for years and years.

He had become the hard man his father wanted him to be— the best, the one who never gave up, who always won through against the odds. It was only much later, when the old man, half-drunk, had come to watch him pass out from Sandhurst, that James had seen him for what he really was. A broken-down, second-rate engineer who had only seemed tough when looked at from the perspective of a small, thin boy. He had never really forgiven his father for not dying before he was old enough to discover the truth.

72

He woke, as he always did on these occasions, feeling vaguely depressed. He did not like the dreams about his father, but he preferred them to the others—the ones about Molly.

This operation was vitally important—and virtually impossible. But he would approach it in exactly the same way as all the others—with the intention of coming out on top. His father had been in his grave for five years now. But Decker still had to prove that he was the best, not a fake like his dad. The desire to win every time still burnt in him. The desire to win alone.

Chapter Eight

Martínez stood in the shade and watched the Englishman stride across the tarmac. He was marching rather than walking, and even in street clothes there was no mistaking his profession. Yet he had been told that this man had lived undercover for months.

Martínez didn't really care for the English character. It was too abrupt—too cold. A Spaniard could derive some pleasure from almost any situation; an Englishman seemed unable to really let himself go even in the most favorable circumstances.

Decker was closer now. He carried no luggage and Martínez could see that his jacket and trousers were old and shabby. He was still in his deep cover clothes, yet somehow he made them seem like a uniform. He was a big man, and broad. His movements suggested power, determination—and a total lack of *joie de vivre*.

"We are both professionals," Martínez told himself. "And that is the most important thing."

He stepped out, extending his hand to greet Decker.

"Inspector Julio Martínez," he said in English. "Welcome to Madrid."

Decker's grip was firm, but he made the handshake brief. He spoke in clipped, precise, South American Spanish.

"Decker." Abrupt. Like the crack of a pistol. "What have we got so far?"

"There are hundreds of men out on the case," Martínez said. The lack of courtesy, the failure to respond to a colleague, grated. "But it's early yet. Nothing concrete has come in. No real leads."

The reply was only what Decker had expected. The Latin attitude of waiting, hoping that things would turn up of their own accord. The Inspector seemed too laid-back, unaware of time. He shouldn't have come to the airport himself, he should have had better things to do. It was action that was needed— not handshakes. And Decker distrusted Martínez's well-cut suit and suave manner which suggested that he put too high a value on the good things in life. He looked like a typical Spanish skirt-chaser. There was no place in Decker's world for women when he was working—not since Molly.

"We've been given an office in the Ministry of the Interior," Martínez said as they walked towards the unmarked car from the vehicle pool.

"I'll need a terminal linked to the main computer," Decker said, "and the facility to tap into London."

"*I'll need. . .*" Martínez noted.

As if he himself were just an office boy, a Third World "gofer," there to attend to the needs of the big expert from London.

"I'm not going to take much more of this shit!" he told himself.

Aloud, he said, "I've booked you into a hotel near the Ministry. I'm told it's a comfortable place."

As if comfort mattered. If Decker cared about comfort, he'd have gone home and packed before he left London. If he cared about comfort, he wouldn't have been in this job at all.

"Where are you staying?" he asked Martínez.

The Inspector shrugged.

"I haven't really thought about it. Only arrived this morning myself. I'll probably move a camp bed into the office."

Decker looked thoughtfully at the Inspector. That was the way an emergency *should* be approached—but he was surprised that Martínez seemed to think so.

"A camp bed will suit me too," he said.

As her car drove down The Mall, the Prime Minister was deep in thought. Her audience with the Queen had been a success—if that was the right word for it—given the circumstances. Until today, their relationship had been merely cordial, but during their tea together, the Prime Minister felt a bond of understanding, perhaps because she too had had a child missing. And although the Queen had behaved with incredible restraint and dignity, the Prime Minister had known just how she must be feeling.

She turned her mind back to political matters. It was not her usual day for an audience with the Queen, but no one could guess what the meeting had been about—as long as the deception worked.

The deception. When the idea was first suggested over the scrambler, she had known that it was brilliant. If they could carry it off—and if the Princess was released unharmed—then there would be no damage done to Anglo-Spanish relations.

Her one worry had been whether Her Majesty was prepared to go along with the plan. It was asking a great deal to expect the monarch to involve herself in a conspiracy to fool the world's press. But the Queen had surprised her. If it would help the safe return of her daughter-in-law, and at the same time serve British interests, then she would take part. Should any rumors begin, she would make it well-known, among her advisors, that nothing was wrong. And if necessary, she would even appear in public with the Spanish girl.

"That will do the trick—if anything can," the Prime Minister thought.

"These sort of questions are rather personal, aren't they, Captain Decker?" the Prince had asked, running his hand through his hair and shifting in his seat.

"I appreciate that, sir, but we need to build up as complete a profile of the Princess as possible. Every single detail, however insignificant it seems to you, might help."

The initial questions had been of a general nature, and the Prince was ready with quick but thoughtful answers. Slowly the picture emerged of an intelligent woman, sometimes high-spirited but with clear understanding of her responsibilities as a Princess, a wife and a mother.

"I am quite certain, Captain Decker, that wherever she is being held, she is thinking of ways to communicate with me. She often talks of our 'vibes.'" He seemed uncomfortable with the word. "They way we seem to connect in our thoughts for each other."

It gave Decker the opening he had been looking for, the invitation to probe into the personal intimate details the Prince shared only with his wife.

"Your closeness has often been mentioned in the popular press, sir. Her jokes, sometimes unexpected, and her comments which appear to me to be spontaneous, so often make headline news. Please don't think I'm out of line, but it's that side of her approach to life that I'm trying to build up a picture of. But I suspect that much of what is in the tabloids is not always totally correct."

The Prince clearly saw the reason for Decker's probing questions. He wanted to—he must—cooperate as fully as possible.

Within the space of a few minutes he gave Decker a score of details, including her taste for special French toiletries and perfume, and her exercise and dietary habits.

"It's one of the things we argue about. I think she takes slimming a little too far."

He was pacing the room now, taking long gangling strides, his hands clasped behind his back.

"How does she get on with people, sir? In private, I mean."

"She can't stand bores or people who keep their thoughts to

themselves. She's so naturally open, you see. And people who fawn simply because she's a Princess soon get short shrift."

"How do you think she will be reacting now, sir? Will she be able to talk to the terrorists?"

A melancholy smile appeared on the Prince's face. It was as if he was remembering someone already dead.

"My wife is very good at talking to all kinds of people. She can make anyone feel relaxed. But terrorists? Won't there be a language problem?"

"No. They'll have someone who speaks English. They always do—even ordinary criminals, kidnapping for ransom."

"Will there be a ransom request, do you think?"

Decker shook his head.

"They don't want money. They don't want *anything* from you. Their demands will be on the Spanish state. The Basque situation is very similar to that in Ulster. ETA is fighting a war for an independent Basque nation."

"And how do they treat prisoners-of-war?" the Prince asked gravely.

Decker was pleased that, at least on this point, he could be reassuring.

"She'll be well-cared for. They'll want her cooperation, if only because a cooperative prisoner is easier to handle."

They'd probably want her agreement to make recordings too, he thought. But there was no point in mentioning that to the Prince now. He had enough on his mind with the coming ordeal at the airport.

"They'll see she has plenty of food and drink and they may even grant little requests if they think that will keep her mind occupied. There's a limit of course. They won't let her see the newspapers, and they certainly won't give her a radio or television. Possibly a book or two. . ."

"Would they let her have music? She spends hours listening to cassettes, particularly when she's travelling."

"What sort of music does she like?"

It was just another detail for the dossier, the mental portrait

78

of the hostage that Decker was building up.

"She does listen to classical music," the Prince said, "but I think it's mainly to please me. She's much more interested, in pop music—disco." Again the word did not sound quite right in his mouth. "I'm trying to learn to enjoy it myself."

The windows shook slightly. The Prince looked up and saw that the helicopters were about to land.

"What else do you want to know? What more can I do?"

Decker sensed the pain and the grief.

"You can help us most, sir, by carrying on as if nothing had happened."

"It seems so much like running away, deserting my wife."

"It isn't, sir. Your part in this is harder than anyone's."

"Thank you for that," the Prince said sincerely.

"The helicopters are here," a voice said from the doorway.

The two men turned to look. The King stood there, a woman at his side.

For a moment, Decker thought it was all over, that the terrorists had, for reasons of their own, released the Princess. The resemblance was amazing.

"We have to go now," the King said gently.

"If there's anything else you want to know, Captain Decker..."

"I'll contact you in London, sir."

The Prince nodded and walked to the door. Then he turned and faced Decker again. He was known to be a shy, undemonstrative man, but the captain felt that at that moment his future sovereign would have liked to embrace him. Instead, he shook Decker's hand.

"Captain Decker, you can't possibly know how I feel, nobody can, but you've been very understanding. I would like you to know that I have every confidence in you."

Decker saw a tear forming in the corner of his eye.

"Please get her back."

A second later, he was gone, leaving Decker alone. The Prince had been wrong when he said no one knew how he felt.

Decker did. An image of flaming red hair, the sound of uninhibited laughter in country lane, flashed through his mind. He had been in the Prince's situation—exactly. And he had failed.

The Prince had touched a nerve, not as a member of the royal house, but as a man who was suffering as he had suffered. Decker would do everything in his power to get him his wife back, whatever it took.

The Palace got smaller, until it was like a doll's house below them. Isabel felt herself trembling.

"Treat it like any other modeling assignment," the King had told her.

And in the Palace, for part of the time at least, she had been able to do so. The King and the foreign Prince no longer intimidated her. But within minutes, she would be at Barajas Airport, in front of the press, in front of the television cameras. Millions of people would be watching her, expecting her to act exactly like the real Princess.

The thud of the rotar blades seemed to be quieter than the beating of her own heart.

This wasn't any ordinary show, and she couldn't persuade herself that it was. She had no idea what was going on, but she knew that it was awfully important. To the Prince, to the King—to Spain. They were all depending on her, and if she made a mistake. . .

She was a working class girl from a small town, who had made money because, by an accident of birth, she looked like a princess. But she wasn't a princess.

She couldn't do it. She just couldn't. She knew that whether she willed it or not, the moment her legs touched the tarmac they would begin to run, taking her away from all this responsibility. She was certain of it.

The Princess still did not feel like food. But if she was to do anything about the terrible situation she was in, she would have to keep her strength up. Besides, by eating, she seemed to be pleasing the young man, and it was very important to keep on his good side.

"What's your name?" she asked, as he nodded approvingly at the sight of her empty tray.

"It doesn't matter, but you can call me Xabier."

She played with the sound, running it around the roof of her mouth.

"That's a strange name. How do you spell it?"

He didn't answer, just picked up the tray. She was losing him. She must keep the conversation going.

"Thank you for what you did this morning. The girl—sorry, I don't know her name—did look away."

"It's all right."

"Would it be possible for me to get some exercise? This room is very cramped and the only time I've been out of it was to go to the bathroom."

"I don't know. I'm not in charge. I'll ask, but I don't think so."

Diana looked up from where she was sitting on the side of the bed, her eyes appealing for consideration.

"I'll go crazy if it goes on like this. Could I have something to read—or maybe a radio? I love pop music, it would help to make all this much more bearable."

Xabier was surprised that the hostage should like popular music. It didn't go with the image he had formed of a royal. It was one of his favorite pastimes, listening to pop. He sometimes felt embarrassed by it, as if it were somehow an unworthy activity for a serious, dedicated revolutionary to indulge in.

"I must have *something*." the Princess said. "You can't expect me just to sit here." The tears that ran down her cheeks were part real, part an attempt to appeal to the better side of Xabier's nature. "How long are you going to keep me here, anyway?"

"Just a few days, until our demands are met."

The sight of a distraught woman always affected him. He tried to banish the emotion. This woman, as Idoia said, had always had it easy. She was the symbol of a class system that he was totally opposed to and was fighting to overthrow.

The Princess wiped away the tears with the back of her right hand, making sure that her jailor was fully aware of her distress. Almost without realizing it, Xabier reached into his trouser pocket and brought out a crumpled, but clean tissue.

"Here," he said gruffly, "use this. I'll get you a box."

He watched her dab her eyes and blow her nose.

"You keep on talking about demands. What demands? What have they got to do with me? And what will happen to me if they're not met?"

"Don't worry. They will do what we say. They want you back very badly."

He left her looking at him. He made sure the bolt was secure and walked through the bathroom, along the corridor, and into the living room.

Guadaña was sitting at the dining table cleaning his automatic pistol, with practiced ease. Xabier stopped, looked at the weapon and wondered. Would the demands really be met, even to free a princess? And what would happen to her if they were not?

"I'm just going to get a box of tissues," he said.

Guadaña did not even look up from his task.

Chapter Nine

Arenas crossed Puerta del Sol, the hub of the capital. The square marked Kilometer Zero in the Spanish highway system, the place from where the roads started to every corner of Spain, including, to the furthest corners of the Basque country. Arenas saw it as the very symbol of the Spanish government's imperialist policy.

He glanced at the clock tower on top of the old police headquarters. He had fifteen minutes to get to the rendezvous.

He hated the city and all it stood for, but he was glad to be there. It was in Madrid where real work was being done. Not planting tiny bombs on beaches, which even the tourists ignored, but hitting at major targets—fighting the real enemy.

He walked along the narrow streets between Sol and the Plaza Santa Ana. It was a warm afternoon and the slight breeze carried the smell of grilled shrimps and boiled squid from the many small restaurants and tapa bars. Cars were tightly parked, their wheels blocking most of the pavement, while their drivers wandered off to meet friends, taste the tidbits, and drink cold beer or wine. He squeezed past a crowd lining up impatiently outside several booths selling tickets for the next day's bullfight and then paused to read the names of the matadors who would be appearing.

"Not a bad *corrida*," he said to himself.

Had he not been on a mission, he would have gone to see it.

In the plaza, old women sat under trees, knitting and watching their shrieking grandchildren; young blue-jeaned tourists wandered in the sunshine, unhurriedly. In the center, a small but studious crowd was gathered around a concrete slab chess board.

Arenas stood next to the white king's rook, as he had been instructed.

An old man in a black beret chewed thoughtfully on a toothpick while his opponent, a bespectacled youth, moved one of the three-foot high chess pieces forward. Arenas looked on interestedly as the older player struggled to contain the two pronged attack of a knight and a bishop.

He didn't notice the man standing behind him until he heard his own code name whispered in his ear. He made no move until several seconds had passed, then edged his way free from the spectators and saw his contact walking slowly towards the *Cerveceria Alemana*.

The beer hall was quite full, the clientele a mixture of locals and tourists who were following in Hemingway's footsteps. The contact was wearing a light safari jacket and jeans. He stood at the marble-topped counter and ordered a half-liter tankard of beer. Arenas, by now at the other end of the bar, did the same.

Safari Jacket was watching the entrance to the toilets. When the door opened, and a man emerged, he immediately put down his drink and made a beeline for it. Arenas followed.

Safari Jacket checked that the toilet stalls were empty, and then turned to Arenas.

"Do you have a good suit?" he asked.

"No. I'm posing as a student and..."

"Get one tomorrow. And buy a briefcase...leather." He looked Arenas up and down. "Have a haircut, too. Where you're going, it will help to look smooth."

He put his hands in his pocket, pulled out an envelope, and

handed it to Arenas.

"Be at the bar five minutes before it starts. Don't wear the suit. Put on a green jacket and white trousers. If you haven't got them, buy them. Get a poster outside, and carry it rolled up under your arm."

"What bar? Before what starts?"

The other man did not answer. Instead, he turned and left the toilet. He walked straight through the bar, not stopping to finish his beer, and was swallowed up in the mass of couple outside.

Arenas went into the cubicle and carefully opened the envelope. It was a ticket for Wednesday evening. A good seat in Tendido Seven. Arenas was going to the bullfight after all.

Simon Hartwell, highly paid professional royal watcher, stood with about ninety other press and TV men on the mobile observation platform at Barajas Airport. They were a waste of time, these departures, but he didn't dare miss one, just in case something unusual happened.

Christ, he needed a new angle. Pregnancy? Exhaustion? Marital problems? He had used them all in the last few weeks. And still the reading public waited ravenously for more details, fresh disclosures.

It wouldn't be long now. Officials were already milling around the red carpet that led to the Royal Air Force jet which would carry the Prince and Princess back to England.

Hartwell thought about the distance.

"They seem to be keeping us well back today, don't they?" he asked the man next to him.

"Doesn't bloody matter, does it? There'd be nothing to see if we were rubbing bloody noses with them."

He was probably right. But there had to be a fresh slant somewhere.

The blue and white helicopters of the King's Flight clattered in low, and touched down near the glass-fronted terminal. The Spanish monarch emerged from the first helicopter and walked swiftly over to the second to greet the royal visitors for the last time.

"The Prince isn't piloting the helicopter," Hartwell said to himself. "I wonder why. 'Is the Prince losing nerve?'" he thought, seeing the phrase in inch high letters.

No good. Anyway, it was the Princess his readers were really interested in.

The Princess stepped out of the helicopter. She wasn't even wearing a new dress; he's seen that turquoise number several times before. He was going to need all his skill and ingenuity to make this story interesting.

As she stepped onto the tarmac, the Princess turned away from the King and in the direction of the terminal building.

"Princess's last fond look at Madrid." Bloody hell, how could anyone get sentimental over an airport? But she was certainly taking her time. It was almost as if she'd decided not to leave after all.

The King was waiting expectantly. The Princess turned, curtsied, and embraced him.

"You're doing splendidly, Isabel," the King whispered.

He embraced his English cousin, then stepped back.

"It's nearly over," Isabel told herself, finally relaxing a little. As they walked along the red carpet towards the waiting plane, she reached out to take the arm of the Prince.

"No!" he said urgently.

Isabel realized she had made a mistake, though she didn't know why. Her hand fell back to her side.

The woman's gesture, although fleeting, had not been missed by Hartwell.

"Christ, they're not the Smiths going back to Birmingham after two weeks on the Costa del Sol," he thought. "But she's bloody well acting like they are."

At the top of the steps, the Royal couple stopped and waived. Then they turned and the Prince ushered his wife past

86

the two Royal Air Force cabin attendants into the plane.

"She nearly took his bloody arm!" Hartwell said to himself.

It was unusual, he had to admit that. But he didn't see how he could make a story out of it.

Now he was no longer in the public gaze, the smile disappeared from the Prince's face. He put both his hands to his face and leaned forward as the aircraft gathered speed for takeoff.

"This just can't be happening," he said.

He heard the wheels unstick from the tarmac, and the plane became airborne—a moment he normally loved. But now it seemed as if he was snapping a cord with the woman he was leaving to her fate.

"I will be back, my darling. I am not deserting you. Please believe me."

He looked down, through the smog that hung over the capital, at the tall buildings and the jumble of streets which stretched as far as the horizon. Within three hours, he would be with the children. He'd hardly thought of them, his thoughts had been so intent on his wife. What should he tell them? Just that Mummy would be away for a few days more. It seemed as if he and Mummy were always away. The children looked forward to their mother's return, to her taking them out on little excursions, but this time, they would have to do without her. Nanny would have to do the caring. He almost wept.

Charles sat upright and took a deep breath. It was vital to remain in control. He turned to the woman sitting stiffly opposite him. She smiled uncertainly. The tension, which had been with her ever since the car had collected her from her flat, slowly drained away.

It was almost uncanny, the Prince thought, looking at her face. And by God, she was carrying it off. Gratitude welled up in him, temporarily replacing the sheer horror of it all.

He leaned forward, and gently gripped her arm.

"Thank you," he said. "You've been so splendid—absolutely

wonderful. You're buying us vital time."

Her smile faded and was replaced by a look of puzzlement and confusion. Then she realized.

"*De nada,*" she said, blusing slightly. "*Gracias.*"

Martínez was watching the television with keen interest when Decker returned from the Pardo Palace.

"It's incredible," he said. "You wouldn't know anything was wrong. Just look at that!"

Decker looked at the screen. The fake princess was standing at the top of the steps, waving and smiling her farewells to the Spanish royal family.

Decker was relieved that it had worked, but it annoyed him to see Martínez jubilant, as if *he* had done something.

The captain had been in Madrid for just over three hours, talked to a man in deep distress who had almost begged for his help—and had no leads. He felt frustrated and angry. It was obvious that the Spaniards didn't have a clue as to where the victim might be.

"The end of a really historic and colorful visit," the commentator said in rich, flamboyant Castillian style, "the first in modern times by an heir to the British. . ."

Decker switched off the set.

"Very pretty," he said, "but it hasn't solved any of *our* problems. At best it's given us a little space to maneuver. Shall we use it?"

It could have been said as a helpful suggestion, but Decker's tone was curt and edge with sarcasm.

Martínez remained silent, staring at the blank screen, his hands thrust deep in his pockets. They must get on, Colonel Valdés had said.

"Fuck it," he thought.

"I don't like sarcasm, Captain Decker. We have men out there busting a gut to get on top of this case. And I have been sitting here, waiting. Not because I am a lazy Spaniard, but because there was nothing else to do. I could be interrogating the prisoners, of course, but since we are supposed to be working as a team, I did not want to do it alone."

Decker was standing absolutely still, saying nothing.

"And if we are to be a team," Martínez continued, "we must have mutual trust and respect."

Respect. There had been a lot of walking and a lot of blisters before the day came when Decker's father stopped on that mountain trail, sat on a rock, wiped his brow and looked up at his son, ready to press on.

"You're a tough little devil, aren't you, Jimmy?"

Respect's got to be earned," Decker said. "And in my book, you and your colleagues haven't done much to earn any bouquets from me."

But Martínez was quite correct. If they were to be successful, respect had to come.

"And I haven't done anything to earn yours either," he added. "Shall we go and interrogate the men your police *did* manage to capture?"

Guadaña snapped off the television set after the farewell coverage.

"The bastards! Do they really think they can get away with that for long?"

But he was shaken by the image of the Princess waving good-bye on the screen when he knew the woman was now lying on a bed in the People's Prison, just ten meters away.

Madrid had scored a point and it stung. But really, they were sinking deeper into their own shit. The coverup, the lies, would just add to the smell when the truth came out.

And the leadership in France wouldn't be fooled for a minute. They knew he didn't fuck up.

The operation had been organized on scientific Marxist-Leninist principles, there was no room for individualism. But secretly Guadaña was proud of his reputation among the

89

activists. His name was being whispered in the bars and other meeting places whenever the Cause was discussed. They would need leaders when the struggle was over, when independence came, and he was more than ready.

His imagination drifted and he saw the Basque flag fluttering over the seat of government in the capital, Vitoria. . .

He was jolted back to reality by the sound of the key turning in the lock. He reached for his gun, then relaxed as he recognized Idoia's footsteps.

"They're checking the street. Two on either side—at least that's what I think they're doing. They're three blocks away. Ordinary National Police."

She was slightly breathless from running up the stairs. She put down her shopping bags and looked at Guadaña, waiting for his reaction.

"If they knew about us, they would not approach openly, in uniform. The first thing we'd know would be when they came through the windows. So, just a routine check."

Guadaña stood up, and stuffed his automatic in the belt of his pants.

Corporal Laborda, twenty-seven years on the Force and close to retirement, had been up since dawn, working slowly down Calle Hortaleza. It was always like this when ETA struck. Check for new arrivals, anyone acting suspiciously. And he wanted the bastards caught—he hated cop killers. But as the day wore on, as he tramped the streets to no avail, his enthusiasm waned. He stopped outside the Cabo de Trafalgar.

"We'll see if the barman in there has got any information," he said to the private who was his temporary partner.

He did not expect to find anything useful, but he needed to rest his feet and slake his thirst.

Ignacio, the barman, treated Laborda and his companion as he always treated policeman, with a mixture of familiarity and respect.

"Warm today, isn't it, *caballeros*?" he said, as he pushed

two free glasses of cold beer across the bar.

Laborda took a healthy swig of his.

"Noticed anything out of the ordinary recently?" he asked. "Any new arrivals—fresh faces among the customers?"

"What, is this to do with the murder of those two officers last night? It's been on the radio every hour. Fucking ETA. Sons of whores."

"I am not at liberty to discuss my investigations," the corporal said, a little pompously. "Just have a think, will you, son?"

The corporal and the private both sat down on the plastic-covered bar stools. The holsters containing .38s hung from their belted waists. The flaps were buttoned down, but in accordance with regulations the weapons were free of their brown jackets, and as usual, they sat half facing the door. Laborda always played it by the book.

"There's some new people moved in just above the bar," Ignacio said helpfully. "Young people. They seem decent types—mind their own business. Third floor, on the left. And two single men down the road—soccer fanatics." He thought for a while. "Couple of tarts, just up from the country. They were asking about an apartment. We've got a new transvestite. He—she—comes in every day. Interested?"

Laborda shook his head in disgust.

"Tell me about that first lot. Upstairs. Where are they from."

"Don't know. The man sounds educated. I haven't spoken to the woman."

It didn't strike any chord with the corporal. He had checked out three couples that morning and had radioed them all in before making the routine approach. A pair of screaming pansies, a mechanic and his wife and two spinster ladies. All a complete waste of time. He would have to fill out a stack of report forms when he got back to the station. But at least it showed he was working hard, which would all help to see that he had a sergeant's pension when he retired.

"Thanks for the drink," he said to the barman. "Keep your eyes open and call us if you think you've seen something."

Laborda made for the street, followed by the private.

"Why am I always lumbered with idiots like this one?" the corporal thought. "He hasn't asked an intelligent question all morning."

Laborda called in to the station to inform them that he was checking on his fourth flat of the morning, the one above the Cabo de Trafalgar.

Chapter Ten

Corporal Laborda paused to catch his breath outside Flat 3B.

"Getting too bloody old 'for this sort of thing. About time they found me a desk job."

As usual, his partner of the day kept silent.

Laborda leaned heavily on the door as he pressed the bell. He ˉheard the tinkling inside the flat and then footsteps approaching.

"Who is it?" asked a female voice.

"Police, señora."

The bolt was drawn back, but the security chain was not unhooked. The door opened a fraction and a woman peered at them through the gap.

"Nice," he thought. Green eyes, black hair, a firm mouth— very tasty. And then she moved her head slightly and he could see the puckered livid skin that covered the left hand side of her face. Christ! Fancy waking up and seeing that first thing in the morning—better his fat old missus.

The girl seemed to read his thoughts in his eyes, and automatically tossed her hair so that it fell into place.

"Nothing to worry about, señora," Laborda said to cover his embarrassment. "We're just making a routine check. Could we please come in and have a quick word with you?"

The woman slid off the chain and opened the door fully.

"Of course, officer. Sorry about keeping you waiting, but you can't be too careful. Only last Thursday, a neighbor opened the door and was mugged by young thugs."

"Quite right, señora. Wish more people were like you. There'd be less crime. It's Señora. . .?"

"Ortega."

She was wearing an apron over her prim blue dress. There was flour sticking to her hands. She had a trim little figure. Pity about the face.

She led them into the hall but did not invite them to go further.

"Just a minute, my husband's working. Miguel," she shouted, "there's two police officers here. Can you come and have a word with them?"

The corporal wanted to be invited in after climbing three flights of wooden stairs. He didn't see why he should conduct the interview in the hallway.

"Don't trouble yourself, sir," he called out. "I'll come to you."

He was already moving towards the lounge. The private stayed at the door.

The husband met him at the doorway. He was intellectual looking, and quite handsome too. Over his shoulder, Laborda could see a table piled with ledgers.

"She landed a good husband—considering," he thought.

Aloud, he said, "Sorry to bother you, señor. I can see you're busy, but it will only take a minute. We're just checking on new people in the area. Can I come in?"

He edged his bulky body past the young man and into the room, flopped down in an armchair and pulled out his notebook. He wished he could take his shoes off.

"Seems you're already in," the man laughed. "I could use a break from all these figures anyway. Now what seems to be the trouble?"

In the next five minutes, the corporal meticulously recorded in his notebook that the Ortegas had been in the rented apartment for about a month and that he was an accountant working up a private business from home. They were from Aragon, had been married for two years and were still childless.

"That just about does it," Laborda said, rising heavily to his feet.

It was just as he had expected, a couple like so many others in Madrid. But there would possibly be a check on their identity cards. He had made a careful note of the numbers.

The beer he'd drunk in the bar downstairs was making him feel uncomfortable.

"Do you mind if I use the toilet?"

"It's a bit of a mess," the woman said. "Just give me a second to tidy it."

She sped past him and made for the bathroom.

Idoia closed the door and put her mouth close to the false wall.

"One of the policia is coming in to have a piss. The other one's at the end of the corridor. They don't suspect a thing."

She scooped up some dirty towels and left the bathroom.

The Princess had again been bound and gagged. Guadaña was wedged between the bed and the wall.

He looked down at her. His gestures were obvious, one hand against his mouth, the other pointing the gun at her. She had only understood one word of the brief message that came through the false door. Policia! This could just be the end of the nightmare.

The corporal stood over the toilet, urinating and considering his immediate surroundings. He had plenty of time to take in the scene. His prostate wasn't what it used to be.

A nice big bathroom, more modern than the rest of the flat. Looked like it had just been done up. The paintwork was gleaming and the sink looked new. He broke wind.

The decorator hadn't quite got the paint mixture right on the far wall. A shame, it would only have taken a little extra effort. He wondered if the couple had done it themselves, as he did. The man looked as if he could be handy around the house and the wife was bossy enough—just like his old woman.

He shook the last few drops of liquid from his penis. As he was zipping up, he walked across the studied the emulsion.

"Doesn't look quite thick enough," he thought.

The Princess watched as Guadaña moved the gun slowly from her head and pointed it towards the door.

"He's going to shoot the policeman," she thought. 'I must warn him."

She was tied up and gagged. She couldn't move her hands or feet. She couldn't even scream. But could she make some other movement? She arched her back. Her legs and shoulders were lifted off the mattress. The pressure on her neck was intense. She hurled herself on to her side.

Corporal Laborda heard the sound of the sudden movement. It was faint, but clear. Where was it coming from? What the hell was it? He ran his knuckles on his right hand down the paintwork, and then from side to side. Part of it was solid and part was nothing but a thin partition. Bloody strange! And that was where the noise had come from.

He opened the bathroom door.

"Private, come here."

He took out his gun and started to hammer lightly on the wall with the butt end of the weapon.

The private reached the doorway. Suddenly, there was a sharp series of cracks which reverberated around the room. The wooden partition splintered. The corporal was lifted off the ground, a look of open-mouthed surprise on his face. Blood gushed from gaping wounds. His body slammed across the toilet seat with a thud.

Terrified, the private managed to pull out his weapon. There was a pounding of feet down the passageway behind him.

He fired wildly into the partition until he had no more bullets left.

The room was square, with a tiny barred window up near the ceiling. Dark brown paint covered the lower halves of the walls, sickly green had been daubed on the rest—it was all flaking.

The only furniture was a metal table and two chairs. Martínez sat on one chair, the terrorist driver on the other. Decker stood in the corner.

"We know all about you," Martínez said. "Your name, your record, everything."

The terrorist stared coldly across the table.

"Not surprising, is it? We set ourselves up. We were meant to be caught."

"We can pin the murders of Civil Guards on you if we want to," Martínez continued. "We could put you away for life, but not until after I've handed you over to the dead men's brother officers for you to give a. . . full statement."

The smile did not waver for an instant.

"I can stand a bit of pain for the Cause."

Decker marched across the room, put both hands on the table and looked the prisoner in the face.

"He's not just talking about a going over, you know," he said, indicating Martínez. "Wait until you've gone a week without sleep, a light shining in your eyes all the time. And then another week with a hood over your head—in complete darkness. I've seen better men than you lose their minds under those conditions."

The driver looked at Martínez.

"Who's your friend with the South American accent?"

Then he turned back to Decker.

"Listen, you foreign cunt. I won't have weeks of *anything*. By Saturday, me and my comrades will be out of this place, back in our own country."

They would get no further than the previous interrogators,

97

Decker realized. Every shred of information that could be extracted had already been taken: the whereabouts of the flat they had rented only a week earlier, the codenames they used and their real identities. Absolutely useless. But that was all they knew. They were ETA's cannon fodder. Dedicated, determined and fanatically brave, but each with knowledge of only his part of the operation.

They were on their way back to their office when the call came through. Martínez took it.

"Yes. . . yes. . . I understand."

"That was the colonel," he said. "Two National Policemen failed to radio in after a routine check. And they can't raise them now. Could be something."

"You're sure that's where they went?" Martínez asked the barman.

Ignacio shrugged.

"That's where they seemed to be going. I'm pretty certain they did."

This had something to do with the snatch, Decker had a gut feeling about it. And glancing at Martínez, he could see that the Inspector seemed to think so to.

"Third floor, you say?"

Ignacio nodded.

"Any back entrances?"

"No, just that front door."

"Right, now forget it all. It never happened. Understand? Just go back to serving your customers."

Ignacio nodded.

"He's got the message," Martínez said when they were outside. "Do we want a full-scale operation mounted on this?"

Decker shook his head.

"Policeman don't just vanish. There could have been shooting. If they've got the hostage in there, the fewer people who know about it, the better. How long will it take to have a back-up in plain clothes in position outside?"

"Five minutes at the most. There's a squad on permanent standby at headquarters."

"Get them in. Lowest profile possible."

"Then we go in," Martínez said. "Just you and me."

"Just you and me," Decker agreed.

They stood outside the door of 3B for five minutes. There was no sound from within. They had waited long enough. The two men stood clear of the door. Martínez rang the bell.

There was no answer.

"Who takes the door?" Decker asked.

Martínez looked at the broad English captain.

"You've got the weight for it."

Decker stood back while Martínez moved into a crouch in front of the door. Decker's right leg shot forward. The sole of his size ten shoe struck the lock. The door burst open and Decker pulled back. The Inspector swept his gun in an arc. across his line of vision, then both were inside, each flattened against a wall.

Only silence greeted them. With the captain covering him, Martínez charged through the half-open door into a bedroom. The bed was unmade. Decker passed him, bending low, and entered the living room at speed. It was then that the Inspector saw the legs sticking out of the bathroom doorway.

"Down here," he shouted.

Decker sprinted down the corridor and with barely a glance at the dead private, stepped over the body. It was the blood on the walls he saw first, thick blotches, where the corporal had landed—the thinner trails which followed his slide down the wall, ending when his body slumped over the toilet bowl.

"We're too fucking late."

The captain stepped through the bullet-riddled door into the cell.

"This is where they were keeping her."

He bent down and picked up a pair of low-heeled ladies shoes. His eyes swept the narrow cell. A strip of plaster lay

99

on the floor. Two lengths of rope had been flung into the corner. Then he saw the dark stain on the blanket. He put a finger in it. It was blood, almost congealed, but still somehow warm and sticky.

Apprehension gripped him like a hot ball in the pit of his stomach. He remembered the cold Autumn night in Belfast, the piles of cardboard boxes in an alley—soaked and crimson. He had failed again!

Martínez picked up the private's firearm and he flicked out the empty magazine.

"He managed to empty this before they got him from behind."

Decker tried to pinpoint the angle the bullets had entered the false wall. It was wild firing, there was even one hole in the ceiling, but what had the other five struck?

"Are you all right?" Martínez asked.

Decker had been cool in action, and Martínez was impressed by the professionalism of the Englishman. He had felt throughout that his back had been covered. But now the captain's face was pale, and there was a faraway look of pain in his eyes.

"I said, are you OK, James?"

The captain snapped back into the reality of the blood and confusion.

"Sure. I . . . We'd better start searching. The bastards went in a hurry. They must have left some clues."

Colonel Valdés stood in the lounge.

"That makes it four officers in less than twenty-four hours."

He made the remark to no one in particular. Around him, the police forensic unit were combing every inch of the apartment.

A young plainclothes inspector came into the lounge. He was holding a lilac sweater. Decker took it. It was very soft and light. There were bloodstains all around the neck. But there were no bullet holes.

The captain looked at the label. The sweater came from Kanga, a top boutique in Knightbridge's fashionable Beauchamp Place.

Chapter Eleven

It was very difficult at first. They could not talk to each other and all communication was by sign language. The Prince explained by gesture—which would have been funny but for his morbid expression—that they were to travel somewhere else by helicopter. And then he pointed downwards with his hand and showed his teeth, to indicate that she should smile when they landed.

The arrival at Heathrow Airport was low-key, with just a handful of freelance photographers hoping to get a picture of the Princess wearing something new. Even the most photographed woman in Britain, if not the world, wasn't big news *all* the time.

When they reached Kensington Palace, the Prince led her to the couple's private apartments. Once inside, he closed the door with a heavy sigh. Then, recovering his natural good manners, he mimed a drinking motion and Isabel, who was getting used to this method of communication by now, said, "Coca-Cola, *por favor*."

The Prince went to fetch it himself. Although the servants were very discreet, he dared not allow them to get close to her—just in case.

They sat in uncomfortable silence. At any other time,

Charles would have found some way to entertain her, but now, exhausted and sick with worry, he could not make the effort.

He wanted desperately to speak to his mother, to listen to her advice and words of comfort. But he could not leave this lady in a strange place. And he would talk to the Queen alone—at Buckingham Palace.

It was an hour before the Duke of Casla arrived. He had been flown to Brize Norton by the RAF and then on to London by car. He was taken straight to the Prince's suite.

"Thank God you've arrived," the Prince said, gladly relinquishing the responsibility of Isabel. He managed a reassuring smile at the girl, nodded his head and left the room hurriedly.

The Duke looked at Isabel—pale, worried and certainly disoriented, but also excited.

"It's all very strange, isn't it?" he asked.

"Yes."

Somehow she had never imagined that a palace would actually look like a palace—priceless paintings, antique furniture and Persian carpets.

"You'll get used to it," the Duke said, reassuringly.

"Used to it?"

She felt the panic rising. All this luxury was too much to absorb. She longed for her cozy little flat.

"How long will I be here?"

"Who knows?" the Duke asked himself. "Until the Princess is safely returned. Or until her body is found."

"Just a few days, Isabel. And you might have to make a public appearance or two."

"In England? I couldn't!"

The Duke reached over and placed an avuncular hand on her knee.

"You've done very well so far. I'm sure you can carry it off."

It was some time before the Prince reappeared.

103

"I've been to see my mother. She is very distressed—naturally—but she would like to see Isabel now, to thank her for all that she has done."

The Duke translated and Isabel rose to go and meet a second reigning monarch in eighteen hours. Surely this was all a dream—and her heart was thumping.

It was Decker's decision not to tell London that the Princess might be wounded or dead. There was no point—not until they had received the blood analysis.

The Princess's blood group was soon established. All it took was a call to the Zarzuela Palace, where the King himself, to avoid bringing anyone else into the secret, checked on the medical dossier that all visiting VIPs brought with them.

The evening sun reflected brilliantly off the white tiles in the Ministry lab. The white-coated police forensic analyst, seemingly oblivious to the three men waiting for results, went about his task of examining the blood samples in a methodical way.

Martínez looked from Valdés to Decker. The colonel was edgy and impatient, and the Inspector knew exactly how he felt. But it was more than that with Decker. Ever since he had seen the blood, the captain had been acting strangely. It was as if he had a personal, rather than professional, interest in the case. And since he had entered the lab, the lines of strain had become clearly visible on his face.

"Do you mind if we grab a cup of coffee, sir?" Martínez asked Valdés.

The colonel shook his head.

Martínez walked towards the door.

"Come on, James!"

Decker stood where he was a moment longer, then followed.

"We'll be in the office if you want us, sir," Martínez said over his shoulder.

The analyst was working with maddening slowness, picking

up each test tube, adding a reagent and examining the result under a bright light.

"There can't be any mistakes," Valdés said. "Take all the time you need—but for God's sake, hurry!" •

If the blood was the Princess', she could be dead or only wounded. But would they have taken away the body if she'd been killed? Valdés could imagine the impact of the corpse of a Princess suddenly appearing in the Plaza Mayor—Madrid's main square—a gruesome symbol of terrorism.

The technician picked up one of the tubes he had examined before, and looked at it again. Then he took a pen from his top pocket and made notes on the yellow pad next to the microscope. Only when he had done that, did he look up at the colonel.

"Those match up with the murdered officers." He pointed to two of the tubes. "The third, colonel, is the same group as that of the unnamed subject whose medical records you gave me."

Unnamed subject! The Princess! Christ!

The colonel ran up the stairs to his office, ignoring greetings, almost shouldering people out of the way. His subordinates followed his progress with amazement—they had never seen the normally unruffled colonel act like this. He flung open the door of his room and slammed it behind him. Decker, sitting near the window, rose to his feet, his face a mixture of expectancy and fear.

"It's the same blood group. . ." the colonel gasped.

Then the Princess was hurt or dead. Decker had only been in the city for a matter of hours. He tried to absolve himself of all blame—and failed.

". . . same blood group," the colonel continued, "but a different *sub* group. Here is sub-group C, the blood on the jersey is sub-group D. That's why it took so long—they had to do the tests twice."

Decker visibly relaxed, the tension draining from him. He sank down into his chair again. But it did not take him long to

105

compose himself. He was soon back on his feet, the crisp military officer.

"So it's one of the terrorists who caught your officer's bullet—or bullets. Now. . . hospitals, doctors. Get a message out to all medics in Madrid that they should ring us immediately and make the treatment last until we get there!"

"That's been done," Martínez said. "And I've sent men to all hospital and Red Cross emergency aid stations."

Decker nodded, again impressed by his new colleague.

"And we've also got men working on descriptions of the terrorists. The young man and the girl," Martínez continued.

"Don't ETA cells always have three members?" Decker asked.

"Sometimes more, but never less. On an operation like this, there's a back-up in contact with the cell, but I'm pretty certain there was only one more person in the safe house. ETA Command would want to keep everything to a minimum."

"They left in a hurry," Decker said, thinking aloud, "in broad daylight. One able to walk, we can assume, but wounded. Are all the roadblocks still up?"

"Yes," said the colonel. "The exit roads from the city are still being watched closely. They wouldn't attempt to leave."

"Other safe houses?"

"The Madrid Command had at least three."

It was just like Northern Ireland. By now, the terrorists would have a new base.

The phone rang. Valdés picked it up.

"Yes . . . I understand . . . you've checked everywhere and you're absolutely sure? I see."

He replaced the receiver and looked at the other two men grimly.

"The flat's been checked thoroughly. The place is clean. No worthwhile prints."

Guadaña was feeling faint from loss of blood and there were spasms of pain every time Idoia swabbed the bullet wound.

106

"Of all the fucking luck. A lousy corporal has to come tapping on the wall after taking a leak. Pure chance."

Idoia could see that the bullet had smashed no bone as it cut its way through muscle and flesh. There was both an entrance and an exit hole, in his right side. At least it was nowhere near his heart.

On the floor lay the heavily stained towels she used to stem the flow of blood. It must hurt like hell, but Guadaña had not cried out once, not even when she had applied the stinging alcohol to the gaping wound at the back.

"I'm no doctor and you need one to treat this."

"There will be no doctor. Nothing. Not until this operation is over."

Diana had never seen so much blood. First it had been the terrorist's, the one with the pale face. When he fell back heavily on her, she had felt the thick hot liquid as it soaked through her jumper. And then the others had come, the girl downstairs and the man—Xabier—who was with her now. They had pulled Pale-Face off her and then dragged her through the bathroom, past the policeman by the lavatory and over the other one in the doorway.

She shuddered, still remembering how her legs had touched the body. She had never seen violent death before.

They gave her no time to recover. Xabier went to collect the car, the girl roughly hauled the bloodstained sweater over her head and threw it aside, giving her another one to put over her blouse. Then the black wig was jammed back on to her head.

When Xabier returned, the girl spoke rapidly and intensely to him, almost barking her orders. Xabier turned to the Princess.

"We're going outside," he said. "If you scream or do anything to attract attention, she'll kill you."

She looked at the woman. The eyes were full of cold resolution and hatred. Diana was sure the warning was a real one.

They walked down the stairs slowly, Xabier linking his arm

107

with hers. Idoia was just one step behind, her light jacket covering the gun which at times jabbed into her back. Pale-Face had gone down before them and was waiting, stiff-backed, in the front passenger seat. It could not have been more than five minutes from the time the policemen died until they drove away.

"Keep your eyes tightly closed. Don't open them until I tell you to. Remember, I'm watching you."

Xabier knew that she was too shocked to do anything but obey.

"She's more terrified now than when I sat with her after the snatch," he thought.

In the driving seat, Idoia, who had only recently shot a policeman in the back, negotiated the mid-afternoon traffic with calm confidence.

It was eight in the evening. Outside, the road was filling as people drove home from work. The sun was setting, casting a pale red glow over the office wall.

Decker looked at the identikit pictures of the two terrorists.

"Could be anybody."

Martínez agreed. It was easier to recognize the photofit from the terrorist than vice versa.

Decker moved across to the computer terminal and printer that had been installed on his desk. He picked up a book lying by the keyboard, and flicked through it.

"DB2 database. Excellent!"

He switched on the monitor and began typing with quick, sure fingers.

"What are you doing?" Martínez asked.

"I want to check up on suspects, correlate their movements," Decker replied. "I'm accessing the data dictionary first, to see what information is stored—and how."

It seemed such a short time ago, Martínez reflected, that a question from him would have received a short, snotty response. Now, Decker seemed almost friendly.

Still, he didn't understand computers himself. He only used them reluctantly, and then through an operator. He turned his attention to the pile of thick plastic files with tangible documents in them. In the background, Decker's fingers clicked away at the keyboard.

After half an hour, Decker looked up.

"This is a massive database," he said. "The amount of information you've collected is incredible."

"It's unfortunately necessary," Martínez replied. "We only got our lead on Commando Madrid by checking on every single Basque student in the capital. What are you going to do with it?"

"I'm working on what you said earlier, about the cell needing back-up. ETA will have had to move extra people into Madrid. Maybe from the Basque land, maybe from operations elsewhere in the country."

"They could be using sleepers," Martínez pointed out. "People who've been lying low in Madrid for years."

"In that case," Decker said, "what I have in mind won't lead anywhere. But it's worth a try."

"What is?"

"On a job of this importance, ETA will try to cut down the risks as much as possible. That means they won't use anybody with a police record. But given that you've got all this material on anyone whose family background, left-wing affiliations or lifestyles—combined with other factors—might make them join ETA, the chances are that the people they're using will be somewhere in the database. All we have to do, is find them."

"How do you plan to do that?"

"I've narrowed down my criteria to all suspects with no official police record who've dropped out of sight in last two weeks. And I'm correlating that with reports of unusual activity in nationalist centers and areas where ETA is known to be active."

He pressed a button, and the printer whirred to life.

109

The printer finally fell silent and Decker tore off the last sheet and handed the wad of wide pages to Martínez.

"On average, ten ETA suspects go to ground every day," the Inspector said. "Either they know the heat's on, or they're off on some mission—usually information gathering. Most of them surface again very quickly, and the ones we pull in usually have cover stories that would stand up in any court."

He ran his eyes down the list. Some of the names rang bells, most didn't. Suddenly, he stiffened. Emilio García. His own request from Valencia to Police Headquarters, Burgos. It had found its way into Decker's web of cross-references because García was not a student, but a middle-aged farm produce salesman, still living in Burgos. The I.D. card number quoted was no longer current. He had been issued with a new one after it had been lost or stolen two years earlier.

The man posing as García could be just a common criminal, but taken in conjunction with the bombings, that didn't seem likely. A stolen I.D., especially one modified by a skilled forger—changing both photograph and age—as García's must have been, was a very expensive item. Chances were that he was the bomber—the beach boy. And he had disappeared just before the kidnapping!

"The University will have a photostat of that identity card," he told Decker. "I'm going to get a fax of it up here as soon as possible. The quality won't be much good, but police artists can sharpen it up."

They spent the next three hours cross-checking the print-out, eliminating those people whom ETA would be unlikely to use on a mission of this nature and importance. They were left with seven. Martínez phoned through a request to Valdés for an overnight sweep and search operation in the Basque country. There was nothing more they could do that evening. They might as well grab a few hours sleep.

The door was swung open and the light switched on. Decker, his instincts in control, was instantly awake. When he

110

saw Valdés standing in the doorway, his body relaxed—but his mind registered the fact that the colonel looked disturbed.

"What's the matter, colonel?" The sleep was still evident in Martínez voice.

"I've just been talking to the Minister," Valdés replied in he tone of a man determined to impose order onto his scattered, agitated thoughts. "He's had several newspapers and radio stations on him. ETA has claimed responsibility for the kidnapping. . ."

"How are the press treating it?" Decker interrupted.

"As a hoax—at the moment. They saw the Princess leave this afternoon. But they are surprised that the caller knew the current authenticated codeword."

"What were their demands?" Martínez asked.

They would be substantial. The Princess was a far bigger prize than the industrialists they had kidnapped in the past.

"The KAS Accords!"

Decker didn't know what that meant, but he saw the look of deep concern on Martínez's face.

"All of them?"

"Yes! The release of all ETA prisoners, the withdrawal of all security forces and the right of self-determination. Up there, that means independence. ETA would win that vote by fear tactics. And they want all their demands met by Friday—four days."

Four days. It was logical. The terrorists must be aware of the fact that the police were mounting a massive operation and were bound to find them in the end. Time was ETA's best weapon.

"And what if the demands are not met?" Decker said.

But he already knew the answer.

"If we have not agreed to everything they ask by midnight on Friday, they will execute the Princess." He looked Decker straight in the eye. "I must tell you, captain, that the government will never accept their terms."

So it was all up to them. Decker looked at his watch. They

111

had no more than ninety-six hours to find the Princess. If they failed, she would certainly die.

TUESDAY

Chapter Twelve

"So what exactly can you do? There must be some room for negotiation!"

The British Prime Minister's hand gripped the telephone tightly.

"Very little at this moment, I'm afraid."

Sr. Gonzalez, the Spanish Premier, was fully aware that in the political sense, he, his government and indeed, the country, owed a massive debt to London for its support over the difficult years. Now the British Prime Minister was calling in the loan. But how could he repay?

"Prime Minister, the military would never tolerate the division of Spain. Even the suggestion of independence for the Basque country would provoke a situation which would be difficult to control."

"I appreciate your difficulties," the Prime Minister said, "but is there *nothing* at all we can do? We do not negotiate with the IRA—*as such*—but we do have unofficial contact with them and often, as a result of these meetings, certain matters are cleared up. Must we, in this case, put our faith entirely in police action?"

The Premier at least had an answer for that one.

"Late last night, I spoke to one of our parliament's most

respected members, a man who has ETA's confidence. We've used him before, with positive results, He can be trusted. He is already at work on my behalf."

The Prime Minister thought carefully before speaking again. This had to be said both tactfully and obliquely.

"If there is any way that a compromise can be reached, if the British Government could, through your good offices, offer something which did not, in any way, endanger the integrity of the Spanish state, then we would be very willing to do so."

The Premier drew deeply on his Cuban cigar.

"Now what's that supposed to mean?" he asked himself.

London supporting the separatist cause at the UN? Giving its members political asylum, as France had done for so many years?

Blue smoke hung heavily over his desk.

"Señora, what would be your reaction if the IRA captured our Infanta and as a result Madrid came out in support of a united Ireland? I don't think the relations between our two countries would remain as friendly and solid as they are now." He paused. "This is such a difficult situation."

"I doubt very much whether we would ever have allowed her to be kidnapped in the first place," the PM thought, bristling. But then she remembered the assassination of Earl Mountbatten, the murder of the British Envoy to Dublin, the car bomb which killed Airey Neave—right in the House of Commons' carpark, the Christmas slaughter at Harrods . . . the list was endless.

"Mr. Premier," she said, "you might consider some concessions we could be prepared to make over the future sovereignty of Gibraltar. We will always respect the Gibaltarians' wishes, but it could be possible to sway a vote in the colony in favor of Spain—as long as there was a complete guarantee of autonomy. It would be difficult—but we are voted into office to deal with difficult situations, you and I."

The premier was jolted. The return of the Rock had been the dream of kings, dictators and democratic statesmen for nearly three centuries. Battles had been fought over it, it had often dictated Spanish foreign policy. The leader who saw its return would be guaranteed immortality.

He was at a loss for words, but the British Prime Minister was not.

"Before we can discuss that in more detail, however, there is the immediate problem to solve. I fully accept that you may well have to take actions which it would not be politically prudent to discuss with me. But I suggest that you take them soon. We must have the Princess back!"

The Prime Minister replaced the phone on its cradle as did the gray-haired man standing next to her who had been monitoring the call. He was in late middle-age. His tie proclaimed that he had served in the Guards and his pin-striped suit identified him as a civil servant. He was the mandarin of a twenty-story glass and concrete building in South London. He drew a handsome salary and lived in a large house in the green belt. His private life was similar, in all respects, to that of nearly every other high-ranking bureaucrat. But the nature of his work was different to theirs. He was the Director of MI 6.

"Your assessment?" the Prime Minister asked crisply.

"However much the Spanish might wish to get Gibraltar back, their scope for negotiation is limited. I do not think that there is anything that ETA has demanded which it would not be political suicide for them to grant."

"What about from our side?" the Prime Minister asked.

"I think I could put a package together that would have the desired effect."

The Director did not go into detail.

"How big a budget would you require?" the Prime Minister asked.

"I would think somewhere in the region of 22 million pounds."

It was a staggering sum, especially as it would have to be raised covertly. The Prime Minister's quick mind flicked through the possibilities. Yes, it could be done.

"I think that will be acceptable," she said. "But you know that on no account do we pay them off." She took his silence as sufficient confirmation. "Could you set the wheels in motion, please?"

Martínez compared the two pictures on his desk: one a fuzzy lift from the photocopy of García's ID card, the other a police artist's impression based on the photostat and his memory of the student.

"Not bad at all," he said.

The two identikit mock-ups of the suspects from Calle Hortaleza were less successful. They had been composed after hours of questioning Ignacio the barman and the other people who had seen the two terrorists. The descriptions had varied considerably and they had had no choice but to select features solely on the grounds that they matched the opinions of the majority of the witnesses.

All three pictures were being shown at roll calls at precincts in the capital and had been sent out to police departments all over the country.

Decker was sitting opposite, in his underwear, sipping coffee and shaving with a portable electric razor. The Inspector pushed over a sheaf of reports that had come in overnight pouch from the Basque country.

"They've detained five of the seven suspects the computer turned up last night. They all have alibis and anyway, their being close to home rules out any connection with the kidnapping."

"So that leaves two, including your friend from Valencia," Decker said. "And any number of others not in the database."

Decker stood up, then hit the ground so rapidly that Martínez thought for a second that he had collapsed. But, as his arms thrust upwards and his muscled body arched, the Inspector realized that it was merely the start of his daily exercise.

"Very impressive," Martínez said, after he had counted the

twenty-fifth push-up.

During the night, Martínez had woken to find Decker turning in his bed and mumbling. He still hadn't settled down when the Inspector had finally fallen asleep again. But he seemed fine this morning. Martínez thought they were beginning to develop an understanding.

"You'll need some clothes," he said. "Give me your neck size and I'll have some shirts and underwear sent in."

Decker was lying on his back, kicking his legs in the air.

"Size sixteen shirts, short-sleeved if possible."

"Colors?"

"Irrelevant. Nothing garish."

"I'll tell Conchita, the colonel's secretary, as soon as she arrives. You'll like her—she's very pretty."

The comment was teasing—suggestive. Decker stopped kicking and sat upright.

"Let's not forget what we're here for, Inspector."

Martínez did not respond.

"Where are the showers?" Decker asked.

"Down the corridor, second on the right. When you've finished, we'll get some breakfast in the canteen."

Martínez watched as Decker disappeared through the door. On the surface, the captain's outburst had been unwarranted, but Martínez suspected that he had inadvertently touched a nerve. He was angry with himself for having intruded on a colleague's private life.

The Princess was haunted by the dreadful belief that it was she who had caused the deaths of the two policemen.

Had they heard her sudden, deliberate movement on the bed? Was it that which made them first tap the wall and then start hammering? Pale-Face had already switched his gun from her head to the hidden door, but would he have fired?

A little light filtered in through the small grimy window set into the roof. The bed, on which she had spent a fitful night, was old, with a brass bedstead, but more spacious and

119

comfortable than the cot in her previous prison. The only other article of furniture was the overstuffed armchair, floral-patterned but stained with grease. She sat in it, and looked round her.

A faded red carpet partly covered the wooden floor which had not seen polish for years. A battered tin trunk of the type that travelers used to take to far-flung corners of the Empire, was nearby. The roof was sharply angled so that in much of the room, she could not stand upright. Cobwebs trailed down from the center beam and the whole place had a musty smell.

As she looked blankly across her new cell, the tears came, uncontrollably. She buried her head in her hands and her body shuddered as she wept.

Xabier could not explain his reaction to the scene he encountered when he unbolted the door. He put down the tray of food on the bed and laid a hand on the Princess's heaving shoulder.

She looked up at him, her eyes red-rimmed and deep with pain.

"It was horrible—what happened yesterday," she said.

"I know."

Up until that moment he had been hiding his feelings of revulsion, even from himself. But now the blood, the twisted limbs, the stink of death, all came back to him.

For Xabier, his part in the Basque struggle, his war, had been fought from the small study in his house in Bilbao, whose window overlooked the golf course, grass, trees and birds.

He had seen the photographs of dead policemen, lying slumped on cafe floors; of ETA comrades caught in Civil Guard crossfire. But to him the violence had seemed far away, not relevant to his contribution to the cause.

But now he had been there when four men were killed—an overweight, middle-aged corporal—polite, doing his job; his rather gormless assistant; the two traffic policemen trying to clear the road. All dead! *And he had seen them die.* Now there was this young woman, a hostage not because of what she'd done—but because of who she was.

120

Then he was overwhelmed with other feelings—shame, and a sense of his own unworthiness.

"It was necessary," he said, as much to himself as to the Princess. "In any war there must be casualties."

"Did *I* kill them? Was it *my* fault?"

Diana felt his fingers squeeze her shoulder.

"No," said Xabier, "You didn't kill them. It's best to try and forget it."

He wished to God that *he* could.

"Let's talk about something else."

But what did one talk about to a Princess? Their worlds were so different. He looked with concern at her puffed-up and pleading face.

"Have you ever been to the Basque country?"

She shook her head and tried to hold back a sob.

Xabier sat down on the bed.

"I once read an article in a British magazine about my country. It said that the history of our people was buried in the mists that shroud the valleys before the sun comes up. You know, that's very true. We have our own language, our own sports, our own traditions—and no social anthropologist has yet been able to give a total explanation of their origins."

He realized that he was lecturing her, and now was not the right time.

"It's a beautiful place too," he said. "High blue mountains and deep valleys. There are pine trees and little meadows, mountain streams and a rugged, breathtaking coastline. You should listen to a Basque choir in a little church in remote village, almost untouched by time. I have, and it touches the soul. I'd like to..." He stopped abruptly. "I'll leave you in peace to eat your food," he said, heading for the door.

She looked up.

"No, please tell me more. Stay and talk."

"What I was going to say was that, one day, when this is all over, I hope you and your husband can see it for yourselves. I have to go now. They want me downstairs."

121

As Idoia stood in the kitchen, unpacking the shopping, she heard Xabier walking heavily down the three flights of stairs from the attic.

"How is Guadaña?" he asked as he entered the room.

"He didn't sleep much last night. He's in a lot of pain. This morning he coughed up some blood." She turned on the tap and held a bunch of carrots under the jet of water. "And how's Her Ladyship today?"

"Very scared. She's been through a lot. I've been trying to calm her down."

"Good for you," Idoia turned her back on him. "It's nice to see you taking so much interest in your work."

There was something new in he voice. Not the professional tone, not the hatred of those more privileged than herself. He couldn't pin it down, but he didn't like it.

"We can't afford to act like this, Idoia," he said, "especially now that Guadaña's out of action. One of us will have to go to the bullring tomorrow instead of him."

"I'll go," Idoia said.

"I think it had better be me."

She glared at him, eyes blazing with anger.

"I'm less noticeable," he said, adding hurriedly, "a man fits more easily into a bullfight crowd."

But it was too late. Idoia was running her fingers, in an unconscious gestured, over her scarred face.

"It's not up to us," Idoia said. "Guadaña is still in command here. And he's *not* out of action," she snapped. "Go into the living room and see for yourself!"

Guadaña was sitting in the corner of a large leather sofa. The arm rest supported his injured right side. He was bare-chested. Long plaster strips held the cotton wool and bandages in place. The dressing was new, but already, blood had seeped through to stain the white pillow that she had placed behind him. He had taken two pain-killers, but they had had little effect.

He winced as he turned his head to look at the two other

122

terrorists.

"You need a doctor," Xabier said.

"No doctor. I can hold out until the end of the operation."

The blood that he had retched up that morning told him that the bullet had done more than just damage flesh and bone. He wondered if the others realized it too.

"It's worse than it was yesterday." Xabier said. "It's not going to get better by itself."

"We claimed responsibility for the kidnapping last night," Guadaña said, changing the subject.

Xabier did not ask how he knew. He was the leader. He would have been told much more than they had been.

"Yes, we claimed responsibility and we listed our demands. We phoned all the major papers and radio stations. And the bastards have said nothing. They're still talking about us as if we were ordinary bombers."

There was a touch of pride in his last few words.

"They can't hope to keep it quiet for much longer," Xabier said.

He could see why they were doing it. As long as it was kept secret, there would be less pressure on both governments. But after the bull fight, no one would be able to ignore their message.

"Since the demands have now been made," Xabier said, "might *we* be allowed to know them?"

"Of course. The KAS Accords."

Xabier was astounded. He had never thought it would be that. Release of political prisoners, a timetable for the discussion of a negotiated settlement—yes. But independence?

Was it possible that the government would give in? He thought of the woman upstairs. He hoped it was.

"What sort of state is Isabel in this morning?" the Prince asked.

"Better than yours, my friend," the Duke of Casla thought.

The Prince's eyes were hollow from lack of sleep but the

123

fight was still in them.

"She was in surprisingly high spirits when I left her half an hour ago," the Duke said.

But it had been difficult to keep up the model's morale. He dared not trust anyone, and so she had been a virtual prisoner, confined to her quarters, seeing no one but the Duke and a foreign prince who could not even talk to her without an interpreter.

"My mother has agreed with the Prime Minister that we are to make a public appearance today. Details are still being worked out."

"Where?"

"An old people's home. It will be an impromptu visit. The press will be informed just before it happens."

"But that's not like the airport! She'll be close to people. They'll speak to her. She won't understand what they say! She won't be able to answer them!"

"The security people have told us that the longer we can keep this a secret, the better chance there is for my wife," the Prince said heavily. "The Prime Minister has made it plain that it is in the national interest that we keep up the deception as long as possible. Last night, ETA announced the kidnapping to the Spanish press. They are still treating it as a hoax, but if Isabel is to retain her credibility, she must be seen at close quarters."

"How are you going to stop people talking to her?" the Duke persisted.

The Prince covered his face with his hands.

"I don't know," he mumbled through his fingers. "I just don't know."

Chapter Thirteen

Big Atlantic waves crashed against the rocks, throwing up spray, and pounding against the sands along the wide Bay of Gascogne. The early afternoon sun turned the white-capped rollers a deep blue-green.

The sight of the French Basque coast usually delighted Augustin Echeveste, but today he had other things on his mind.

He had been adamant, when the Premier called him at his home in Vitoria, that if there was any hint of his being followed, he would turn around and return to Spain. The Premier had given his word.

Even so, he had made the calls setting up the meeting from a public telephone booth. Despite many protests at the highest levels of government, his private and office lines were continually tapped.

Some 30 kilometers after skirting Biarritz, the signpost to Capbreton appeared. The pine forests that stretch almost as far as Bordeaux shaded the sun from him as he drove to the quiet resort.

A gendarme cycled past the yacht marina at the mouth of the River Boudigau. Facing the scores of small sailing boats and cruisers moored to pontoons, were cafes, hotels, holiday apartments and villas. Capbreton was a peaceful resort, untouched by factional violence and major crime.

The *Cristina* was berthed discreetly in the center of the third pontoon jutting out into the river, almost concealed by the masts and hulls of other leisure craft.

He only knew one of the three men who were waiting for him in the cramped cabin...Iñaki Irribar, iron-gray hair, lined face, body, even when sitting, slightly lopsided because of his limp—an injury inflicted by the Guardia Civil.

The two had known each other since their late teens. They had been founder members of ETA, then a group of young militants who considered that the traditional Basque Nationalist Party was too complaint to the Franco dictatorship. They were idealists and it was only in response to the brutality that was meted out to them that they carried out their first assassination—shooting down the police chief of Irun.

Echeveste had slowly come to realize that negotiation was the only way. He quit the movement to form a far-left democratic party. Iñaki had not, and as their political paths separated, respect disappeared—and now only trust remained.

The other men were younger, in their early thirties. One was obviously a bodyguard, the other an aide. Not even their aliases were given as they shook hands.

Irribar was the first to speak after an uneasy silence.

"Well, we're here. I understand that you are now an envoy for the central government. Say what you've been instructed to say."

Echeveste had expected the animosity.

"No, Iñaki, I've not come to represent Spain. I've never been a lackey of Madrid. I'm here to speak for *our* people, to save the Basque country from irreparable damage. To make a plea for peace. What you have done will set back the cause of freedom twenty years. All our negotiations, all the compromises we have managed to squeeze out of Madrid, will be swept aside."

"What compromises? What progress?" snapped the aide. Irribar glared at him and the man lapsed into silence.

"We will become an occupied territory, with half the Spanish Army quartered in our homeland," Echeveste continued.

"If the Spaniards agree to our legitimate demands," Irribar said, "there will be no problem. the woman will go free, I promise you."

"After all these years," Echeveste thought, "Iñaki is still playing games."

"You know they will not give way," he said. "Why pretend?"

Irribar smiled.

"Then they must take the consequences."

"No! *We* must take the consequences!"

It was what he wanted, Echeveste realized. The born revolutionary. For him, change could only come through violence. As long as Madrid was making compromises and moving towards gradual reform—more autonomy—ETA's support was waning. In the last elections, their political wing had got no more than fifteen percent of the vote. But move in the army in force, and they would have the whole of the Basque people behind them.

"You've lost your path," Irribar said. "We haven't. There is only one way to force Madrid to yield the right of self-determination and we have taken it."

He stood up to signify the brief meeting was over.

"Go back and tell the Spanish government there will be no negotiations. Our demands must be met by Friday midnight or we will exercise People's Justice upon the woman."

It was hopeless, Echeveste realized. The terrorist had been involved in the war for so long that now it was the struggle itself, not the result, that mattered to him. Waging armed conflict justified his existence, made him come to life. Echeveste suspected that if Madrid had, against all probability, agreed to the demands, Irribar would have been disappointed.

"Be it on your head. If sanity returns, you know how to contact me."

Echeveste strode down the pontoon, onto firm land.

"Such a beautiful day, but there is madness in the air."

"Tell me more about the Basque country," the Princess said.

Xabier was surprised and pleased. The hostage had recovered her composure. The puffiness had gone from her face. She had no make-up on, but she didn't need it. Her complexion was pale, the delicate smooth shading of an English rose, he thought.

"Are you really interested?"

"Yes, Xabier. You have kidnapped me because of your feelings about your homeland. If I have to stay here, I want to know why. I want to know everything."

Diana was fighting back again, in the only way she could—through the young man. Their relationship was undergoing subtle changes. She was grateful for his kindness when she was full of grief and remorse. But she also realized that she had touched him in a way that she could never have done with a calculated, cleverly worked out approach. Now she had a little power over him, and she intended to use it. It was her only hope of ever seeing her husband and children again.

The fact that the kidnappers had never worn masks told her that they had no fear of her identifying them—and that could only mean one thing!

She would not give in! The dreadful deaths of those two policemen proved that everyone was looking for her.

How could she help them find her? There had to be a way.

"If your land is green and lovely—and peaceful—why is there all this violence?"

Xabier sat down on the bed again, and faced the Princess.

"Ireland is pretty, isn't it? But there is violence there too. It's just the same thing—the people struggling to be free, to throw off their capitalist oppressors."

The conversation was moving in the wrong direction. As long as he had political slogans to hide behind, he was protected.

"What about you? You haven't told me anything about

yourself, not even if you're married. After all, you know everything about me."

What harm was there in telling her a little? They were going to need her cooperation in a short while.

"I've been luckier than most—a comfortable home, enough money available to give me a good education. I'm not married, but I have, as we say a *novia*—a fiancee."

"Is she pretty?"

"I think so. She's not fair, like you, she has lovely black hair, and her eyes are brown, not blue. I haven't seen her for quite a time."

Xabier was far away.

"What do you do...when you're together?"

He laughed.

"We certainly discuss politics but not too seriously. We like walking in the mountains. Sometimes we go with friends for a drink, or to a disco."

"It sounds wonderful. I'd like to do that sort of thing too. I love music, but it's very difficult for me to just go to disco without being recognized and bothered. At least, that's what my husband says." She laughed sadly. "I suppose I'm always a bit of a prisoner really."

She stopped talking, leaving an embarrassing gap for him to fill. She had given him the lead on music—she hoped he picked it up.

"Have you ever heard the sound of a flute?" he asked. "Of course you have. To the Basques, it is as important as the guitar is to the Spanish."

"I don't really..."

"Don't get me wrong," he said, eager not to give a false impression, "it's not all folklore and tradition. Our discothéques are some of the best in Europe. But I'm not one for hard rock, and neither is she. We love ballads, soft music—like the flute."

"Really! We have that in common at least." She looked him in the eyes. "I think we're both rather sentimental, don't you?"

129

He was melting to her. She had found a chink in his political armor—his romantic nature. She pressed home her advantage.

"One of my favorite records is called *The Power of Love*." She started to hum.

"Do you know it? It's by Jennifer Rush."

His answer came as he started to quietly sing the opening bars in Spanish. He became aware of Idoia standing in the doorway, and stopped singing immediately.

She made no comment, but he could see that she was furious. In her hands she held the Polaroid camera and the newspaper.

"Time for the photograph, Idoia?" he asked.

He had meant it to sound friendly, but it sounded ingratiating, like an apology. Yet he had only been doing his job.

"Tell the woman to hold the newspaper in front of her, so that we can clearly see the front page," Idoia said.

"I know what to tell her."

He translated for the Princess.

"Why do you want me to hold the paper?" she asked.

He didn't know how to answer her. She looked at the date.

"It's today's edition. It's to show I'm still alive, isn't it? To show that you haven't killed me yet?"

"Yes, you're right," he said quietly. "But we're not going to kill you—it's just that they might think we have."

The process took several minutes. After each flash, Idoia waited until the color photograph emerged. Each time she studied the result, then blew on the print to speed the drying.

"That'll do," she said.

She snatched the newspaper from the Princess and left.

"I don't think she liked you singing. I don't think she sings very much."

They both laughed. It was the first time that they had shared a joke.

"Xabier, do you think I could listen to some music? It really would help me so much."

The terrorist said nothing. He turned and left the room. She

130

heard the key turning in the lock and the bolt being rammed home. The sound of his footsteps receded down the stairs and she was alone again.

Xabier had said earlier that he didn't think music would be allowed. If he brought her some now, he would be breaking one of the rules. And the first time you did something was always the hardest. If he took that step, maybe he could be persuaded to do something else.

He was a nice man—a nice boy, really.

She was exploiting him—but she was fighting for her life.

The Mayor, warden, matron and one of the more sprightly patients—holding roses—waited on the lawn and looked up, as the helicopter banked over Exeter Cathedral. The rest of the old folk, and most of the nursing staff stood or sat, some in wheelchairs, on the terracing in front of the big house. What a rush it had all been: they had only been told about the visit an hour earlier. They had known that the new extension was due to be opened—but not that day, and certainly not by the Prince and Princess!

The helicopter settled gracefully beside the flowerbeds. Clapping and cheers greeted the royal couple, as smilingly, they stepped from the machine.

The handful of local reporters confined to a roped off area, scribbled down details of the Princess's new dress—a flared blue and white creation.But she had on the same hat that she'd worn for her departure from Spain. They hoped she would come nearer so that they could perhaps hear what she was saying. They were keeping her so far away.

The pensioner stepped forward, curtsied and with slightly trembling hands, offered her the roses.

"These are for you, my love, and God bless you and the Prince."

Isabel accepted the flowers and smiled.

"Thank you," she said. Her voice sounded a little strange. She pointed to her throat and said the only other English word in her vocabulary, one she had been practicing all morning. "Laryngitis."

The Mayor and the other dignitaries were introduced, then the royal couple were lead on to the terrace. The Prince chatted with old people, shaking their hands and leaning close to hear what they had to say. He was a past master at this sort of thing. The Princess just smiled and looked beautiful. She was constantly flanked by Lady Margaret and the Duke of Casla.

After a brief welcoming speech by the Mayor—he'd been told to keep it short—the Prince went to the microphone.

"As you know, this visit comes at short notice. But in these days of modern travel, decisions can be made quickly and it is with great pleasure that my wife and I are here in Exeter, a city which has done so much to help the aged..."

As the royal party moved into the extension building, one of the old ladies watching them turned to her companion.

"Don't say much, do she?"

"Milly said she's got larry...larry...a sore throat."

"Has she? Poor little love. And she still came to see us. Isn't she wonderful!"

Already the Press Association stringer was in a booth in the street outside, telephoning in his copy.

"Princess Di shook off the effects of a sore throat and delighted three hundred old folk with a surprise visit to their residential center in Exeter today..."

The pretty nurse was confused.

"Milk or sugar, Your Highness?" she had asked.

"Thank you," smiled Isabel.

"Sorry. Did you want milk—or sugar? Or both?"

"Thank you."

The Prince appeared from nowhere.

"I say, that looks most welcoming. Yes, I'll have a cup. Thank you. So refreshing. Tell me nurse, do you enjoy working here? What exactly do you do?"

132

"Yes, I'll... it's very... I work mainly with those confined to their beds..."

The Prince devoted *a whole five minutes* to her. She basked in the glory, even more so when she saw the matron's encouraging smile. His Highness had really been *interested* in her work.

She forgot all about the misunderstanding over the tea. Nor did she notice that the second the Prince began talking to her, the Duke and Lady Margaret moved in and steered the Princess away.

Half an hour later, the visit was over and the helicopter was taking the royal couple back to London.

Princesa por un dia! Isabel smiled as she remembered the television program that had captured a huge Spanish audience several years earlier—a program in which an ordinary working girl was granted every wish she had ever dreamed of. For a day, she became a princess.

For her it had come true. And she was beginning not only to be relaxed in the role but to enjoy the sheer luxury of it all. The nerves, so shattered when she had been summoned to the palace in Madrid, were still there at the old folks' home. But the almost continuous attention given her by the Duke of Casla and the kind Lady Margaret who, as she had said with a smile, was her lady-in-waiting, had given her confidence.

Now she was back in a guest room in the large apartment where the Prince and Princess lived in Kensington Palace. The place was nearly empty of staff. The Duke had told her that they, or most of them, had been sent off to the royal couple's country house in the Cotswolds on the pretext of preparing a big weekend party.

She hadn't seen the children. They must have gone too. It was just as well—she might have fooled the old folks, but she would have had no chance with the Princess's kids. She wondered about what sort of children they were and how it must all be so different for them being raised amid so much

133

luxury—and so little privacy.

The Duke was sitting with her on a large sofa. He poured them both a coffee and asked if she wanted cream or milk.

"Cream, please."

Luxury all the way!

"You love the world of fashion, don't you?" he said.

The girl nodded, puzzled, not knowing quite where the question was leading.

"When you return to Madrid, I think you'll find that the way will be cleared for you to have a prominent role in promoting Spanish styles throughout the world. And I think you'll be back in London again quite soon."

He poured the cream over the spoon and let it flow into the coffee.

"There will be other rewards too. One of them will be a new apartment—a very large one. But Isabel, we do ask one major thing—and that is your complete silence about the events that you have played a part in over the last few days and..."

Isabel cut him short.

"I don't know what all this is about, but it must be very important. Whatever it is, I pray that it all works out. A happy ending will be reward enough for me."

From the look in the Duke's eyes, she knew that he now trusted her completely. She felt a warmth sweep over her and relaxed into the cushions.

When Arenas read about the previous day's shoot-out, he phoned in the number of the small hostel where he was staying to his contact in Bilbao. Then, he waited in his dingy airless room for new orders. When none came, he knew that the operation was still on schedule.

He stubbed his Ducados cigarette resentfully into the small tin ashtray by the side of the bed. He had come to Madrid with high hopes of an important role in this operation, but it had not worked out.

"I don't know a bloody thing about it," he said to himself.

134

"All I am is a courier—a messenger boy."

He was hot, sticky and hungry. He looked at his watch. If he went out now, he could have lunch, preferably in an air-conditioned restaurant.

He played it safe, mixing with the afternoon pedestrian traffic, heading for the busy Opera underground station. He changed trains several times, and selected his exit point at the last minute.

He didn't know Madrid. He had no idea where he was, but that didn't matter. It had been even hotter in the metro than it was on the street and he wanted a beer. He looked to the right and saw Don Sancho's Restaurant. That would do fine.

If he had continued to walk down the street, he would have come across the red-bricked complex surrounded by a high wall and guarded by white-helmeted military police. It was one of the capital's most important army command posts.

The two detectives assigned to watch the area around the military complex in the wake of the ETA killings were not sure that the man entering Don Sancho's was the one they'd seen in the mock-up photo at rollcall that morning. But their radio message was put through to Martínez even before the suspect had had time to order lunch.

"Sit tight. Make no move to unsettle him. We'll be there in a few minutes."

"Something at last?" Decker asked.

Frustration had gripped both men all morning.

"Certainly worth checking out. A possible sighting."

While Martínez drove, Decker studied the photofit, committing every line to memory.

"I don't know if he'd recognize me," Martínez said as they pulled up at a red light, "but it's not worth the risk. You go in. If you think it's him, stay there. If you're not out in five minutes, I'll call in a surveillance team. We'll put a box around him."

The captain sat down at a table just vacated by two

135

overweight businessmen and waited for the dirty coffee cups and wine glasses to be replaced. It was a small restaurant, and although the suspect was at the other end of the room, he had a clear view of him. He couldn't be sure—but he was! His instinct told him that this was Martínez's Beach Boy. It was the suspect. He had to be connected with the kidnapping. ETA wouldn't be running a second operation in Madrid at this time.

Emilio García, real name unknown, working alias unknown, mission unknown, was ladling into his onion soup with gusto. Decker would be there for a good hour. He picked up the menu. If he was to stay there, he would have to eat—but he didn't feel like food.

Chapter Fourteen

It had been the brainchild of a young Australian—a small army of photographers spread out all over the United States, taking pictures in one twenty-four hour period. Every camera enthusiast in the country was urged to join in, with prizes offered and the chance of seeing their work next to that of famous photographers. The result was a thick, glossy, expensive coffee table book called *A Day in the Life of America*. It's success was phenomenal. So the idea was tried in several other countries, also with excellent results.

Which was why, on this particular Tuesday, there were internationally known and amateur photographers in every corner of Spain, recording the doings of the rich and poor, rural and urban, which made up twenty-four hours in a nation's life.

Richard Bond had been in the massive El Corte Ingles' store near the New Ministries since it opened at ten o'clock. He had taken shots of an elegantly dressed housewife buying clothes; a young couple in the furniture department planning their new home; a blonde-haired woman—obviously foreign—accompanied by a little old lady (perhaps her Spanish mother-in-law) dressed in black; two children enthusiastically arguing over the merits of different model cars. All these—and many more. He had used dozen rolls of film already, but was fully aware, as he pressed the button yet again, that only one—at best, two—of the hundreds of pictures would be included in the book.

He looked at his watch. School would be out soon, and the teenage buyers would be swarming into the basement area, eager to send their money on computer games and videos. He made his way downstairs.

Arenas paid for his meal and folded the bill neatly away in his wallet, knowing that he would eventually have to submit chits justifying what he had spent, right up to the last peseta. Just as if he was a businessman on the fiddle. He left an acceptable tip—standard procedure to avoid being noticed—and left.

The bright light outside hurt his eyes, and the heat beating off the buildings soon had him perspiring. He walked back towards the metro station. The four agents, one in a suit, another in overalls, the others dressed casually, formed a box. All had minute radio transmitters wired inside their clothes. All carried the standard .38s.

Arenas got off the subway car at Avenida de America, waited until the doors were closing, then stepped back on. It did not faze the agents. Two of them had stayed on the train, the others were already moving towards the two possible exits and didn't even break their step. Arenas switched trains twice more, but by the time he emerged at Opera, he still had two shadows with him. Totally unaware of their existence, he returned to his hostel.

Once in his room, he looked around at the cheap wallpaper, the heavy wooden wardrobe, the iron bed. What a crummy joint! He had an expensive new briefcase and suit. Wherever they were sending him after the bullfight, he would be staying in a place considerably better than this.

Outside, the detectives took up position and radioed their location in. The box-type surveillance re-formed—two agents fifty paces down, one on each side of the street, two others fifty paces up, facing the door but ready to turn smartly and walk away if the suspect chose to head in their direction.

The suspect's hideout was probably just what it appeared to be, they thought—an ordinary hostel. They would have to wait patiently for him to lead them somewhere more significant.

"He's back at his hostel," Martínez said, putting down the phone. "And he's been employing standard evasion techniques."

"Then that means he's definitely on a mission. Any chance he spotted your men?" Decker asked.

The Inspector shook his head.

"Shall we increase the vigilance?" the colonel asked.

Martínez and Decker considered it. It was vital that they didn't lose the Beach Boy. But the more men they moved into the area, the greater the chance of one of them being spotted. And once the suspect knew they were on to him, he would either do nothing or lead them on a false trail.

So what was the bigger risk?

"No. Let's keep the low profile," Martínez said finally. "He won't get away. We've got him sewn up tighter than a duck's arse."

The colonel sniffed.

Decker grinned, but hoped and prayed that his partner was right.

Xabier left the safe house and walked along the Calle Nuncio. He liked the street very much, with its old three-storied terraced houses, many now turned into individual apartments. There weren't many pedestrian streets left in the bustling capital. Probably the only things that had saved this one were that it was too narrow, and was blocked at one end by the Army Bishop's Palace.

He walked for fifteen minutes before taking a taxi to a busy hotel in the center of the city. Once there, he went to a pay-phone and called one of Madrid's many motorbike express delivery services.

He waited outside the hotel. The motorbike pulled up and Xabier handed the youth the white envelope marked "Urgent and Confidential," addressed to the editor of El Mundo, Spain's most important paper.

The young man had not even look up. He logged the delivery, pocketed the cash and was away. Xabier would bet money that he never saw faces—just hands.

He had been meaning to return immediately to the safe house as instructed, but as he crossed the broad, tree-lined Avenida Castellana and saw El Corte Ingles, he had an idea.

"Why not?" he asked himself. "The store's big enough—there's no risk. And a little music will help to keep her calm."

The Etarra stepped into the crowded ground floor and rode the escalator down to the music department. He knew what tapes he was going to buy.

The editor's secretary slit open the envelope, but did not extract the contents. Instead, she took it straight through to her boss.

"Another 'Private and Confidential.'"

Carlos Rodriguez wasted a lot of time reading letters marked confidential. Any number of cranks wrote in with all sorts of libelous nonsense. Some threatened; some asked for advice, even about their sex lives. Many complained about government, neighbors, anything and everything. But there was the occasional nugget, sent to him, rather than any other editor, because he dealt personally with such mail.

He took out the photographs and looked at them. His expression did not change.

He turned to his secretary.

"Could you give me a few minutes alone, Dolores? I just want to make a phone call."

As she went to close the door, the editor stopped her.

"Dolores, did you look at the contents of the envelope?"

"You know I never look at anything marked confidential," she answered, slightly hurt.

She had been with him since he became editor and he trusted her implicitly. But it was as well that she hadn't seen the photographs.

He dialed a number he knew well, the Interior Minister's private line.

"Miguel? About the missing Princess hoax. I have some photographs which look very much like her."

Guadaña was muttering in an uneasy sleep and Xabier could see that his condition was getting worse—but even so, the automatic was still tightly clenched in the sick man's hand.

"Did it go all right?" Idoia demanded as soon as he came in.

"Yes," he said, his fingers brushing against the cassettes in his pocket. He didn't mention them to her. She would only accuse him of having gone soft on the Princess.

"Have you checked on the prisoner?" he asked.

She shook her head.

"I've been too busy with *him*," she pointed at Guadaña. "That wound's getting worse. He really needs attention."

"What about a doctor?"

"How do we get one, for God's sake? And where from?"

"We can't manage this with just two," he thought. "We've got to keep Guadaña active."

"I'll think about it," he said, as he went up the stairs to the attic.

Xabier had done it! He had broken the rules and brought her the tapes. A battle won—the Princess felt triumphant. Yet at the same time she was deeply grateful to the young terrorist for his kindness and consideration.

"Thank you, Xabier."

He was embarrassed. The look on the Princess' face had given him unexpected pleasure.

"Any prisoner-of-war is entitled to a few home comforts."

141

"And you remembered the Jennifer Rush record."

"You said it was your favorite. And I thought you might like to listen to the Basque music. You won't understand the words, but it should give you a feeling of my homeland."

He asked himself why he was saying all this to her. Why did it matter that she should understand? Wasn't it enough that she was, however involuntarily, furthering the Cause?

"A feeling of your homeland," Diana said. "Misty valleys and high mountains. I'd love to listen to it."

She put the cassettes and Walkman down on her lap, looked up at the filthy ceiling and the small skylight, and sighed deeply.

"When do you think this will all be over?"

Xabier saw little point in making her depressed.

"I think that something definite will be happening quite soon. The newspapers have your photographs by now. They will force the government to take action."

He wished he could offer more assurance. The lines of their well-defined relationship, jailer and prisoner, were becoming blurred.

"Won't you listen to your music and try to relax?" he suggested.

She had not answered by the time he left the room.

As he walked down the stairs, an idea formed of how to get Guadaña the medical aid he needed. He was thinking like a freedom fighter again.

The Minister and the editor faced each other across the former's plush office. It was Santana who moved, hand outstretched, to greet his old school friend.

"Good to see your, Carlos."

"It's always a pleasure, Minister."

So that was how he was going to play it—formal, rigid.

The Minister did not know how to begin. He didn't have to.

"Last night when I phoned you up, you said the ETA claim was a hoax." He held up the photographs. "Now I have these.

142

Are they genuine?"

"Yes."

"So you didn't tell the truth to me—or to the other newspapers."

The Minister spread his hands in a gesture of helplessness.

"For reasons of state, Carlos, I had to deny it."

The editor was angry.

"I might just mention that when I run the story."

This was not going to be easy, the Minister thought.

"I don't think you quite appreciate what the effect of publication would be," he said. "Sit down, Carlos, and I'll explain it to you."

The Minister talked quietly, a sense of urgency, but reason, in his voice. When he had finished, Rodriguez sat there in silence, weighing his duty to his readers and to his professionalism against that to his country.

Finally, he said, "What if one of the other newspapers publishes?"

"They haven't got the pictures, Carlos. They'd have been on the phone immediately if they had." He tried a little flattery. "The terrorists sent the photographs to you because you edit the best newspaper."

"We're the best because we always print the facts!"

Another silence. Rodriguez drummed his fingers on the arm of his chair. He was deep in thought.

"When this is all over, then can I print the story and the pictures?"

It was all Santana could do to hold back a gasp of relief. The hardest part was over—but the rest would be tricky enough.

"If the Princess is killed, yes, you can publish the pictures. If she is rescued—quite frankly, Carlos, I don't know.

"But I'll promise you this—the King, this government, the British royal family and the Premier owe you and your newspaper a favor—no, a debt. I intend to make sure that it is paid."

"Miguel, I am sacrificing what is the story of my career—a

143

story that would scoop the world. But I will."

"There's another way you can help us," Santana continued.

"How?"

"The terrorists never expected to have to move. They're safe enough for the moment, but they're edgy. Like rats, they don't like being disturbed. It's important to keep them jumpy, to prove to them that things are not working out the way they planned. Force them to provide more evidence—because then they just might make a mistake.

"What do you think their reaction would be if they found no photographs in tomorrow's newspaper but a tough opinion piece accusing ETA of making false claims in a desperate attempt to retain its credibility? And to back if up, you could even print a photograph of the Princess at an old people's home in England today."

It had been Valdés' idea to rattle the terrorists, but Santana had immediately seen the political value of it, too. It would appeal to the editor to be playing a part in events of national importance, rather than just commenting on them. And once he agreed, he would be caught up in the conspiracy.

"Then they'll just send the photographs to the other newspapers," Rodriguez said.

"I'll handle that," Santana assured him. "Though, of course, I won't take the other editors into my confidence as I've taken you."

He could see that Rodriguez was about to protest that it wouldn't work.

"And if any of them do intend to print, I'll let you know immediately and give you all the details they won't have."

More silence. Santana wondered if he had overdone it. Should he have taken a tougher line, threatened Rodriguez with the consequences if he went ahead and put the state in an impossible position?

"All right, Miguel," the editor said at last. "I'll do it. I'll even write the editorial myself."

The man known—for the moment—as Harding, caught the shuttle service to Bruxelles and stationed himself outside the offices of Kalsell well before the close of business. He had never met the Belgian, but he had seen his photograph, and as Delgarde emerged from the foyer and waddled down the street, he fell in behind him.

Delgarde descended the steps to the underground parking lot, breathing heavily, and made for a shiny Rolls Royce.

"Nice," Harding thought to himself. But he wasn't surprised. He already knew how much money Delgarde made.

He walked over and tapped the Belgium lightly on the shoulder.

"Monsieur Delgarde, we need to talk."

"I do not discuss business outside the office," Delgarde snapped.

"I think that this time you will have to make an exception."

Delgarde stared at the man. Tall, with unexceptional features, he would blend easily into a crowd. But beneath the well-cut jacket was a body that looked iron-hard. And the voice had a cutting edge that conveyed both the certainty of his absolute right to do as he wished and the ruthlessness that would follow if anyone tried to stop him. Delgarde was used to dealing with ruthless, unscrupulous characters, but he didn't think he had ever come across a tougher one than this man.

Delgarde felt his heartbeat increasing. This Englishman—he was sure from the accent that he was English—was too dangerous to become involved with. He tried to bluster his way out.

"You must make an appointment with my secretary."

"Monsieur Delgarde," Harding said quietly, "I come armed with the carrot and the stick. The carrot is that the job I am about to offer you will only take a short time, and will earn you two million pounds. The stick is the information I have on your dealings and your bank accounts. There are several governments that would be very interested in it." He quoted a few examples. "You could go to jail for a long time—unless

145

we decide to punish you in other ways."

With that much money, and those intelligence sources, the man could only be representing a government. Delgarde realized, as Harding had known he would, that there was no choice.

"How long will the business take?"

"Not long. It will be over by Saturday."

The whispers in the morning
Of lovers sleeping tight
. . .
As I look into your eyes
I hold on to your body
And feel every move you make

The Power of Love. The song reminded her of times so different from the present, of places that seemed in another world, a million miles away from this room. Evenings in discos, *Tramps* and *Annabel's* in wonderful, safe London; the holiday in Majorca with the Spanish royal family. She had been singing it on the back of the King's motorbike as they sped along the country lane, just before...it happened.

From now on, she would associate the song with Xabier, too. Xabier, the terrorist who sometimes treated her as a human being instead of simply a pawn in a vicious struggle which she had played no part in creating.

Would she ever hear this song again in happier circumstances, with the children, with her husband, surrounded by her friends? And if she did, what memories would it conjure up? Sun-drenched Spanish beaches, a disco after midnight or this dreadful room where, each time the bolt slid back, she feared her last moment had come?

She had never felt so far away from Charles and there were tears forming in the corners of her eyes. Ballads always made her feel close to him, or sad if he was not there. The words to this one seemed so appropriate.

146

The Walkman prevented her from hearing the bolt and the keys, nor she did she notice the two of them standing there, until Idoia shook her.

"Where did she get that from?"

"It's mine. I lent it to her." Xabier did not want to admit that he had bought it. "I thought it would help."

Idoia was enraged at such softness, but she knew she mustn't argue or remove the Walkman...not for the moment, at any rate.

"Tell her what she has to do."

Pedro Gomez, sitting on his rickety cart, gave his donkey a tentative flick of his whip.

Bloody police, always moving him on. Holding up the traffic, they said. As if they expected a donkey to go as fast as a car. And as if he didn't have as much right to work as anybody else.

Calle Nuncio was coming up. There were no bloody cars on that street. And it was a good hunting ground, too. People were always throwing out beaten-up refrigerators or ancient bedsteads. The gypsy whacked his donkey on the back and the cart turned into the pedestrian-only street.

As the animal clipped along past the three-story houses, Pedro filled his lungs with air.

"*Chatarra*," he shouted.

It was the traditional call to alert housewives that the junk man was around.

"*Chatarra*."

The cry brought an immediate response. A third floor window was opened and a woman, her hair in curlers, poked her head out.

"Come on up here. I've got an old sofa you can take away."

If it was in fair condition, he could trade that. If not, there was always the scrap from the metal springs. And he could sell the wood.

147

Xabier handed the Princess a single sheet of paper. The words on it were in English, printed in block capitals.

"It's very simple. We want you to say this slowly and clearly. Study it for a while, read it through."

The Princess looked at the message and read it silently to herself.

"Take your time," Xabier said. He brought up a chair and placed a tape recorder on it.

He was worried that the Princess would refuse to record it and they would have to get tough with her.

I am being held in a People's Prison and I am being well taken care of. There is every justification for this measure. I freely admit that I and my family represent a class system which has sought to repress the power of the people, their love of legitimate rights and freedoms. The system must be changed. Capitalism must be overthrown by revolution if necessary. The claims cannot be ignored any longer. The right of self-determination for the Basque people and their occupied home-land must be granted now. This is the just price of my freedom and one with which I am in full agreement. I plead with the Spanish authorities to do what is right so that I can be returned to my family. Long live the Basque People—Gora Euskadi.

Her heart beat faster as she read the words. There was a way to get a message out. She mustn't let her excitement show!

She turned to Xabier

"Is that last bit Basque?"

Xabier breathed a silent sigh of relief. She was going to do it.

"Yes. It means 'Long Live the Basque Country.' Try pronouncing it after me. *Gora Euskadi.*"

She repeated the two words several times.

"That's it—not bad at all."

Even Idoia looked pleased at the way the prisoner was pronouncing the phrase which meant so much to patriots.

"Will this help get me free?" the Princess asked.

"Of course it will."

"All right, I'll do it. Start the machine."

Her voice quavered at first but gained strength as she went along.

"I am being held in a People's Prison...and I am being well taken care of. There is every justification for this measure. I freely admit that I and my family represent a class system which has sought to repress the power of love of the people... their legitimate rights and freedoms. The system must be changed. Capitalism must be overthrown by revolution if necessary. The claims cannot be ignored any longer..."

She was doing well, Xabier thought.

"...I plead with the Spanish authorities to do what is right so that I can be returned to my family. Long live the Basque People—*Gora Uskadi.*"

He pressed the stop, rewound the tape, and listened. It was not perfect, but the little hesitations, the failing of the voice, added to the poignancy of the plea.

"You did that beautifully," he said.

He broke into Basque.

"How did it sound to you?"

"I didn't understand it, but she made no attempt to disguise her voice and she certainly sounded pathetic and worried enough."

"I'll be up later with your food," Xabier said. "Now I'll leave you to your music."

Diana sat still for several minutes. The tight knot of fear in her stomach slowly uncoiled, leaving her temporarily spent. She had been terrified in case Xabier noticed her slip, and realized that it was deliberate. If he had *done*, he would have felt that his kindness had been betrayed, that she had been using him. There would be no more talks, no more little luxuries. Worse still, he would have told the girl about the trick, adding fuel to what was now an obvious and burning hatred. The Princess paced her prison, ten steps one way, four the other.

"I wonder, oh I wonder, will they get it?" she said in a desperate and low whisper, which echoed around the room.

The thick walls seemed to mock her, and she struck angrily with her first. A pain, starting in her knuckles, shot rapidly up her arm. She clamped her hand underneath her armpit to ease the hurt. There was not even the trace of a mark on the wall where she had hit it.

She looked up at the skylight, far beyond her reach. Escape from this room was impossible. She prayed that the people who received the tape would understand her message, or, if they did not, that they would let her husband hear it. He would understand—he would have to!

It was her only hope.

Chapter Fifteen

He was with Iñaki again, on his first mission, yet somehow they both seemed much older . . . and it was so hot, even though the snow came up over their ankles. He wasn't called Guadaña—The Scythe—though he didn't know why. The policeman was totally unaware of their presence. He even had his back to them. It was very, very hot.

"You take him," Iñaki said.

Young Tomas walked quietly towards the Guardia. The man heard his feet squelching in the snow and turned—still unsuspecting. Not many policemen had been killed by then—so long ago. He turned again, to watch the traffic. Tomas stopped a meter away, drew his gun and aimed slowly and carefully at the back of the oppressor's head. His hand was steady. He pulled the trigger, and even before the man fell, he was walking back to Iñaki.

He felt a strange surge of fulfillment as if all his life—his school days under the hectoring parish priest, the early years sweating in the steel mill, the poverty and grind in the shadow of the big houses on the hills—had all been leading up to this, his first act of political violence.

But he showed none of this to Iñaki. He was cold, matter of fact, as if it was any other job, like driving home a rivet or helping his uncle to bring in the harvest. He hoped that his face was not flushed, because it was so very, very hot.

The Guardias had come in the night, through the rolling fog. The blows—first from fists and then rifle butts! They knew he was a terrorist . . . just sign this paper. More blows. The grinning sergeant, the menacing captain, telling him the garrotte would be his end. The pole, the steel collar and screw being tightened. Five weeks at police headquarters, lights glaring in his face, kicks in the night to keep away the peaceful shroud of sleep. Still no confession, and in the spring, they took him from his cell and all but hurled him out into the street.

Why was it so hot?

"The bastards!"

The Scythe—cutting down the weeds that choked the Basque nation. The name had become known. Guadaña, the hit-man, the revenger, the executioner, carrying out the sentences of the People's Court to cleanse the nation.

Sweat rolled down his neck, staining the bandages. He was lying full length on the couch. The sheet that Idoia had put over him lay crumpled on the floor.

"Don't ever repeat any of that," Idoia said fiercely. "Don't tell anyone what you've just heard."

Xabier was angrier than he could ever remember being before. So angry that he did not dare to reply. What kind of man did Idoia think he was? He had worked hard on this operation and was running exactly the same risks as the others—could end up dying with them. And yet he was not to be treated as an equal. In Idoia's eyes, his part was nothing. He was not even to be trusted to keep quiet about Guadaña's private thoughts, his secret inner-life, spilled out in a bout of delirium.

"You heard me! I said keep quiet about it," the girl persisted.

He could stand no more.

"Stop treating me like a bourgeois individualist. You've no

need to lecture me on security, particularly when it comes to a comrade. And we are all comrades; all part of the same struggle."

She fought back.

"Struggle! What do you know about struggle? What have you ever done for the Cause?"

"Whatever I was ordered to do. Wherever those in command felt I could make the greatest contribution. There are other ways to serve, apart from firing a gun." His voice became withering. "But I can't talk about it, because, unlike you, I *do* understand the meaning of security."

Idoia was speechless. She had never heard him talk with such passion. She had no idea that there was so much power in him.

Guadaña started coughing like a heavy smoker drawing on his first cigarette of the day. Specks of blood lined his bottom lip.

Xabier reached for his jacket.

"Where are you going?" Idoia asked, almost meekly.

"We can't get him a doctor, but at least we can get some drugs."

"Where from?"

"A pharmacy, using whatever means is necessary. You know—direct action. What you're always talking about."

Beach Boy had been quiet since lunchtime, seemingly content to remain in the hostel. The computer had given them no fresh names. The policemen on the streets were still checking on new arrivals—but they would have needed an army to check the whole of the city.

The valuable hours were ticking away, and nothing new was turning up.

"We should get some action tomorrow," Martínez said hopefully, "when *El Mundo* hits the streets and there's no picture of the Princess."

"When does it come out?" Decker asked.

153

"The first edition appears in the city at six o'clock in the morning, but there are special editions before that for places like Catalonia and Andalucia."

Special editions! An idea came, already completely formed, into Decker's mind.

"Do you think *El Mundo* would do something else for us?"

"Sure! I don't know what Santana said to the editor, but he's got him eating out of his hand. Why? What have you got in mind?"

"When there's no photograph tomorrow, ETA will try again. Only this time, they'll send them to other newspapers."

"Yes?" Martínez said.

That much was obvious.

"If they do it the same was as before," Decker said, "I think I've found a way to pin down the area where the safe house is."

He outlined his scheme to the Inspector.

"Brilliant!" Martínez said.

He picked up the phone and cleared it with the Minister. He had only just replaced it when the bell rang again. He listened.

"That was surveillance. Beach Boy is on the move."

Xabier traveled to the northwest sector of the city by a No. 7 bus. He sat halfway down and pretended to read a magazine. No one paid any attention to him. He alighted in Calle Uruguay and headed for the late-night pharmacy.

It was one of a row of small stores. The green cross of the *Farmacia* was lit up—all the other businesses were closed. The street was deserted.

Xabier stood outside and rang the bell. The white-coated pharmacist was arranging tins of baby food. She looked up, saw a well-dressed, respectable looking young man outside, and pressed the button to open the door.

Xabier smiled at her, and the woman smiled back.

"I've just come from the doctor's," Xabier said.

"The doctor's! At this time of night?"

154

"Yes, it was packed, so I didn't wait. I hope you can help, even though I don't have a prescription."

The smile was replaced by a look of uncertainty. It was not going to work. Xabier lowered his voice, although there was no one else around.

"Look, that's not strictly true. My elder brother's wife caught him in bed with a neighbor. She stabbed him in the shoulder with a pair of scissors. We don't want it to get out. The police would probably arrest her, and the scandal would kill my poor mother. Could you let me have a few things, just to ease his pain?"

"What about the family doctor?"

"The wound's not that bad, just deep. It'll heal itself, but in the meantime it hurts a lot. Could you let me have some painkillers?"

The pharmacist looked dubious.

"I can't let you have anything strong. Not without a prescription. We get inspected all the time and we have to account for everything. It's because of the junkies."

Xabier put his hand in his pocket and pulled out the gun.

"Don't scream," he said quietly. "Just get what I tell you to and you'll be all right."

Keeping the gun trained on her, he backed away, closed the door and reversed the "open" sign.

The pharmacist wanted no trouble.

"What are the symptoms?"

"A high fever, delirium, some internal bleeding, a large wound in the chest, a lot of pain."

He followed her around the counter. She assembled the things he needed.

"Can you use a syringe?"

"Yes."

"These will ease the pain and clean the wound, but they aren't a cure, you know. The ampules are very strong. Be careful. You really should get it seen to by a doctor."

Xabier took out his wallet with his free hand. With some

155

difficulty he extracted two five-thousand peseta notes and laid them on the counter.

"I want to pay. This is not a robbery."

The woman stared at the money.

"Go on! Take it!"

The woman pressed a key on the cash register, picked up the money, and put it in the drawer.

"Now give me your I.D. card."

With trembling hands, she opened her bag and handed the card to Xabier.

"Listen carefully. I know your name. If you go to the police, I will come back—and if I can't somebody else will. You and your family will be shot. So just forget that all this happened."

Xabier put his gun back in his pocket and moved towards the door.

Pepe, the fruit and vegetable seller, hauled the last sack of potatoes on to the pile at the back of his store. He had already cashed up. Time for a drink. But first, he would go and say goodnight to his neighbor in the pharmacy. She was a very attractive woman; he must get around to inviting her out some night.

He looked in through the window and saw the man just putting the gun away. A robbery. He hugged the wall and waited. He was sick to death of young thugs, high on drugs. This little bastard would get his comeuppance—and not from some soft-hearted judge who would only give him a slap on the wrist.

As Xabier left the shop, Pepe swung him round, clasped him in a bear-hug and kneed him in the stomach. The terrorist's legs collapsed underneath him and he gasped for air. The storekeeper hurled him against the brick wall.

"You son of a bitch!" he said, lashing out with his boot.

Xabier sank to the ground and struggled for his gun as successive kicks jarred against his spine, side and stomach. His senses were fading and he could hear the pharmacist screaming for the police. He rolled away. As he looked up at his assailant again, the gun cleared his jacket. He fired once.

The bullet caught the storekeeper on the inside of the knee of his raised right leg—just as another kick was on its way. The metal burst through cartilage and bone, ploughing a furrow through the upper part of the thigh and exited, shattering the glass shop window.

Pepe was knocked back several yards, finishing up sitting on the concrete, looking with glazed eyes at his right leg. A fountain of blood, pumped out by his furiously beating heart, squirted into the air.

Xabier climbed shakily to his feet. He pointed his gun at the storekeeper, then saw that the man would cause him no more problems. Half-running, half-limping, he crossed the road and made his escape through the park.

"How long's he been here?" Martínez demanded. "What's he told you?"

The owner of the hostel, bony elbows poking out of holes in his cardigan, shrugged his shoulders.

"He arrived on Sunday. Paid a week in advance. Told me he was looking for work. It's none of my business."

Beach Boy had gone straight to a small restaurant and ordered a beer and the menu of the day. One of the surveillance team had followed him in. Decker and Martínez took the opportunity to visit his hostel.

"Now, señor, listen carefully," Martínez said to the owner. "This is an important police operation. If he ever gets even a hint that we've been here, I'll have this placed turned over by the Hotel Squad. All your guests bothered, checked—every single day. And if that doesn't ruin you, I'll get the health inspectors, building inspectors, every bloody sort of inspector down here, and make sure you're closed. Understand?"

The man ran his hand nervously through his stringy gray hair and nodded.

"Yes, sir."

"Right. Now show us his room."

At first glance, it was just like the room in Valencia. Aside from the clothes, there were no personal possessions.

"New green jacket and white trousers. New suit and briefcase—and they look expensive."

Now why would someone posing as an unemployed man need those?

They examined the rest of the room quickly and efficiently, found nothing, and were out on the street again in five minutes. The surveillance team reported that Beach Boy had eaten a leisurely meal and spoken to no one but the waiter. When he returned to the hostel, he seemed to be settling down for the night.

The report of the pharmacy raid was on their desks when they returned and the woman was waiting upstairs. She had been treated for shock. The wounded man was in a critical condition, undergoing surgery for a severed main artery and could not be questioned for at least twenty-four hours.

A female inspector brought the pharmacist up to them.

"I don't know if this has anything to do with your operation, but we were told to report all cases involving gunshot wounds to you immediately. The man who attacked this woman wasn't looking for hard drugs, like an addict. Or money. He wanted strong painkillers and antibiotics. And he paid for them."

"Thank you," said Martínez.

She was really rather pretty. Perhaps when all this was over . . . He helped the victim into a chair.

Decker held the photofit of the young terrorist compiled from the barman's description.

"Is this him?"

She shook her head, hardly glancing at it.

"Look at it carefully," Decker said.

"What did he say to you?" Martínez asked gently.

The woman started to sob.

"That if I said anything, he'd kill my family."

"He won't," Martínez reassured her. "He'll be locked up

158

soon. And until he is, we're going to give you round-the-clock protection." He picked up the phone. "I'll give the order now."

They talked to her for twenty minutes. She told them all she remembered. The photofit lay in front of her. She never looked at it directly and her description of the attacker was not only vague but inconsistent.

Decker picked up the photofit again, as if to take it away. Suddenly he spun round and thrust it under her eyes.

"This *is* the man, isn't it!"

The woman dissolved into tears, dropping her head into her hands. The agents barely heard the whispered, "Yes . . . yes."

"Thank you, señora," Decker said, all hardness gone from his voice now. "We'll arrange for someone to take you home."

One of the kidnappers was seriously wounded, so badly that they risked a raid on a pharmacy. The police had an Etarra who must be connected with the operation under surveillance in a seedy hotel. Progress had been substantial, but it was nearly midnight on Tuesday, Day Three of the kidnapping. And every minute that ticked away was precious.

The last time Decker had checked his watch, he had noted there were ninety-six hours to go until the threatened execution time. That had now been sliced by twenty-four. The Madrid edition of *El Mundo* would be coming off the presses now. It was the paper the Princess had been holding up in the first picture ETA sent. He hoped to Christ the terrorist would stick to the pattern and use *El Mundo* next time as well.

Xabier lay on his head, his body aching. They had swabbed and cleaned Guadaña's wounds and given him an injection. He was in deep sleep for the first time since being wounded.

Xabier thought about the storekeeper. He had not wanted to fire, but there had been no option. He had never shot anyone—it had been his baptism and he didn't like himself. If he had not been a dedicated Marxist, he would have prayed for the man not to die.

159

His hands felt his thighs, then he lifted his shirt and probed the rib area. Nothing appeared to have been broken, but by tomorrow he would be stiff, with ugly brown bruises all over his body. At least his face had escaped; at least he was still operational. The big problem, he thought, was that the police would by now have another eyewitness description. He was thankful that he had no record on police files.

He dozed and then became aware that someone else was in the room. Idoia! Leaning against the doorpost, her scarred cheek turned away from him.

She looked exhausted, yet he sensed a coiled up tension in her, screaming for release.

"When she's like this, she just has to hit out at somebody," Xabier thought, "and I'm the only one available."

She would attack him, mock his intellectualism, jeer at his concern for the hostage. He would not fight back, he would let her catharsis run its course.

But Idoia didn't say anything. Instead, almost shyly, she turned out the light so that the only illumination was the pale glow of the street lamps. He could see her shape, but nothing more. For over a minute, she simply stood there, as if she was watching over him while he went to sleep. Then she began to move across the room. Not as she had moved in the country lane outside Brunete, submachine gun in hand, eyes fixed on the Guardia Civil patrol car. Then, she had been swift, surely, deadly—a panther stalking its prey. Now she was awkward, touchingly graceless.

She knelt by the side of the bed.

"Xabier . . ."

"Yes?"

"Nothing, I . . ."

He felt her hand touch his knee, felt her fingers slowly, laboriously, climbing his thigh. Until they reached his crotch. The fingers probed and pummeled at the space between his legs where his hard throbbing penis should have been straining for release from the confinement of his pants. He was ashamed

160

of his limpness, his lack of response.

"You're still tense," she said with a kindness and understanding he had never heard from her before.

"For once," he thought, "we are partners in uncertainty."

"Try to relax," she soothed. "It's all right. You did very well out there."

He had almost killed a man out there!

"Let me take your clothes off," Idoia said. "You'll feel more comfortable with your clothes off."

She unfastened his pants.

"Lift a little so I can pull them down," she told him.

And like a small, sick child he did as he was told.

His pants were round his ankles, his underwear over his knees. Idoia leaned forward. Her thick, black hair tickled his naked flesh. Her tongue began to play along the shaft of his penis, light, delicate strokes, and then her wet lips were around its head—teasing, encouraging. As his penis hardened, she took more and more of it into her mouth, until her nose was touching his pubic hair, brushing it back and forth with each new suck, each new gulp.

His body was ready, but his mind was not. He felt strangely detached, as though he were in the corner of the room, watching the scene.

Idoia stood up, and he heard the rustle of clothing being discarded, then her shape silhouetted against the window. Her breasts were small and firm, her stomach slightly, erotically, curved.

She straddled him and began to move up and down, slowly, rhythmically. He reached out, stroked her hard, jutting nipple and then began to massage her breasts with his hands. She was breathing more heavily now, and her movements were getting faster.

And nothing was happening to him!

He could feel his member wilting. She knew it too, and her throaty gasps stopped abruptly.

He moved his hand to stimulate her clitoris, but she was

161

having none of that. She pulled herself off him and rolled to the other side of the bed. Her body was shaking slightly, and he was sure that she was crying.

"I'm sorry," he said.

"Is it because of my face?" she asked. The sobbing was louder now, punctuating her words. "Is that what it is?"

"No . . . I . . ."

"I used to be pretty. I used to be beautiful! There was a fire . . . I was only twelve."

He didn't want to hurt her.

"It's not because of your face. You're still pretty. I have a *novia* at home. Maybe that's the reason."

"Liar!" Anger had replaced pain. "It's because of that woman upstairs."

It wasn't like that at all. He had never looked at the Princess with desire, never imagined her in bed. He simply could not conceive of such a thing.

Yet in a way, Idoia was right. His emotional life was becoming centered on the Princess, all his normal reactions and feelings seemed to be losing their importance.

"She has everything, and I have nothing." Her tone was almost a hiss, the sound of a snake about to strike. "I hate her. When we execute her, I want to be the one to do it."

Xabier felt suddenly cold. He knew that killing her was a possibility, but had managed to thrust it to the back of his mind. Would the government give in to the demands? They must do! But if they did not, he would have to obey his orders.

He turned on to his side and placed a hand on Idoia's naked hip.

"If *anyone* has to shoot her," he said, "I will do it."

WEDNESDAY

Chapter Sixteen

Guadaña was fully dressed and sitting upright. The pain in his right side and chest varied in intensity and location—sometimes it was like hundreds of red hot needles running up and down his body; at others, it was as if someone had stabbed a knife in his wound and was twisting it around. But at the moment, he was aware of nothing but his rage. With his left hand he flung that morning's copy of *El Mundo* across the low coffee table.

"Not a bloody mention—never mind a photograph. They're pretending the whole thing never fucking happened!"

The terrorist leader had woken up after ten hours solid sleep determined to take command again.

"It's Day Four of the operation," he thought, "and apart from the capitalist authorities in London and Madrid, nobody knows we've got her."

They had been depending on the general public, particularly in England, to force a reaction—get results. The kidnapping had been a brilliant success, a personal triumph, and no fucker knew about it, despite the claim, despite the photographs!

Idoia and Xabier sat watching him. A strained atmosphere seemed to exist between them today, not antagonistic, as in the past but a more intimate one, the sort that hangs in the air after a family row. He wondered what had been happening while he had been out of action. Whatever it was, it was time for him to take re-establish control.

"The man you shot yesterday is still alive, critical but expected to pull through. It would have been safer to finish him off. The pharmacist too. The police must have a fair description of you now."

Xabier had bought three papers from the kiosk on the corner and he didn't tell either of the others that he had felt a surge of relief at the news.

"How many copies of the tape have you made?" he asked Xabier.

"Six, as I was instructed. I'm keeping the master copy."

"As a souvenir?" Idoia asked acidly.

Guadaña interrupted sharply.

"I don't know what's bothering you, but you can stop the snide cracks.The tape is even more important now that they've managed to block the other messages. I expected Xabier to keep the original."

Idoia bent her head slightly, registering the rebuke.

"Xabier wants to deliver the tapes, but I think I should do it," she said, more reasonably, "particularly after what happened at the pharmacist's."

Despite all her efforts, the bite was still there.

"No, I shall take it. Xabier's job is here with the woman and I've got an important task for you."

The two accepted Guadaña's decision without question. He was, if only temporarily, back in command.

"Should anything go wrong at the bullring today, you two will follow the operation to the letter. When the demands are met—and the games they're playing now are only a desperate attempt to avoid the inevitable—the woman is to be tied up and her whereabouts kept from the police for twenty-four hours. That call will be made by somebody else."

"And what if the demands are not met? Will there by any extension?"

Guadaña glared at Xabier.

"Midnight Friday is the deadline. My orders are—no extensions. Our credibility is on the line. If we do not carry out our threats in this operation, we will be seen to have suffered a serious defeat. Governments usually try to stall with hostage situations—it's a well-known strategy. If they hold off long enough, they know resolve will be weakened. It has worked too many times. It will not with us."

Guadaña clenched and unclenched his right first, but his face did not register the pain.

"Because of the wound, I've decided to break silence. The situation merits it, and you are to handle the communication, Idoia."

As Xabier went to the kitchen to prepare the hostage's breakfast, he heard Guadaña begin... "First, call and book..."

"The tapes have got to work," Xabier thought as he poured the coffee. "We must get this whole thing over and done with."

He's known there would be pressures, but never imagined it would be like this. Thinking of his novia and the peaceful, beautiful scene from his study window, he sliced the bread.

The Princess was up. Xabier saw that not only had she tried to clean up the room, but she had made the bed. Her hair was brushed and she looked fresh.

Xabier was moving stiffly.

"What's happened to you, Xabier?"

There was concern on Diana's face.

"I got beaten up last night."

"I'm so sorry."

And she was. She had manipulated him, but she still liked him.

"I shot a man," he said.

A surge of revulsion swept through her. Not at a shooting,

167

she had become more hardened to that in the last few days, but that Xabier that become like the other two. She would expect anything from them, but not this boy with the serious brown eyes.

"Don't show it," she told herself. "Don't alienate him. He's the only ally you've got."

She kept her voice calm as she asked, "Why?"

"I went to get drugs for Guadaña. I was attacked. He was a big, strong man. There was no way I could fight him off. You may not believe this, but that was the first time I've even aimed a gun a anyone."

He paused for a second.

"I don't want him to die—really I don't."

He could never have said it to the two downstairs, there was only the Princess he could talk to. He looked at her face, anxious for her reaction.

She looked serious, and said quietly, "I know that, Xabier."

"Thank you," he said.

Delgarde had only just settled into the suite of his Biarritz hotel when the phone rang.

"Monsieur, your property deal is of interest."

The voice was businesslike, and Delgarde could hear the sounds of a cafe in the background and knew that the call was coming from a public telephone.

"Does your room overlook the beach?"

"Yes.

"*Bien*. If you look to your left, you will see a line of rocks jutting out into the sea. They are connected by a walkway. Be there at midday."

There was a chill wind blowing in from the sea and only a few vacationers had chosen to brave it. On both sides, the Atlantic swell broke heavily against the rocks.

"Monsieur Delgarde?"

The Belgian nodded, but did not offer his hand. The contact

was in his mid-thirties. His eyes were hard, his stance was that of a man always watchful, always prepared for an attack. Even before he made the approach, Delgarde knew that this was the man he had come to meet. He had no difficulty in recognizing terrorists.

"You have certain goods which my client is interested in," Delgarde said carefully. "I do not know what they are, nor do I care. I am authorized to tell you that on the delivery of these goods in a satisfactory condition, I will give you merchandise of your own choice, from my warehouse, to the value of twenty million pounds."

The wind ruffled Delgarde's sparse hair. Both men turned to face the land, their backs leaning against the iron railings. A mother screamed at her child for leaning too far out through the rail. Seagulls glided close above them.

"How do I know you're not a plant?" the man asked. "How do I know you can fulfill your part of the bargain?"

"My identity is easily established," Delgarde said. "Call my office. You can look up the number yourself. Mention to my secretary that you represent the Pyrennean Mineral Water Company. She will reply that Monsier Delgarde is staying at the Royal Hotel here in Biarritz, and will give you the room number.

"As to the other matter," he took out his wallet and extracted a card, "ring this Swiss bank, quote the number and password that I've written down, and you will be told that the account contains the money I spoke of. Does it really matter who I am, as long as the money is real and the goods can be supplied?"

The man nodded. It was not a nod of acceptance, merely an acknowledgement that what he had heard had been understood.

"I will deliver your message and if my superiors are interested, we will re-establish contact. *Au revoir.*"

As he started to move away, Delgarde grasped him by the arm.

"Do not take too long to make a decision," he said. "My

client has informed me that after Friday, the goods will no longer be of value to him."

"You see that bar over there, that's where I first met my wife."

Martínez said it casually, but Decker felt his voice was tinged with emotion. Nostalgia? Sadness? And he was surprised to hear that Martínez had ever been married. From his breezy attitude and roving eye, the captain had assumed that he was a bachelor.

They were waiting. Waiting for more results from the street searches, waiting for more photographs to appear. But most important of all, waiting for the one solid link they had, García, the Beach Boy, to do something. If he didn't make contact by late afternoon, they had decided, they would pick him up.

"It never really had much of a chance of working out," Martínez continued. "Her family would have been happier if she'd married a business man or a ministry official. I think probably, after the first golden days, she would have been too."

Decker didn't speak.

"Never show your pain," his father used to say. "It's a stinking world and if you once let it see your weakness, you're lost. Keep it in, boy, keep it in."

"It was the Basque situation that led to the final breakdown. When I was posted up there, Ana went with me. Wives of serving officers did. It's a strain, but most of them learn to cope with it. She didn't. End of a marriage!"

"Does it still hurt?" Decker asked.

"Not really. Sometimes I think I still love Ana. But then I tell myself that it was doomed."

He thought of the past three years, the constant stream of women who had shared his bed.

"I'll tell you something, I've never fallen in love again. Ana used to say I was really married to the police force. If it wasn't

170

true then, it is now. I throw myself into the job, and try to keep my memories at bay."

"Doesn't always work though, does it?" Decker asked.

Martínez looked again at the bar across the road. The two men lapsed into silence, each with his own thoughts.

The car was parked on double yellow lines around the corner from he Beach Boy's hostel. Apart from breakfast in a nearby bar, he hadn't moved all day.

Decker checked on the time. It was just after three. The Inspector saw the gesture, but made no comment.

Then the radio came to life. The suspect had just walked out.

The two agents left the car, Martínez adjusting his sun glasses. Decker thought that even with the sharp parting gone, and the hair brushed straight back, he still looked like a playboy on the prowl.

Idoia closed the heavy blue door firmly. As she walked up the narrow road which had been turned into a pedestrian precinct, she swung her fashionable leather bag, feeling happy to escape the close confines of the house.

She was wearing a well-cut gray outfit as a disguise—the revolutionary dressed as a bourgeois. Part of her hated it, but there was a little corner of her that knew she looked good, and she rejoiced in it. She could see men in the distance watching her—young handsome men like Xabier. Ah, but when they got closer—when they could see her face! All that was so superficial, so unimportant, she told herself. It was only the Cause that really mattered.

She dialed Bilbao from a public telephone. She had a message, she said, for Head Office. She read the number from the piece of paper in her hand. It was vital that the sales department ring her there in the next two hours.

"Ask for Señora Benitez."

She hung up.

171

It had been a leisurely lunch. Arenas had finished eating an hour ago, and was now on his second coffee and brandy.

"That's the first time he's been seen to drink anything else but a glass of beer. Is he celebrating something or is he nervous?" Decker said.

But he had done nothing to celebrate, not in all the time they had been watching him.

The Beach Boy called for his bill, and the team was on the move. Once again, the agents noticed that he was careful to fold up the receipt and put it in his wallet.

"Now why would any man keep his bill?" Martínez asked softly, "unless he was on expenses? And who would pay the expenses of an unemployed man? It stinks of ETA."

The suspect left the restaurant and strolled down Calle Fuencarral.

"He's going back to his hostel," Decker said in disgust. "Let's pull the little shit in now."

Martínez nodded. He was tired of this game, too. The agents quickened their pace. They were not more than ten yards from their quarry when Arenas reached the Gran Via. Decker signalled to Martínez to move. In seconds they would have him, and because they were both pros, it was unlikely that anyone would even notice it. In fifteen minutes, he would be in the hot seat at the Ministry.

At the corner of the busy main street, Arenas turned left, in the opposite direction to the hostel. The two officers dropped back instantly.

"He's going for a stroll."

Decker nodded and noticed the front half of the box moving forward to get a good fifty yards ahead of the suspect.

The Beach Boy stopped occasionally to glance into shop windows. Once he consulted his watch, but there was no quickening of his pace.

"He's meeting someone," Decker said. "That's why he's got that new jacket and trousers on—so his contact can recognize him. But he's early."

Two back-up cars leapfrogged each other, stopping at intervals as Gran Via dipped down past the expensive stores and the cinemas, into the banking and insurance zone.

At Plaza Cibeles, the big four-faced clock, high in the tower of the city's ornate post office, chimed 5:30. The Beach Boy crossed at the green pedestrian lights and walked on the sunny side of the avenue, up Calle Alcala.

He paused at the Independence Gateway, as if making up his mind. Then he swung right and entered Retiro Park.

"It's a good place for a meeting. Let's separate." Decker said, taking off his jacket and slinging it over his right shoulder.

Arenas felt a tinge of envy as he passed a young man and woman embracing on the grass, his hand easing its way slowly under her jumper.

"Lucky bastard."

It seemed like weeks since he had last touched a woman. But there would be plenty of time for that after the operation was over.

The suspect reached the other end of the park without any contact. The agents, fifty paces apart, crossed Calle Menendez Pelayo and rejoined Alcala. By the time they arrived at the large roundabout at the Plaza de Roma, it was just past six, and the traffic had been reduced to a crawl.

The suspect crossed over and began to walk with the thickening crowd down the Avenida de Toreros.

Martínez beckoned Decker.

"He's going to the bull fight."

"That means crowds."

Thousands of people, all moving towards the bullring. There for a couple of hours and then surging out again. The perfect place for a meeting—and an escape.

The two narrowed the gap between themselves and the suspect to a few paces at the same time as moving further apart from each other.

173

Even bending to get into the taxi hurt. But Guadaña couldn't travel any other way, couldn't risk being jolted in the crowded underground or on a bus. The wound was dressed and he had taken a mild painkiller, strong enough to give him a little relief, but not enough to blunt his edge.

He had placed a weapon in his pocket where he normally kept his wallet. In the left hand pocket of the jacket was a bulky, well-sealed, brown envelope. It had been folded several times.

"Where to?" the cab driver asked.

"The bullring, please."

Chapter Seventeen

Idoia hated Alonso's. It was full of bourgeois women wasting their time and money and chatting inanely. But Guadaña had been right. Who would ever think that an Etarra would go there?

The hair dryer brought relief from the conversations around her, mostly concerned with the beautiful English Princess who had just visited Spain—her flair for fashion, her style, her poise.

"Oh yes, but it's so easy for her," Idoia thought. "Her eyes are no prettier than mine, my hair is thicker, glossier. But she has the skin, the wonderful unblemished skin—and that counts for everything. It's the skin that Xabier notices—and all men notice. And that's why, whatever he says, he's being nice to the bitch."

As assistant tapped her on the shoulder.

"Señora Benitez? There's a phone call for you."

"Can I take it somewhere quiet?"

She was led to a small, elegantly decorated cabin. Mirrors covered the walls. At first, Idoia saw her hair and that part of her which made her a woman and not a soldier. She admired the craft of the stylist. But the mirrors reflected the disfigurement. She could see her face from all angles. She quickly turned away and picked up the phone.

The line from the salon would not be tapped, but it was perfectly possible for calls from France to be bugged. She had no idea how to conduct a coded conversation with someone of importance in the Movement.

The voice on the other end immediately set the tone.

"Señora Benitez, how nice to hear from your. Now what seems to be the problem with the sales campaign?"

"Everything is on schedule, but the sales manager caught the flu last Monday."

"Oh, I'm sorry to hear that, but I have every confidence in you and your team. Is it a bad attack, or should he be back on his feet soon?"

"He is working at the moment, although I really think he needs to rest. But he is very worried about the publicity angle."

Idoia glanced round angrily as another client came in to use the phone. Seeing the withering look and the wave of the hand, the woman mumbled an apology and quickly closed the door.

"Yes, I've noticed that the advertising and expected free publicity have not come up to expectations. I think you need to re-launch the sales brochure."

Idoia fully understood the orders.

"If the sales manager isn't fit enough, then I suggest you take over. But please keep pushing our brochures. You'll find the media will accept them in the end, particularly from a persuasive woman like you. My regards to the manager, and tell him to get better soon."

The line went dead.

Iñaki left the phone booth and entered the bar section of the general store, the only shop in the cluster of houses that comprised the hamlet.

As he ordered a wine, the gaunt, limping man realized that, at the age of 52, after what seemed a lifetime of struggle, he had reached a pinnacle. For he had no immediate superior to

176

contact and discuss the situation with. The leadership was dead, in exile or in custody. He himself had only missed the dragnet because his cover had held up.

Iñaki drove out the village in his battered Citroen. The springs groaned in protest against the rutted road. He was deep in thought and driving slowly. There could be no retreat. With their hostage, it would be all or nothing.

He was worried about Guadaña's wound. They were both veterans, even though Guadaña was ten years younger. A bloody good operative and, he had to admit, as cold as ice. He was certain that Guadaña would see it through—or die attempting it.

The telephone had had to be dealt with first—the situation in Madrid had priority.

Now his mind turned to the fat man waiting in Biarritz, waiting for a meeting. Twenty million English pounds was a massive fortune. But he was not interested in money, only what it could buy. He would listen to what the man had to say.

"No hay entradas" was plastered across the bullfight posters which listed the matadors for the afternoon—Espartaco, Jose Antonio Campuzao and Pepe Luis Vazquez. The bulls, from the ranch of Victorino Martin, were reckoned to be the bravest and the biggest in Spain.

Light reflected off the copper domes that topped the main columns of the red-brick Plaza Monumental de las Ventas, the most important bull ring in the world. The crowds were immense.

Arenas stopped to buy a bullfight poster, looked at it, then rolled it up and carried on walking through the throng of *aficionados* making for the entrances. It was 6:45. The fight would start in another fifteen minutes.

The Madrid ring is sliced up, like a cake, into ten sections, with upper and lower rows of seats, making it easy for fans to find their way into their particular sector, where their tickets are checked and they can be escorted to their seats. Tendido

177

Seven was the entrance to the sector which had both sun and shade on any fine summer afternoon.

The ticket tout had never met an easier pair of mugs than Decker and Martínez. Fifteen thousand he asked for, and fifteen thousand he got. No arguments, cash in hand. And all the time the transaction was taking place, the two buyers never took their eyes off the man in the green jacket and white trousers.

Arenas entered at the block of turnstiles under the main gate. Tendido Seven was to his right. Around him, fans were renting cushions to make the numbered concrete slabs more comfortable. Others were hurrying from the wide circular ground floor to the galleries above.

He noticed the distinctive smell that every bullring exhuded: a damp mixture of straw and manure from the corrals, sweat, black tobacco smoke, perfume and deodorants—and even of blood.

The bar at Tendido Seven was lined three or four deep in places—a long counter with five waiters in attendance.

"Where the hell do I stand?" thought Arenas, as he tucked the bullfight poster under his arm.

He moved to the far end, and as he did so, contact was made, so quickly that it could have been a pickpocket. But instead of something being taken from his coat pocket, a package had been put in. Arenas only caught a glimpse of the pale man, his face screwed up as if in pain. But it was enough. They had never met, but he had seen him from a distance. Guadaña—almost a legend. Then the man was gone, swallowed up in the crowd.

The transfer had gone unnoticed by the agents. Decker had seen the bustle of a thirsty, fast-drinking crowd and he was worried that the surveillance team might have lost contact. He and the Inspector had to keep close in such a mass of people.

178

He spotted Martínez at the end of the bar, standing just away from the counter, glancing round as if waiting for a friend. Decker also stood back. The suspect was between them and any escape route out of the plaza was blocked.

The rows of customers thinned out, the stairs leading to Tendido Seven were solid with people going to their seats. The minutes ticked by. Suddenly, the ground floor walkaround was almost deserted. Amidst the excited hubbub of the huge crowd above them, came the *pasodoble* music announcing the entrance of strutting matadors, their entourages of *bandilleros*, assistants and mounted *picadores*.

There were no more than a dozen drinkers left, timing the emptying of glasses with the air of bullfight veterans who knew exactly when the ceremonies would end and the first fight of the afternoon begin.

Arenas had been about to move when he saw the man at the other end of the bar. There was something familiar about the face, but he hadn't seen it in the last few days. Valencia? It was probably a different man. Or just a coincidence that they should both turn up at the same corrida, in the same tendido. He would wait until the man had taken his seat, then slip through the exit and out into the street.

But more people left, hurrying up the stairs, and still the man remained where he was. Soon there were only three of them—Arenas, the man from Valencia, and a tall, broad, foreign-looking man at the other end of the bar.

Arenas made a mistake. He unconsciously patted his pocket, then slipped his hand inside.

Decker and Martínez knew what that meant. Contact had been made, and they had missed it. There was no point in waiting any longer.

Above them, the rumble of voices, the stamp of feet, turned to roar and then fell away to an almost eerie quiet—the hush of expectation as the heavy red door of the passageway to the corrals was pulled open.

179

The two agents closed in from opposite directions, reaching for their concealed weapons.

Arenas stood sideways to his oncoming adversaries, knowing that he could not bolt to his left or right. With the speed of a sprinter, he took the only escape open to him—and started up the dozen or so concrete stairs that led the packed seats and the ring.

Last minute *aficionados*, waiting patiently to be shown to their seats, blocked the entrance and the narrow gangway down to the ringside. Arenas hit the backs of the waiting fans, low and hard, with his right shoulder, sending a mass of people tumbling into each other.

"What the fuck"... *"Cabron"*... *"Coño"*... *"Maricon"*... *"Hijo de puta"*... *"Sin verguenza"*...

Arenas was past the clutches of two National Policemen and running down the steps, his speed, and the strength brought about by desperation, clearing a path.

"Police!" Martínez yelled as followed by Decker, he jumped over sprawled bodies and elbowed his way through the shocked spectators. Slowly, faces switched from the corral gates to the confusion that was taking place next to them.

The agents had Arenas trapped. He wasn't going anywhere. Only meters separated them. The big thing was to get him without disturbing the crowd too much. Firearms were definitely out.

Pepe Luis Vazquez peered across the top of the wooden barrier inside the ring. He nibbled the top of his heavy yellow and red cape, eyes only on the entrance from the corrals. It was the moment all matadors tensed for, the arrival of the Iberian fighting bull—said to be the most powerful animal in the world. One mistake and he could be like a rag doll, tossed high in the air, fatally gored.

Tormento was, at six hundred and thirty-seven kilos, the

heaviest of the six bulls due to die that afternoon. And its horns were wide, up-pointed and wicked. It had been bad luck to draw the jet-black beast.

Arenas did not slow down. He could see only one way out—across the sanded ring and through the crowd on the other side to an exit. The unexpectedness of his move would get him through.

He put one hand on the top of the thick wire strand in front of the first row of seats and vaulted across the *callejon*—the last sanctuary, from where the doctors, the managers, the assistants, the bullring officials, the vets and the press, watch the action in the ring.

As his feet hit the ring, he stumbled, but quickly regained his balance. He heard several voices shout *"Espontaneo"*—a lad leaping into a ring to face a bull in a bid for fame.

The voices were lost in a roar, as Tormento, all muscle and fury, thundered into the ring. The bull stopped, its head high, horns pointing to the sky, looking for movement.

The terrorist was halfway across the ring when Tormento spotted his fleeing figure.

Arenas glanced over his shoulder to see if the policemen were up with him. He saw instead the huge black beast thundering towards him at an angle. In the flash, his mind registered the eyes fixed on him, horns glinting in the sun. He almost fell. His heart was pounding, his lungs were on fire. Ahead of him, he could see faces in the callejon, frozen in horror and he heard the warning cries of *"Toro! Toro!"* Five more steps and he would be there, over the protective fence—safe.

The bull was closing the gap. Arenas could sense the vibrations of hooves biting into the sand. He wanted to turn again, to see how close the horns were. But he kept his eyes on the fence and the desperate leap he was preparing to make.

He was so near the barrier now that he could see even tiny details—rings on fingers, gold teeth in mouths held agape. He was going to make it! He started his jump. Only one foot had

181

actually left the ground when he felt himself being lifted high into the air, so high that he was above the *callejon*, looking at the spectators in the first few rows of seats.

He saw the mass ranks rising to their feet. It was then that he realized that he was impaled on the end of the horn.

The bull tossed to its right, the muscles in its neck bunched and quivering. The right horn had caught Arenas in the small of the back, the other rammed into the *callejon*, splintering the thick top plan of the protective barrier with the force of the charge. The bull turned.There were blurs of movement—the color of sequinned gold and silver, of red and yellow as matadors and assistants reacted and set out to try and rescue the *espontaneo* from the beast.

For several seconds, Arenas hung on the horn. Then another toss of the huge head, and the bull sent him spinning into the air, the body somersaulting once before it landed with a sick thud, full length on the sand.

As the terrorist's eyes glazed over and the blood came up through his throat, he was trying to mouth into the sand the ETA battle hymn. . .

We are Basque soldiers. . .

The capes of the matadors swirled through the air as they attempted to lure Tormento away from the fallen man. One assistant raced in while the bull was distracted and dragged Arenas by his feet—away from the danger of the horns. Six red-shirted *monos* held the terrorist, three on either side, as they raced along the *callejon* past the front rows of spectators looking down at the bloodied body.

The surgeon and his medical back-up were putting on their green gowns in the operating room. The doctor, one of the country's foremost horn-wound specialists, slit open Arena's shirt. The terrorist's jacket lay crumpled in the entrance.

"What are these men doing here?" the surgeon demanded,

182

hardly looking up from his task.

"They're police, sir," the nurse said.

"They have no right to be in my operating theatre."

"Will he live?" Martínez asked.

"I'm not God," the surgeon said angrily. "I don't know." He turned to the nurse. "Get these men out of here!"

But they had already gone. They had seen the green jacket in the corner, a huge hole sliced through its back.

Decker extracted the envelope and opened it.

"Jesus!" he said.

There was a first class air ticket for the London plane later that evening and six cassettes, each neatly labeled for one of the major news agencies—two American, French, German, British and Russian.

"We'd never have been able to keep the lid on it if these had got out," Martínez said.

But it was a negative achievement. There were no further in their search for the Princess.

Decker looked anxiously towards the operating table where the gowned figures were bent over the half-naked body of the Beach Boy. He was obviously only a courier, but he could have some information which would set them on the right track. He might not know where the Princess was being held, but perhaps, through him, they could trace a chain right back to the people who were coordinating the operation. And he must have seen his contact who had to be, Decker was sure, one of the Princess's jailors.

"What do you think?" he asked Martínez.

The Inspector did not need to ask about what. Both men had a vivid image in their minds of the green and white figure, high in the air, his body pierced by the horn.

"He may have a chance," Martínez said. "These doctors can do marvels with gorings."

"Indeed we can," said a voice behind them.

They turned to see the surgeon, his gown, like the Beach Boy's jacket, soaked in blood.

183

"Sorry I ordered you out earlier," the surgeon said. "You've got your job to do."

Martínez looked at the operating table and then back at the surgeon.

"Worst goring I've seen. You're right. We can do marvels—but not miracles! Stupid bloody *espontaneo*."

"Yes," Martínez agreed bitterly. "Stupid bloody *espontaneo*."

Chapter Eighteen

"...so that I can be returned to my family. Long live the Basque People—*Gora Euskadi*."

Decker clicked the replay for the tenth time.

"There's something wrong with it," he said to Martínez. "Something that doesn't quite fit."

"I am being held in a People's Prison..." the voice began again.

"She's tense," Martínez said. "That's understandable."

But it was more than that. The Princess obviously was under strain, but there was a note of determination in her voice that had nothing to do with the actual message.

"...I freely admit that I and my family represent a class system which has sought to repress the power of the love of the people...their legitimate rights..."

"That's it!" Decker said. "The rest of the piece flows. Whoever wrote it had an excellent command of English. But that jars. It's inelegant. And its not Marxist jargon. 'The Power of the Love of the People'?"

"It could be just a slip of the tongue," Martínez suggested.

But Decker was thinking back to his conversation with the Prince.

"I am quite sure, Captain Decker, that wherever she is being

held, she is thinking of ways to communicate with us. . . she often talks of the 'vibes' we have. . ."

The King listened grimly to the message. His face was strained, he had hardly slept since the snatch, four days earlier. The Prince had not blamed him. The Princess had wanted to go, and he had agreed, he said. The King's friends had not blamed him either—terrorists could strike anywhere and even members of royal households were entitled to a small slice of normal life. *No one* had blamed him—but he blamed himself. His sense of responsibility, which had driven him to lead Spain, weighed heavily on him now.

He had been in constant contact with Valdés and Santana, and had made daily calls to London, relaying every scrap of information as it came to hand. He still felt he was not doing enough, and was desperate with worry.

"What do you suggest we do now, Captain Decker?" he asked.

"I think, sir, that we should let His Highness hear the recording."

"You're absolutely certain that it's the Princess's voice?"

"No, sir. Only the Prince can tell us for sure."

"Then I agree," the King said, "although it is bound to be very distressing for him."

"I am sorry to have to ask you to do this," said the voice on the phone.

The Prince stiffened his shoulders and prepared himself for the ordeal. He had only just returned from another official function, an address to a meeting of international environmentalist. All the way through his speech, he had had to force his mind away from his wife's predicament, so that no one would see his anxiety and realize that anything was wrong. Thankfully, the meeting had not required the presence of the Princess.

And now there was this! A recorded message from his wife

which might be the last words he ever heard her speak.

"I'm ready," he said, moving to his private desk.

He swallowed deeply several times as he listened. He had a vision of a terrorist with a gun pointing at his wife in some barred room, as she stumbled through the message, a fist gripping a microphone in front of her mouth. He trembled and then pulled himself together.

"Captain Decker has something he would like to ask you," the King said. "I'll put him on."

"Good evening, sir."

The Captain's voice sounded firm and confident. The Prince was thankful that he had insisted that this man be involved.

"Most of the message was the usual terrorist ideological jargon. But there was one section that puzzles us. It's the bit about the power of the love of the people. It doesn't fit. Does it mean anything to you, sir?"

"The power of the love of the people? No . . . it doesn't ring any bells. I'm not an expert in this sort of thing, Captain."

He could almost feel Decker's frustration.

"No sir, what I mean . . . what I'm trying to suggest, is that there could be a hidden message in it somewhere."

"Play it again," the Prince said.

"The power of the love of the people. . ."

Click.

"The power of the love of the people. . ."

Click.

"The power of the love of the people. . ."

He had it!

"Yes, Captain. I think I know exactly what it means."

He had not had a drink since he began watching for the Target. He badly wanted one tonight, but he knew it would be a mistake. There had been two weeks' preparation. First, reconnaissance of the area until he found exactly the right spot, then lining up the scope of the bolt-action Enfield Envoy by practicing on deer, almost as difficult to kill with one shot as humans.

As dusk fell, he abandoned his vigil. It was the ninth day he had waited. But time did not matter, he would be in position for as long as necessary. The day had been no different from any other, but tonight there was a tingling in his neck muscles. He recognized the signs, the old hunter's instinct. Tomorrow the Target would appear in his sights, he would gently squeeze the trigger and the job would be over.

Guadaña refused a morphine injection from Idoia but took two painkilling capsules.

The wound had bled slightly during the two hours it had taken him to get to the bullring, pass the package to the courier and return through the crowds to a taxi stand. It was obviously infected. Yellow tinges stained the bandages.

He looked so white-faced that the taxi driver had twice asked him if he felt all right. He didn't. He had almost collapsed onto the sofa and sat for several minutes in silence.

Idoia and Xabier had said little to him, except to suggest rest and food. He couldn't eat, he would never keep it down, but he had accepted a glass of brandy.

He asked Xabier to turn the television on for the evening news. It was too soon for the courier to have delivered the tapes, but perhaps by now the government had broken, and admitted that the woman had been kidnapped. But there were no reports—nothing.

He picked up the half-finished tumbler of brandy and hurled it against the wall, the glass shattering into tiny splinters.

"The fucking government and their cover-up. Help me upstairs. I'll shoot her now and leave her body outside the Ministry. Then let's see the bastards deny it!"

He was only saying it because of the pain, Xabier thought. Guadaña knew better than any of them that orders were orders and had to be obeyed. But still, he felt that he had better say something.

"We're still on top," he began, calmly, rationally. "They found the People's Prison, they have blocked our messages to

188

the world, but we still have the Princess."

"The Princess," Idoia snorted. "The beautiful, flawless Princess. Can't you see she's nothing but a capitalist leech?"

He realized he had made a mistake in using that word. Now that Guadaña seemed to be losing his grip, it would be up to him, Xabier, to take control and see that the mission was brought to a successful conclusion—whatever it was. And that meant treating Idoia—emotional, unstable Idoia—carefully. He had to keep the cell together.

"Call her whatever you wish," he said, attempting to cover his gaffe. "It is the title she is given in her own country. It shows her importance to them.

"She is our ace, our winning card. They are holding out at the moment, but only because the British people do not know about it. When they do, they will demand action. And they will find out tomorrow. I am going to take the photographs now, and then I will distribute them. Not just to *El Mundo* but to the rest of the national newspapers as well. The government can't buy them all off."

Guadaña looked calmer, almost happy. Xabier suddenly understood that what the older man wanted was immortality as the man who had held a princess prisoner.

"You can't go out, Xabier," Idoia said. "After what happened last night, they must know what you look like." She turned to Guadaña. "Let me go?"

The pale-faced leader nodded his head.

Xabier didn't argue. Idoia was right, it was not safe for him to leave the house. And anyway, he wanted to keep an eye on Guadaña. He picked up the polaroid camera, a copy of the day's *El Mundo*, and walked upstairs.

It was almost midnight. The Minister of the Interior looked across his desk at the six men sitting in a semi-circle. They were all powerful figures; shrewd journalists, opinion makers—and he had to con them. He had thought carefully about what he was going to say, but he did not know if he could pull it off.

"It seems, gentlemen," he began, "that having failed to fool *El Mundo*, the terrorists are now seeing if any of the rest of you is more gullible."

"Since you requested that we show no one the photograph until after this conference, I haven't sought the opinion of my photographic editor, Minister," interrupted the editor of *Ahora*, "but it looks like the Princess of Wales to me."

The other editors nodded.

"Indeed it does look like her," Santana replied smoothly. "But you can do so much with a montage. You know that the history of journalism is studded with fake pictures and documents. Look at the Hitler diaries. The German media was turned into a laughing-stock over that one. I'd hate that to happen to my friends in the Spanish press.

He paused for a while, to let it sink in.

"The Princess is in England, going about her normal duties." He laughed. "Do you think that everyone, including the British royal family, is involved in a conspiracy of silence?"

Some of the editors joined in his laughter, but not loudly enough for his liking.

"Now I will tell you gentlemen, what we think is going on, and why. There has been a split in ETA."

The editors were not surprised, the history of ETA was a history of schisms. Old ETA and Young ETA, ETA 5 and ETA 6, ETA Militar and ETA Politico-Militar. It all made little difference. The terror continued.

Santana had expected just this reaction—curious, but not excited.

"I must stress this is off-the-record for the moment. The big difference with the split this time, gentlemen, is that the breakaway faction is in the majority—and they wish to negotiate a peace settlement."

He had the full attention of the editors now. The end of terrorist violence would be a major leap forward. Not only that, but a story of colossal proportions.

But editors are not to be easily sidetracked even by major stories.

"What's all this go to do with the Princess?" the man from *El Castillo* asked.

"A very great deal," the Minister replied. "The hard core cannot maintain either their credibility or their support if negotiations go ahead. They are, therefore, attempting to create an atmosphere in which nothing anyone associated with ETA says or does could be trusted, and one in which it would be impossible for us as a government to negotiate with them."

"The Princess," said the editor of *El Castillo* softly, but not so softly that anyone in the room failed to hear it.

"They have launched a two-pronged attack. On the one hand, there is a massive disinformation campaign of which these photographs are only a small part. On the other, they have moved in a new commando group to kill and bomb indiscriminately. I need not remind you, gentlemen, that four brave police officers have been killed in the last few days.

"Those negotiations could start soon. I have no need to stress how important the success of them would be to all of us. But first, we must find these fanatics from the hard-core. We are getting close to them, but your help is vital. The more ETA fail in their campaign of disinformation, the more frustrated they will become, and the more they will expose themselves in an attempt to gain attention."

He had not risked looking at them for several seconds. Now he favored them with his full, sincere, politician's gaze. Heads were nodding in agreement and acceptance. He had almost pulled it off, it just needed one last element.

"This is a free country," he continued, "and we have a free press. Print if you wish, I cannot stop you. But to publish such disinformation is playing into ETA's hands. It is a time for careful consideration and responsible action, particularly from you, the leaders of the press. I've never considered any of you to be irresponsible or foolish."

191

Then he offered them a bonus.

"I am sure that following the success of her son and heir's visit, the Queen of England would be delighted to have your London correspondents or special reporters at the palace for an exclusive interview to the Spanish press. The Prince and the Princess could be there too. Then you could ask her herself for her reaction to this preposterous ETA claim."

"When, Minister?"

"Well, there is court protocol to go through but relations are so good between the royal families that the premier could ask the King to fix things quite quickly. Say by... Saturday."

The Minister ushered the editors out, shaking hands and patting shoulders. Then he poured himself a stiff whisky, took a large gulp and looked around his office.

"In three days, I could be out of here, ruined."

If they found the Princess in time, he could keep his promise to the press. If they didn't, she would be dead, and all that he had just said would be revealed as a tissue of lies. After that, the editors wouldn't even give him a job as a copy boy.

In the photograph, the Princess looked tired, but there was no sign of defeat on her face.

"She got guts," Decker thought, "like Molly."

He moved the magnifying glass down to the copy of *El Mundo* that she was holding spread before her.

"We had to make it a headline," the editor of *El Mundo* said. "Anything else would have been too small."

Decker could see what he meant. Even under the glass, the banner was just readable.

"We chose the lead story. In the editions going out to the provinces—that's the first four of the print run—and the two Madrid province editions, it read "Changes in the White House." The city edition, the final run of two hundred thousand copies, comes off the press at four a.m. and is taken immediately to the eight distribution points so that it reached the kiosks by six."

Decker did not want to know these details, but forced himself to be patient.

"I can tell you that stopping the presses eight times and putting a new front page plate on the machine took a lot of explaining. The supervisor got round that by saying he was unhappy with the quality of the print. But even he thought I'd gone mad."

The editor picked up the photograph.

"We had 'Reagan's White House Changes,' 'Staff Changes in the White House'—all possible variations on the theme. This one just says, 'Reagan's Staff Changes.' That means it was bought in the center, somewhere near the Gran Via or Puerta del Sol."

"The old part of the city," Martínez thought, "literally thousands of apartments and houses, and hundreds of streets."

They could have bought the newspaper somewhere other than the area they were holed up in, but would any terrorist in hiding walk too far from a safe house unless he absolutely had to?"

"We've got to check out the kiosks and news vendors," Decker said. "There could be a lead and we must check every street." He turned to the editor. "Señor Rodriguez, you've really helped. What you've done has cut down the area of our search to one-eighth of a big city."

"Which only leaves us with about half a million people to check out." Martínez said drily.

"We'll saturate the place with men tomorrow," Martínez said when the editor had left. "The problem is, we haven't really got a very good description of any of the people we're looking for. Even the pharmacist didn't really add much to the photofits of the man who raided her shop."

"Then there's the woman Etarra," Decker said. "That's even vaguer. And no one seems to have even seen the one who's wounded."

"We might have done."

"Where?" queried Decker.

"He could have been the bullfight fan."

The Inspector grinned.

"Come on, James, we're hot on the trail."

"Thanks to the message from the Princess," Decker said, "we just might have a better description of the young man tomorrow."

"Let's go for a nightcap." Martínez said. He noticed Decker's hesitation. "We've got our beepers. The office will know where we are."

Decker could do with a drink. Unless something unexpected happened, it was only a camp bed to look forward to. A few minutes relaxation would do them good. He nodded.

"There's a disco-pub just down the road," Martínez said. "I'll see if I can get them to play our tune."

THURSDAY

Chapter Nineteen

The sniper rose well before dawn. He ordered black coffee in a workers' bar and watched the overall-clad men around him swallowing their first brandies of the day and coughing on early morning cigarettes. Dressed as he was, in work trousers and a green lumberjack shirt, he blended in well. Even his face seemed to fit—coarse, lined, suggesting a lifetime of hard, unsatisfying toil. No one would remember him an hour after he had left. Nevertheless, he had never used the same cafe twice.

He hid his car and was in position by the time the sun rose. It was going to be a fine, clear day. That was good. Twice he had had to give up his vigil because of rain. He would get one shot. Conditions had to be near-perfect.

He slid the 7.62 ammunition into the rifle's breach and brought the weapon up into position. He could see the door through which the target would emerge.

A hunter needs not only to know where his prey will be, he needs to understand how it thinks. That was why he spent a long time studying his victims. He could predict how his target would stand, how and when he would walk. There would be no sudden moves, because all had been anticipated.

He felt very close to the target, almost like a brother. And that was a good sign too. He only usually felt like that just before a hit. Some time today, the door would open, and the target would be standing there, exposed, vulnerable—and then dead.

There are one hundred and ninety-three record shops listed in the Madrid Yellow Pages, but that does not include the large department stores. Nor does it take into account the primitive stalls in the Plaza de Castilla and the Rastro flea market. If necessary, they would check them all.

They started with the big shops, the ones with a large enough budget and turnover to still have stocks of records that were no longer the hot favourites. Sergeant Urgell, who hated crowds at any time, had the misfortune to draw the Corte Ingles near the New Ministries.

There were ten members of staff on duty in the record department, and it was not until the fifth that Urgell struck lucky. She was a pretty, confident girl in her early twenties. Urgell, ten years married and happily settled into stodgy domesticity, told himself there was no harm in just looking while she answered his questions.

"Oh yes, I remember him," she said. "Only it was a cassette, not a record. And I had to go right to the back of the drawer to find it."

It was all too easy, and Urgell, like most policemen, had a naturally suspicious mind.

"Why do you remember him? You must have hundreds of customers every day."

"Well, *The Power of Love*'s an old record, you see. That's why I had to search for it." She blushed. "And besides, he was quite cute. A little serious, but that makes a pleasant change, doesn't it?"

Urgell pulled the photofit out of his pocket.

"Is this the man?"

The girl squinted at the picture.

"Well if it is, it's not a very good likeness. The eyes are much nicer than that. This makes him look like a criminal."

The obvious struck her. "He's not done something wrong, has he?"

"Don't you worry your head about that," said Urgell, avuncular now.

"Only he did seem nervous, as if he thought everyone was watching him. I put it down to shyness at the time. And when he saw the photographer, he nearly jumped out of his skin."

Urgell felt the hairs on the back of his neck stand on end.

"Photographer?"

"Yes, he was in here for about half an hour, taking pictures for a book about Spain."

"Did he take a shot of the customer?"

"I couldn't say really. He was clicking all over the place. He took several of me, I think he rather fancied me. Just think, I could be in a. . ."

She trailed off as the detective turned his back and hurried away. He was off to find someone in authority who could tell him the name and address of this phantom photographer.

"What are you offering?" Iñaki asked coldly.

The fat Belgian shifted in his chair, making himself more comfortable.

"My client. . ."

"Who is?"

"I don't know who he is," Delgarde thought, "except that he's British, and even that could be a fake."

Aloud, he said, "In my business, confidentiality is everything. You know that. All I can reveal is that I have a client, and that for reasons of his own he is prepared to give you twenty million pounds worth of fire power."

"In return for what? How much do you know?"

Delgarde made a show of pushing his podgy fingers tightly into his ears and shaking his head so that his chins wobbled.

"I do not know anything," he said. "It is enough for me that I supply you with your needs."

"Is there any guarantee that when I have fulfilled my half of the bargain you will come through with yours?"

"My business depends on trust," Delgarde said. "If I renege on you, no one will buy from me again. Which will not really matter because, let's be honest, if I don't meet my commitment to you, I am a dead man."

Iñaki nodded his agreement.

"And what exactly can you give me?"

Ears unplugged, the fat man spread his hands expansively.

"What do you want?"

"Uzi submachine guns, assault rifles. . ."

"M 16s?"

"No good!" Iñaki snapped.

"They are standard issue for the American Army," the fat man said.

"They jam too often. Make it Kalashnikov AK 47s instead."

Delgarde nodded his head.

"And I want .357 Magnum revolvers and rocket propelled grenades."

"All possible," Delgarde said. He could see the glow of expectation in Iñaki's eyes. Now was the time to offer the sugar on the cake, the thing that would clinch the deal. "I can also provide you with Blowpipe and Stinger ground-to-air missiles."

With twenty million pounds worth of arms, he could wage a war that would make Madrid tremble, Iñaki thought. With Blowpipes he could bring down helicopters—planes, even. Madrid would have to increase the occupying forces in the Basque country, just as surely as if they'd actually killed the Princess. Only this way, ETA would have more arms with which to fight them.

Here was a man totally dedicated to a cause, Delgarde thought to himself; it ruled him to a point where most people would brand him as being mad. He studied the silent terrorist, a leader anticipating an armed revolution as other men did sex or money. But was he any more insane than the men who had bought arms from Kalsell in Asia, Africa and South America?

200

"How will the deal work?" Iñaki demanded.

"The money has already been paid into a Swiss bank account. Once you tell me you have completed your part, I will ring my principal and ask him for verification. If he supplies it, I will arrange for an immediate shipment of the weapons."

He could contact Guadaña within the hour, the woman could be released by the afternoon; the Belgian already had the arms in some warehouse, they could be dispatched tomorrow under phony shipping orders. There would have to be considerable planning to get them safely stored. But a new and ferocious campaign could begin by the autumn.

"Very well," Iñaki agreed. "We have a deal."

"The films will be processed in the States," Martínez said. "Each photographer is responsible for delivering his own."

"And this Bond chap?" Decker asked.

Martínez spoke rapidly down the line, then covered the receiver with his hand.

"The job's over. They saw him last night and he said something about taking a few days' holiday—touring."

Touring! No contact address, no set plans. They could broadcast an SOS, but there was no guarantee that he would hear it. And in thirty-six hours he would be of no use to them.

"Did he say what part of Spain?"

"Just a moment... yes... I see. Not Spain at all. Canada. And they think he was going back to New York first."

Decker looked at his watch. 11:03. He reached for his phone.

"I'll call TWA," he said, "you ring Pan-Am. The one who finishes first can get on to Iberia."

At 11:15, Robert Bond was just settling back in his seat ready for take-off. He had one short business meeting in the States, then he would take a well-earned vacation. But instead of taxiing along the runway, the plane seemed to be returning

201

to the gate they had started out from. It stopped completely. He looked out of the window and saw a number of groundstaff running towards the hold.

"This is the Captain speaking," said a voice of the P.A., reassuring, calm. "We are experiencing minor technical difficulties but we expecting only a short delay."

But why did they need to bring out the passenger steps for "minor technical difficulties," Bond wondered.

The door to the first class section was swung open and a man in a smart suit came on board. He talked quietly to the chief purser, and was then led him down the aisle to where the photographer was sitting.

"Mr. Bond? I would be grateful if you would come with me," said the man, discreetly showing his police badge. "Don't let's cause the other passengers any concern. I can assure that you have done nothing wrong, but you must come."

"I have an appointment in New York in twelve hours," Bond said, exasperated.

"I am afraid you will have to miss it."

The voice was firm without being threatening.

"But I'm not under arrest?"

"No, sir, we merely wish you to help us with a matter of security." Bond was about to tell him that in that case he could go screw himself, when the policeman added, "although, of course, if you do not come voluntarily, I have it in my power to detain you."

"You can't fight city hall," Bond told himself.

He rose reluctantly to his feet and took his hand baggage out of the overhead locker.

As they went down the ramp, the officer stopped.

"Are your cameras and all the film you took on your assignment in Spain in your camera bag?"

"Never anywhere else."

"Good, then we needn't unload the hold to look for your luggage."

"Hey, what about my grip, for Chrissake!"

"You can collect that, sir, in New York."

"Thanks a lot, buddy," Bond said. "Thanks a helluva lot!"

The fat man and Iñaki hammered out the terrorist's shopping list. It was unlike any of Delgarde's normal business dealings, because there was no bargaining; he was Santa Claus, giving out presents. He offered some advice on the suitability of weapons, but the Etarra did not need it; his knowledge was extensive, and he knew exactly what arms he needed for the conflict he was about to stage.

When it was over, they shared a bottle of wine, and Iñaki was almost convivial, though his 'small talk' consisted mainly of the history and struggles of the Basque region, its beauty, its culture, its sports and the bright future that one day would be theirs.

Although the arms dealer was bored, he thought it prudent to display an animated interest. He just wished that, in compensation, the terrorist had given him a decent wine instead of this garbage he was being forced to drink.

Finally, when he could stand it no longer, Delgarde stood up and moved heavily towards the door.

"I will go back to my hotel to wait," he said.

Iñaki was on his feet, too.

"It will not be long. I am going to the village now, to make the call that will give the British what they want."

Delgarde winced at the direct reference to his supposed client, but let it pass. He was feeling good—bloody good. He had earned two million pounds for two days work. Both men stepped out into the sunlight.

It was almost perfect conditions. A slight wind, perhaps four miles an hour, but the sniper had adjusted his sight to compensate. No shadow at all. And the target standing against a white wall, talking to the other man.

From the way he had walked out the building, the killer could tell that he was slightly drunk. Excellent. Men with too

203

much alcohol inside them tend to linger, reluctant to break off their conversation.

He lifted his rifle so that he would see the target's white face in the scope, then lowered it down to the trunk. At the moment when the cross hairs were over the center of the chest, he squeezed the trigger once. The target spun backwards, a red stain spreading out across his shirt. The assassin put down the rifle on the ground, rose to his feet, and began to walk, with no particular hurry, back to his car.

Delgarde's first reaction, after hearing the crack of the rifle and seeing Iñaki jerk backwards, was to find cover behind his car as quickly as his clumsy body would allow. Once there, he calmed down, although his heart continued to beat heavily. It had been a sniper—a pro. The bullet had been meant for the terrorist, there would be no more. He gave it five more minutes before cautiously clambering to his feet and getting into his car.

It was only as he was driving away, putting distance between himself and the farmhouse, that the awful truth hit. No Iñaki—no two million pounds! But he still had to tell the man in London—he dared not do otherwise.

He stopped at a bar just outside Biarritz and rung through on the pay telephone.

"Inter-Europe Haulage," a bored female voice said on the other end of the line.

"Can I speak to Mr. Harding, please?"

There was no code, probably the name 'Harding' itself was a password.

The dullness disappeared from the girl's voice.

"Putting you through," she said, and a second later, he heard the strong voice of the man he had met in the Bruxelles car parking lot. "Harding here."

Even speaking to him over the phone disturbed Delgarde. His hands had begun to tremble and he had to grope for the right words.

"I am afraid. . . Mr. Harding, that the deal is off. The client has succumbed to heart failure."

There was a heavy silence at the other end, then Delgarde thought he heard a muttered oath.

"Thank you," Harding said, and hung up.

The girl in the *Corte Ingles* uniform had just left. Decker looked at the photographs with satisfaction. One showed the suspect in profile, another almost the full face. There was only a vague resemblance to the photofit picture.

The Captain studied his expression.

"He doesn't know for sure he's been photographed," he said to Martínez, "and he's probably been telling himself ever since that even if he was, it didn't matter. Because the picture wouldn't mean anything to anyone."

"It wouldn't have meant anything to us," Martínez said, "if it hadn't been for the Princess."

"But even the slightest doubt will nag at the back of his mind," Decker continued, "unsettle him, give us an edge."

Martínez picked up the full-face photograph.

"Every man on the street will be issued with a copy of this. If the bastard moves at all, we've got him."

Colonel Valdés suddenly appeared in the doorway. Decker had not seen the old soldier look so agitated since the time he had brought the news that the blood in the Hortaleza flat did not belong to the Princess.

"We've just had a report in," he said. "Some peasant in southern France came across a corpse. Shot—still warm. The French police did their normal fingerprint check and it appears that the dead man is Iñaki Irribar."

Martínez looked as if someone had slapped him in the face.

"Iñaki Irribar?" Decker asked the Colonel.

"We believe that he is—was—the probable head of ETA, certainly one of the top command. If any single person was in direct control of the kidnapping, it was likely to be him."

"GAL," Martínez said savagely. He turned on his superior

in a way Decker had never seen him do before. "How did it happen? How as it *allowed* to happen?

Instead of taking offence, Valdés was apologetic.

"We do not control their operations. This was probably planned weeks ago, long before the hostage was taken."

"Is there any way of keeping it quiet?" Decker asked.

Valdés shook his head.

"No. It's already on the French radio. The news agencies have sent it on the wires as a bulletin. United Press International, Associated Press, Reuters. It'll be on our radio and TV in the next newscast. No—we can't keep it quiet. No way!"

"So," Decker said, spelling it out, "the man in charge is probably dead. Who's going to give orders to the kidnappers? They're on their own—no instructions, no support. They'll feel isolated—they may panic. And then God knows what they'll do to the Princess!"

Chapter Twenty

Iñaki had been like an older brother to him, and now he was dead! It wasn't propaganda put out by the Spanish government—Guadaña could see the stone farmhouse where he had spent many evenings alone with his mentor, drinking wine and talking about the Cause.

He had warned Iñaki about Spanish Intelligence and GAL. But Iñaki had nothing but contempt for the paid fascist assassins. He had thought he was safe. And now they had killed him. The bastards!

The image on the television screen faded, became strong again and blurred once more. It had started to happen the previous night; now it was occurring frequently. Was he dying? Guadaña wasn't frightened of death, but when he died he wanted it to be as a fighter—in a shoot-out with the police. Not now, for God's sake! Not like this! Another spasm of pain shook him.

His fevered brain made a promise to his dead comrade. The mission would be a success. It would end the way Iñaki had wanted it.

He was ankle-deep in snow again and yet it was so hot. He saw the back of the head of the policeman he shot on that first mission, while Iñaki looked on. The black hair turned fair and reached the shoulders.

Xabier and Idoia were watching the mumbling, disturbed man on the leather sofa.

"GAL, assassins... government blood-money... patriots die for the Cause... she dies, she dies. Iñaki, have another glass of wine... one day we'll be drinking it in Vitoria... she dies..."

The girl bent low over him and gave him another injection.

"He'll be all right again in a couple of hours. He's only got to hold out until midnight tomorrow. Then I'm going to drive him to San Sebastian."

"There are probably other arrangements," Xabier said.

But he didn't know what they were. The plans were all in the wounded man's head.

"To hell with other arrangement," Idoia said. "When we've finished this business, I'm getting him out." She looked at Guadaña, the drug was already having an effect. "I'm going north."

Oh, to be driving north, Xabier thought. He longed for the cool mountain streams, the sound of birds in trees, the clean air.

The sweet, sickly smell of Guadaña's infected wounds filled the whole room. It stuck in Xabier's throat and made him want to retch. But Guadaña had refused to go to bed. He would not leave this room. He sat staring at the television set, waiting for an announcement that never came. It was as if he felt that his very presence in the room meant that he was still in command.

But how much longer would he have even moments of lucidity? How much longer would he be alive?

It was up to them now. An intellectual terrorist who had nightmares about shooting a man in the leg, and a volatile woman, her mind scarred and bitter. Well, if that was the team they had, that was the team they would have to use.

Iñaki's death had brought home to him forcibly that this was total war. ETA had only become extremist because the government was extremist. And nothing had changed—the assassination proved it. If ETA was ever to win, then they must all obey orders without question. And there could be no mercy.

"I'm going north."

Idoia's words, her article of faith, echoed through his brain. He had a premonition that after it was all over, after midnight on Friday, he would never go north again.

The Prince, as he was now doing almost subsconciously, added up the remaining hours to the terrorist deadline. Twenty-eight!

The Queen had consulted the Prime Minister and then talked to him. Unless there were any new developments in the intervening period he could fly to Madrid the following afternoon.

"Everything's arranged, sir," said the Duke of Casla. "We will be using the Spanish/US airbase at Torrejon. Much more discreet that Barajas."

"There will be no press coverage," the Prince said. "If anyone in the media is curious, it will be announced that my wife and I," he looked pained as he spoke, 'are attending a private dinner with the King and Queen of Spain."

Charles had kept his emotions under control when in the company of his family or aides. It was only during the long nights, when half-sleep he reached across the bed to touch his wife and found she was not there, that fear gripped him. Then he turned to bury his face in the pillow or stare at the ceiling, sensing the time slipping away until the first touch of light penetrated the curtains to tell him that dawn was breaking— another day.

He had had no contact with Decker since the phone call about the tape. But all the time, the tune played over in his mind. He thought of the whispers in the morning that he had not heard for so long.

The Duke sensed a emotional crisis building up.

"Getting the photograph of one of the terrorists is a big step forward, sir," he said. "It means the police are getting close."

"Could they really carry out their threat?"

The Duke had feared such a direct question ever since he

had begun shepherding Isabel. He had thought that when it came, he would play it down, minimize the risk. But now, looking at this strong, intelligent man who had carried out his tasks of the last few days with courage and dignity, he knew there could be no evasion.

"Yes, sir. From all reports, ETA is desperate. I think they would."

"If my wife is to die," the Prince said quietly, "then I want to be as near to her as possible when it happens. She may not be able to see me, but she will know that I am there."

"More photographs, Xabier?" the Princess asked, forcing herself to sound bright and cheerful.

The Etarra closed the door and went to his now-familiar seat on the edge of the bed. Guadaña's fever had subsided. But the Princess must have heard them and he was surprised that she did not look worried. Thank God she did not know Basque.

"No. They're finished. No more posing."

He had tried to match her mood, but noticed an instant change in her.

"That means it'll soon be over, doesn't it?" the Princess asked.

"Yes, it will. All being well, you'll be back with your family by Saturday."

"But it isn't all going well, is it? I can tell."

"No, it's not. The man downstairs is very sick. That bullet wound has not responded to treatment and he's in great pain. He should be in hospital, but that's impossible at the moment."

"That's not what I meant, and you know it. Xabier, we've always spoken openly to each other before. Don't lie to me now. The Spanish government is refusing to negotiate, isn't it?"

Xabier leaned forward and looked directly at the pale and worried face.

"That's not strictly true. We have had no indication of the Spanish government's attitude. But that is quite normal in circumstances like this. They will wait until the last minute."

He knew he had made a mistake as soon as the words had left his mouth.

"Until the last minute?" The Princess braced herself and a surge of rage swept her. "What the hell is that supposed to mean, Xabier? Tell me! I demand to know!"

The Etarra remained silent.

"And if they don't give in, you'll shoot me! Isn't that true? And it's quite soon. Come on Xabier. You're talking about me being free on Saturday. You mean free or dead—dead if the government doesn't give way."

"They will. They have to."

"Have to? Am I worth what you call your Basque nation? Do you think I'm an idiot? Have to? Will they sacrifice the political future of Spain for one woman? And I am just one woman."

"No, you're not. You're an English princess."

"English princess! Don't be bloody stupid!"

She rose to her feet, her face now more white with rage than fear.

"You're mad. You're all mad. You snatch someone from the streets, take them away from the people they love, and who love them, and you think that everyone will cave in to your absurd demands. We'll they won't. Don't you know, Xabier, because I do—governments do not give in to terrorists."

Tears rolled down her cheeks.

"You and your lovely Basque country! How the sound of a village choir touches the soul. Oh yes, Xabier, I remember every word you said. Such a peaceful place. Yet you're here planning to kill a helpless woman. Not a Princess, Xabier, not a symbol of a class struggle, not a defender of privilege—a woman!"

She collapsed back into the old arm chair. It was the second time since they had brought her to the attic that he had seen her weep.

Xabier made a move to comfort her, as he had done before.

211

But this time he stopped himself.

The Princess did not look up as she heard the door close and the familiar sound of the bolts being slid across from the outside.

Xabier was right. She was a Princess, and not a normal woman. She hadn't been born to it, but over the last few years had tried her best to live up to the role. If she had to die, then she would do so bravely, playing the part to the end.

"The machine the recording was made on was not studio quality," the police audio expert said. "It hasn't even got a Dolby unit—you can tell that from the background hiss. I would say it's a medium-priced family model, the sort that you can buy in any shop."

That didn't help, Decker thought. He didn't want to know the ways in which it was ordinary, he needed to know what was different about it.

'There was some echo. Possibly it was made in a largish room, but one with a sloping ceiling. An attic? anyway, there was certainly very little furniture or padding."

Decker was disappointed at how little information they were getting. But what had he expected, he asked himself, angrily? The sound of heavy breathing in the background, so that he could search the database for details of asthmatic Etarras? A church clock with a distinctive chime suddenly sounding off the hour?

It was just that the other enquiries were leading nowhere. All the newspapers kiosks had been checked, but none of the vendors recalled serving a young man like the one in the photofit. Maybe they would have more luck the next day, with a real photograph. But the next day was Friday, the final day.

"No other sound at all?" Martínez asked.

"Only one, right towards the end of the message. In fact, just before the 'Gora Euskadi." There is some interference—brief and almost inaudible. I've put the tape through every conceivable test to try and establish what it was—magnified it to the limit."

"And?"

"I can't be certain. It seems to come from some distance, and from a lower level than the one where the recording was made. The best I can do is to tentatively suggest that it's a shout from the street or somewhere. It could be a boy playing, or possibly a *chatarrero*."

"What's that?" Decker asked.

"A gypsy junk collector," Martínez explained. "I believe in England you call them rag-and-bone men."

The expert had no more to offer. Martínez thanked him for his work and ordered him not to say a word to anyone. The audio specialist nodded as if the warning was uncalled for.

"How many of these *chatarreros* are there in Madrid?" Decker asked hopefully, after the audio man had gone.

"Nobody really knows. There are thousands of gypsies living in shacks on the outskirts of the city."

They were like Romanies everywhere—the police had no real records on them.

"I think there just might be something in the *chatarrero* theory." The Inspector continued. "Their voices penetrate anything. You can hear them in the top floor of a ten-story apartment block. Anyway, if that's all the tape has to offer, then every gypsy community in Madrid will be checked out."

He picked up the phone and issued his instruction to the duty Inspector. It seemed to Decker that he was getting nothing but flak in return.

"I know that . . . Yes, I'm fully aware that it's a tall order." Martínez voice rose, and there was authority and determination in it. "But it's got to be done and done quickly. I don't care how many men have to be taken off normal duties."

He slammed down the receiver.

"I've just been told that gypsy communities are clannish," he said angrily. "That they believe that the police hound them and that the sight of a uniform makes them dry up immediately. It wasn't news to me."

He walked over to the percolator and poured himself a cup of coffee.

"He *could* also have told me that trying to pin a gypsy down on time is almost useless. They have no idea of it. You see them with mouths full of gold teeth—they've got plenty of money to spend—but have you ever seen one with a watch?"

He knocked back the strong black liquid.

"My dear colleague could also have added, for good measure, that unless they have a set route, like the ones who collect paper at night, they don't work regular pick-ups. They just go where the fancy takes them. So he's right when he says it's difficult. In fact, it's almost bloody impossible—but we have to try everything."

He lapsed into silence.

"Nearly ten o'clock," Decker said finally. "There's nothing else for it, that photograph has got to go out to all the newspapers and to television."

Martínez was alarmed.

"The terrorist will see it. It'll scare them to discover we have positive identification, especially coming on top of Beach Boy's goring and the shooting of Iñaki. It might just put *too* much pressure on them. They could crack, and that will further endanger the Princess."

"You think I haven't already weighed up the odds?" Decker asked. "But if we don't get a lead in the next few hours, she's dead anyway. It's my request and my responsibility. I don't want you dragged down by my mistakes."

"You're right," Martínez said. "We don't have any other choice. And that's *our* decision. Let's go and see the colonel."

The sound of powerful engines reverberated around the Ministry courtyard. The dispatch riders rode through the gates and pulled onto the Castillana Avenue. For a few hundred meters, they were bunched together, then some peeled off at the lights while others carried on. They were driving skillfully and carefully, within the speed limit. They were not aware that it was the photographs of a wanted terrorist they were carrying, but they knew that it was important that their packages reached the various radio and television stations and the national newspapers. As soon as possible.

Even when he was unconscious, Guadaña's body was working steadily, destroying itself from within. Twice during the last hour, Idoia had tended the wounds, gently turning him on his side as she did so. She wiped up the pus and traces of blood which were seeping out, dropping the alcohol-soaked cotton wool pads carelessly onto the carpet. She tried to ignore the smell.

Xabier watched her. Surely she could see that Guadaña was useless now. But she didn't want to see it.

For the sake of the mission, she had to be made to face facts. She must take control—and he must guide her.

"He's finished," Xabier said, and then, seeing the look on Idoia's face, added quickly, "at least for this operation."

Once again, he found himself facing a woman's fury.

"I'll tell you something. Guadaña is twice the man you are. He's wounded badly, but when the time comes, he'll do what he has to do. He'll perform." There was contempt in the girl's voice. Xabier knew she was referring to the bedroom again. Her voice became steel-cold. "If he cannot, then *I* will not let *him* down."

As with the Princess earlier, Xabier made no reply. Instead he turned up the sound on the television, as the second hand on the screen ticked away the last few seconds before the late night news bulletin began.

Suddenly the screen was full of his face and the sound of a tickertape with the word 'Wanted' stamped across his image. Idoia and Xabier were as frozen as the picture on the screen.

Then came other shots. Xabier leaning across the counter, a full-length photograph of him, then back again to the face.

"The Ministry of the Interior tonight issued these

215

photographs of the man suspected of being involved in the murders of the four police officers in Madrid in the last week.

"The authorities believe that he is still in Madrid and have asked for the urgent cooperation of all citizens in locating him. A special telephone line has been opened."

The newscaster read out the number, then it was repeated on the screen under Xabier's face, just below the word 'Wanted.'

The moment the first picture had appeared, Xabier knew where it had been taken. His disgust with himself was replaced by fear.

"How the hell did they get that?" Idoia demanded.

"I don't know."

"They know nothing about you. They haven't even identified you by name." A sudden insight struck her. "You're lying to me, Xabier. You do know how they got the photograph. That shirt you're wearing now is the same one as in the picture. The shot was taken in Madrid, wasn't it? Recently!"

"Yes. It was taken in a department store. I went there to buy tapes and that Walkman for the Pr. . . prisoner."

"You stupid bastard!"

"I just believed that some music, some songs would help to keep her calm. I told you about it at the time. You didn't object then."

"I didn't know then you'd endangered the whole operation. What the hell was the photographer doing there?"

'I don't know. But it could have happened to you or Guadaña. They still don't know where we are, or my name. If they did, they wouldn't have had to put the photograph on the television."

"But someone could have seen you coming down the street, or even entering this house. They could be outside now. Until Guadaña comes round and takes over again, I'm going upstairs, to sit outside *her* room. If they come in, I'll do what I have to do."

The hands clicked and jumped slightly as they reached the

216

top of the wall clock. Twenty-four hours left. There was nothing more the investigators could do that night. Exhausted and demoralized, they undressed and climbed into their army cots. But sleep refused to come.

Decker tossed and turned, then saw a flame flare up as Martínez lit a cigarette. The Inspector inhaled deeply and then said, "Tell me about your girl."

"She's dead now."

"I know." Martínez's voice was full of sadness for the man he had come to regard as his friend. "Was she pretty?"

Decker thought of the flaming red hair, the deep brown eyes, always so lively, the small, perfect mouth.

"She was beautiful," he said, then relapsed into silence.

"How did you meet her?"

"On a job."

It was Military Intelligence's first—and last—attempt to run a woman in deep cover. Molly and Decker had started out as colleagues—partners trapped in a web of deception and fear—and had ended up as lovers.

It was in a bar that Decker heard the whisper.

"The Provos have taken Molly Fitzgerald in."

His heart raced, his hands felt cold. He wanted to grab his informant by the throat and shake out of him everything he knew.

"Steady, James, steady," said the quiet voice in his head. "If you blow your cover now, you're dead. And then who will save Molly?"

He forced himself to feign only casual interest.

"Where have they taken her?"

"Don't know." The man gave him a hard look. "It's not really my business. . . or yours."

He went from pub to pub, listening, asking oblique questions. It was only after four hours that he got a lead.

"Who took her in? Sean Liddy?"

No, Sean's down in the South. It'll be Liam O'Cafferty, like as not."

If it was Liam, Decker knew where he would have taken her.

It was an inconspicuous dwelling, just one of a row of terraced houses blackened with a century of industrial grime. O'Cafferty himself answered the door.

"What are you doing here, Mick?"

"I need to talk to you."

O'Cafferty took him into the front room—faded striped wallpaper, tiled fireplace, plaster ducks flying up the wall. Two other men sat in old armchairs, drinking tea.

"I hear you've been interrogating Molly Fitzgerald. Where is she now?"

Even as he asked the question, he knew he was too late. There was something about their eyes, a heaviness, but also a sense of relief at an unpleasant job unfinished.

"You've been very useful to us, Mick," O'Cafferty said, "very useful. But I don't think it gives you the right to ask that kind of question. Besides," voice changing from annoyance to suspicion, "how did you know about it?"

Before his gun cleared the shoulder holster, Decker fired, causing a small red spot to appear in the center of O'Cafferty's forehead. He swung round and took out the other two men. Their weapons fell from their hands and clattered onto the floor.

They found Molly in an alley, her body tossed casually on a pile of battered cardboard boxes. There was a black hood over her head. At the back there was a small hole, and dried blood, like gaudy lipstick, ringed it. Her breasts and thighs bore the scars of cigarette burns. Yet she had not talked, even under torture. Had she done so, Decker would have been a dead man the moment O'Cafferty saw him.

And now he was in another hunt, another race against time. What if the terrorists had bought the copy of *El Mundo* in a district far from the safe house? What if the Etarra in the photograph stayed safely hidden until after midnight on Friday? Then the Princess, like Molly, would be dead, and he would have failed again.

FRIDAY

Chapter Twenty-One

Xabier didn't make his move until three o'clock in morning, when he was sure the streets would be deserted. Guadaña would not have noticed an earthquake and he was almost sure that upstairs, outside the attic, Idoia was dozing. But the slightest noise could disturb her. He would have to be careful.

Since his photograph had filled the television screen, Xabier's feeling of doom, of the inevitability of his own death, had increased. Every twenty minutes or so, he had gone across to the window looking out on to the narrow street, to check that the house was not under surveillance. In each shadow, he detected a waiting man. A footstep, the occasional laugh or snatch of conversation, seemed to echo Idoia's warning that they could be outside now. Outside now. . . it was becoming an obsession. He thought about running—but to where? He didn't know. If he ran, he would be a marked man for ever.

But fear was soon replaced by his patriotism, for the Cause, for the Basque country. He could not let down his wounded leader who had taken a police bullet but was still determined to see the operation through. He could not desert Idoia, whom he both pitied and disliked, but who was a brave fighter for the Cause—braver than him.

As the clock chimed three times, he quietly opened the front door. The hinges groaned a small protest, and cool fresh air rushed into the hallway. He stepped out into the street. Slowly, he inserted the key on the outside of the door and eased the catch back. The click sounded sharper than a pistol crack and he paused, listening for any movement inside the house.

The phone booth was only fifty yards away and not a light shone from any window of the houses on his journey.

The occasional taxi, green light on, prowled, looking for late-night customers on the road that intersected with the pedestrian street. Even the bars had closed for the night and the few whores who plied their trade in front of them had moved elsewhere or just given up.

He dialed the Bilbao number that he knew by heart. She answered the phone immediately, as if she had been sitting beside it, expecting the call.

"Xabier! Is that you?"

He hadn't even said a word.

"Marta, darling."

There was a gasp that could have been relief or despair.

"I saw it... Wanted for murder, it said. Xabier, what's happened? Where are you? Is it true? Tell me, darling..."

"You know I can't talk about it," he said.

He didn't *want* to talk about it, there was only one reason he had phoned.

"I love you."

"Oh, Xabier." Again, the plea. "Where are you?"

"I can't talk much longer," he said urgently. He glanced out through the grimy window and saw no one. "I just want you to know I haven't killed anyone. And I want to hear you tell me you love me."

"You know I love you. Xabier, the police have been here. Two of them. They're still outside, in a car... what's happening."

He had known they would be there by now. At his parents' house, too. All their lines would be tapped. He had to put down the phone now.

"I love you, Marta, I always will. . ."

Doña Carmen didn't sleep much. She didn't leave her tiny flat much either—at least not in the daytime. There were too many people, rushing, bustling about. But at night it was quiet, and that was when she and her true friends came out.

She hobbled over to the vacant lot, an old shopping bag in her hands containing milk and scraps. The rubble had once been infested with rats, but they had long gone, driven away or killed by her friends.

She was surrounded by them, purring contently or rubbing against her thin, woolen-stockinged legs, when she saw the young man. He looked respectable enough, but you could never tell these days. She moved into the shadows and watched him pass by. There was something familiar about him— or was there? He certainly looked worried. One of her neighbors, one of the night people? She wasn't sure, and the moment passed. Her friends, tails pointing stiffly in the air, were waiting. She had given them all names. She talked to them and she knew they talked back. That was what friendship was all about. She spread the scraps on pages of old newspapers and poured the milk into tin cans until there was no more.

Five minutes after the call to Bilbao, Decker and Martínez were awake and at their desks.

"The call came through, sir, at exactly 3:06," the duty inspector said. "The transcript is on its way to you."

"Where's he made the call from?"

"We're still checking, but it's unlikely we'll get any positive results. It didn't last more than a minute."

"Fuck it!" Martínez said. "Just another sixty seconds and we'd have had the exact phone."

At least the decision to release the photograph had led to the terrorist breaking cover. That was a bonus, but anything was a bonus. Decker was till deeply depressed.

Police headquarters in Bilbao had received more than a

225

dozen calls before the news bulletin had finished, giving the identity of the Etarra. Xabier Mitxelena, aged 26, law student, upper class background. The computer could not find even a traffic offence, never mind a separatist demonstration, against him.

Phone taps had been installed immediately on any lines the Etarra might use.

The Inspector and Decker studied the transcript.

"Three times 'I love you.' Why the hell didn't the little bastard spend another minute or so talking about how he'd *show* her he loved her when he got back?"

"Because he doesn't think he's going back," Decker said softly. "And anyway, it's not the sort of thing he'd say."

For the first time in the operation, he had an image of one of the terrorists. The young man's words of love were deep and sincere, he could tell that, even from the manuscript. And Decker believed that he had had no part in the murders. He wasn't a gunman.

He picked up the photograph of Xabier and looked at it. Deep-set, intense eyes, serious expression. He had sacrificed his passionate love for the girl to his dedication to the Cause. He was an idealist, not a killer. If he had to execute the Princess, he would never be at peace with himself again. But if he thought it necessary, Decker was sure that he would do it.

Martínez opened the window and breathed in the cool night air. It was one of the few times of night when the city was quiet, when the sound of the traffic didn't penetrate, even through closed windows. There was only a slight hum of noise and the night sky was lit by stars.

Decker joined him.

"The heat of summer can be unbearable, but some nights are soft, like this one."

The captain thought of the hours closing in, to almost single figures on the deadline.

"Yes, it is quiet. Let's get some coffee. We're not going to sleep any more tonight."

Dawn was just breaking over the Moncloa Palace when the Premier received the call from Echeveste. They had been in regular contact since the Communist politician's meeting with Iñaki in Capbreton and he had constantly urged the Basque to make every effort to break the deadlock—to at least get a time extension.

"I have been in touch with many sources since Iñaki was murdered, Señor Presidente, and I have found only confusion. No one appears to be in control, no one seems to have authority to make decisions."

"There must be a leadership structure," the Premier protested.

"You have done a very good job of smashing it," Echeveste said. "Everything hinged on Iñaki, and now he is gone."

The Premier's hands were sweating, despite the cool of the room.

"But surely, ETA will not collapse just because of one man's death?"

"No," the Basque replied, "but if you resigned tomorrow, how long would it take *your* party to select a new leader?"

"But we're not talking about a democratic party. ETA is a terrorist group."

"It is an still an organization, and as with any organization, there is an infrastructure. But it will take time to operate. The leadership is dispersed and will take time to regroup.

"There is one other point," Echeveste continued. "I have heard the Iñaki was not alone when he was assassinated. he had just had a meeting with a Monsieur Delgarde, an international arms dealer."

"And?"

The Premier did not see how this could possibly be relevant.

"Apparently he was not buying the guns for himself. They were a gift from an unspecified source."

227

The British! Had they been conducting a clandestine deal, a deal that could have cost a good many Spanish lives? He was furious, but this was something to discuss with the British Prime Minister, not the Basque politician. He returned to the original subject of the conversation.

"How long will it take the leadership to reform?"

"A week at least."

"And what will happen to the operation that Irribar was controling?"

"The cells are trained to operate without central control."

"Are you are saying that even if we were to give in to all ETA's demands now, there is no one with the authority to accept the offer and no one to countermand the order for the execution?"

"At this moment, that's my information. Absolutely no one," Echeveste replied.

Questioning the *chatarreros* was a hit-and-miss affair from the start, just as Martínez had predicted it would be. Romany settlements all around Madrid were visited by police inspectors; and rag-and-bone men and scrap metal dealers had been questioned throughout the night. To a man, they had been evasive, convinced that the police were, as usual, looking for stolen goods.

Pedro Gomez had missed the police visits simply because his shack was on the edge of a gypsy encampment and the sheer pressure of the task had made them overlook it.

It wasn't until after nine a.m. that the dark-tanned scrap merchant came into the police net.

"Morning, Pedro," said the prowl car policeman as Gomez pulled his donkey-drawn cart into the curb on a main road leading to the city center.

"I've not done anything wrong," the gypsy said defensively, "not since the last time."

"We knew that, Pedro. We just want a little help. It's what you might have seen or where you were at the beginning of the

228

week. Say Monday, Tuesday, or even Wednesday."

Monday, Tuesday, Wednesday. He had been in the old part of the city, but he wasn't going to volunteer that information. Pedro didn't know exactly what game the policeman was playing, but he knew it was a trick to catch him out—they were always up to this kind of thing.

"I was round and about, *jefe*," he said. "I just go where the donkey takes me."

"We could make life very difficult for you if you don't tell us, Pedro," the traffic cop said. "We could take you down to the station. You might be there all day."

But his heart was not in it. It was ridiculous to expect these people to remember where they'd been this morning, let alone yesterday.

"I think I was on Calle Arturo Soria," Pedro said unconvincingly. "Or it may have been Calle Pio XII."

That wasn't the area they were interested in.

"All right, Pedro, you can go. But don't let me catch you obstructing the traffic."

The gypsy flicked his whip and the donkey began to clip-clop away.

"What exactly has been going on?"

"Are you really sure you want to know, Prime Minister?" the head of MI 6 asked.

"I have just been talking to the Spanish Premier. It seems that you have failed in whatever you did to get the Princess released."

"That's not quite true," the man protested. "The deal would have gone through but for the actions of GAL, which, it is widely believed, has strong connections with the Spanish government."

"Whatever the case, since it never happened, I think I can safely know about it. Don't you?"

The MI 6 chief could see that she was in no mood for evasions. He sketched out what had occurred. The Prime Minister listened silently, and when he had finished, she told him coldly that he could go.

She had given her chief of security considerable freedom. But weapons for terrorists! That was too much! The assassination of the Basque had been a lucky escape. The whole deal had been wrong from the start. And if it had worked and then the Spanish government had found out about it...

Heads would have to roll, and it would take careful negotiations to patch up the relationship with Madrid—she heard the clock strike ten—if there was any relationship to patch up after midnight.

When the old lady in black entered the Latina police station, it was already packed with victims waiting to report car radio thefts, break-ins and stolen wallets—a normal night's crime in the old part of the city. The desk sergeant was taking down details while his three assistants typed away furiously, filling in the official forms.

Another dissatisfied customer moved away, and the sergeant, looking up, noticed the old woman in the doorway.

"Good morning, Doña Carmen," he said jovially.

He knew her well. She was of a group of aging eccentrics who were always reporting things to the police. Maybe they just liked the company.

"What is it this time?" he asked. "More robbers in the night rounding up all your stray cats to make fur coats of?"

"It's much more important than that," the old woman said with dignity.

"More important than your moggies. Must be a matter of state security. Or is it a bank robbery?"

Doña Carmen was just about to speak again when the sergeant pointed to wooden bench.

"Just sit down, there, and I'll deal with you as soon as your turn comes up."

She wouldn't mind waiting, he thought, she had all the time in the world. And if she got fed up, well, she could always leave as she had done several times before.

Martínez examined the large-scale map on the wall.

"Absolutely hopeless," he said. "None of the chatarreros can remember where he was clearly. We could pull them in for interrogation, of course, but that would take time, and we haven't got much left. And anyway, we still might miss the one who is actually on the tape."

Decker got up and stood next to the Inspector. The central area, where the *El Mundo* had been bought, was circled. Within that circle were thousands of houses, hundreds of thousands of people. Even if the manpower were made available, house-to-house searches were impossible. If the terrorists were cornered, he was sure they would kill the Princess.

"We need something else," Martínez said, thinking along the same lines. "Something to pin it down more." he sounded as tired as Decker. "There was something wrong with that taped message, and I can't think what."

Outside, there was that typical Madrid sound, a screech of brakes, and that only slightly less normal thud as metal hit metal.

"I can't bloody think with all this noise," Martínez said furiously. He marched over to the window and slammed it shut. The buzz outside decreased, but did not disappear.

"I can't bloody think at all," he said. "That's the trouble."

Then he stopped, midway between the window and his desk.

"That's it!" he said. "The *chatarrero* has been of some use after all."

He rushed over and, almost elbowing Decker out of the way, began staring at the map.

"What have you got?" Decker asked.

All signs of exhaustion had disappeared.

"We know she didn't make the recording in a soundproof room," Martinez said. "We wouldn't have heard the *chatarrero's* cry if that had been the case."

"So?"

231

"So why was the rag-and-bone man's voice the only sound we heard?"

He started making pencil marks along certain streets. There was obviously some logic behind them, but Decker could see no pattern.

"We were listening for what was on the tape," Martínez explained. "we should have been listening for what *wasn't* on it. What can you hear out the window. Traffic! Bloody cars! You can hear them in every room of every house in the city. Unless there aren't any running past outside. Unless the house is situated on a pedestrian-only road. And James, there just aren't that many of them in this area."

Chapter Twenty-Two

"Now look here, young man, I've been here three hours and no one's paid any attention to me."

"It's been one of those days," the sergeant said, looking across at the seated old woman half way down the room. His tone was not sharp, he had a grandmother of his own and she had little idiosyncrasies too. He looked at his watch. Another hour and he'd be relieved. As fast as he and his men took down the details of one theft, another victim would arrive. "A lot of robberies today."

"It was much safer under General Franco," Doña Carmen said. "There was no trouble in those days."

She half-turned to see if the rest of the room heard her. Her audience, all victims of petty crime, were inclined to agree at that particular moment. Several heads nodded.

"Now come on, Doña Carmen," the sergeant said, slightly waspishly, "let's keep politics out of this. We've got enough work to do, without that."

He could have done without *her* today, particularly when half the force appeared to be out on some mysterious emergency. He recalled Doña Carmen's spate of complaints—for a long time hooliganism had been her favorite theme, stones thrown at her cats; then homosexuals meeting in corners of the

233

derelict site where the animals lived; and finally it was drunks, staggering about, disturbing her little friends because, she reckoned, the bars were staying open later than they should have done.

"Come on then," he leaned forward. "It's your turn. What's it about this time?"

Doña Carmen rose stiffly to her feet, making a little more of a show out it then was strictly necessary, just to emphasize how long she had been waiting. She hobbled over to the desk, then turned back, walked to where she had been sitting, and picked up her old string bag. The sergeant drummed his pencil on the counter. She returned to the desk and plonked the bag down in front of the sergeant's face.

"Now about this young man," she said.

"Not someone else disturbing the running of the Doña Carmen Home for Retired Cats?"

"No," she said. "It's about the one who made the telephone call."

"The one who made the what?"

"Yes, the telephone... No, I mean the young man they're all on... you know..."

"Fucking bastards! Son of Bitches!"

The sergeant looked sharply over Doña Carmen's head at the sudden disruption of his domain.

"The fucking streets are not safe for anyone, not even in broad daylight."

The middle-aged man with a wide girth was holding a bloodstained handkerchief to the crown of his head. He was white-faced with anger.

"Now just a minute, sir. You can cut out the foul language."

The man elbowed his way down the room to the desk, all but pushing the old lady to one side.

"Cut out the bad language? Well why don't you bastards cut out the crime in the street? Two little fuckers have just mugged me, snatched by briefcase, right in front of your police station..."

"Calm down, sir. This isn't getting us anywhere. That wound needs tending to."

"The fuck it does. . ."

The sergeant nodded to one of his assistants.

"Take this gentleman to Criminal Investigation."

"First it's my fucking shop, then its. . ."

The man was led firmly out of the room.

The sergeant smoothed back his hair and sighed deeply. This sort of thing was happening far too often.

"Now where were we?" he asked, turning back to Doña Carmen.

But the lady had gone.

The two cars had sped along the road, keeping just under the speed limit. The back vehicle, containing the security men, kept a respectable distance, far enough behind to avoid a collision if the Prince suddenly braked, close enough to come to his aid if he needed it.

The Prince had turned down the idea of a chauffeur, despite his mother's anxiety over his fitness to drive. He needed to be in control of at least one thing. And he didn't want any strangers in the car, only these three people who had been with him since the nightmare started.

He glanced in the rearview mirror and saw the image of his wife. Then his eyes picked out the differences. Isabel wasn't her double, but she was close enough to make it painful. If the Princess had been with him, she's have been in the front, where the Duke of Casla was sitting now. He wondered if she'd ever sit next to him again.

"Take the next left turn, sir," Lady Margaret said.

The Prince indicated, checked in his mirror and swung the wheel.

The special Queen's Flight had been routed from the Royal Air Force station at Abingdon to the Spanish/US military base at Torrejon. It was unlikely that even an RAF fitter had spotted the small group that boarded the aircraft at the far end of the

235

apron in front of the control tower.

The squadron leader and his co-pilot had flown the Prince back from Madrid a few days earlier. They thought it strange that the royal couple should want to return again so soon, but their job was to fly the plane, not ask questions. Although they did wonder why, for the second time, the Prince had declined to take the controls.

As the aircraft taxied, the Prince looked at his watch. He didn't really need to; since the ETA demands his brain had become a perfect timepiece, ticking off the seconds. One o'clock. That meant two in Madrid. Ten short hours to the time set for the execution.

"I suppose this is the last meal? Doesn't a condemned person get a choice?"

That woman, that horrible woman, had escorted her to the bathroom. And she had felt the eyes piercing her back as she took longer than usual at her toilet. There was no make-up, or she'd have put that on too. She had used the clothes that they had brought to her as sparingly as possible, so that if a time like this ever came, she could look her best.

Xabier put down the tray on the bed.

"No, it's not a special meal. This is not a special day."

"Like hell, it's not! Just look at your face. You haven't slept all night. You look worse than I do."

A barrier had grown up between them. It was the same as it had been on the first evening, except then she had been terrified and now she wasn't. Could she really believe that her life would almost certainly end that night and yet accept it so bravely?

He didn't know what to say, so played for time, sorting out the two plates and the cup on the tray.

His life had become dominated by three women, and all of them were brave. His lovely Marta, so far away, sitting by the phone, knowing that he would probably never return, and yet offering no rebuke when he called her, just saying that she was worried and that she loved him. There was Idoia, who would kill without compunction, but would just as easily give up her life for the Cause if she had to do so. And there was the Princess, sitting and waiting. Without hope—but without tears either.

"No, I haven't slept," he said finally.

"When are you going to do it?"

"Do what?"

Xabier knew that his hesitation, the way he was trying to bury his feelings, was confirming everything the Princess suspected.

She looked up and he saw the sadness in her blue eyes, not just for herself, but for him too.

"Xabier, you're a decent, good man. Have you thought what this will do to you? Have you thought about your novia?"

The Princess had touched the chord. She saw the moisture in his eyes.

"Her name's Marta. We're planning to get married in the autumn."

He did not know why he had told her, except that, ever since the phone call, he had wanted to tell someone.

"You are planning it? Or you were?"

His whole body winced with pain. She saw it, and felt pity for him, but at the same moment she twisted her knife in the wound.

"Does she deserve all this? If I was Marta, I'd be wondering if I wanted to spend the rest of my life with a murderer."

Xabier looked down at the captive. Did *she* deserve all this? But for his seizing of the intelligence report, suggesting that it be looked into more closely, she would never have been a prisoner in this attic.

"Xabier, it's not too late. There's only three of you here. You must have a gun. You could take me out of this. Do it for yourself and Marta. It's not too late."

Xabier thought of running on the beach with Marta, her long black hair streaming in the wind. That was only a few weeks ago. He remembered humming that tune with the Princess. But there had been hope then.

Finally, Xabier thought of Guadaña, lying to the couch; and he thought of the brave but fanatical Idoia. They were all fanatics. Even he.

"No, I'm afraid it *is* too late."

In the areas surrounding the pedestrian streets of the old city, there was a great deal of activity. Men just in from the countryside talked to janitors of apartment buildings about their cousins who had just moved into the district but whose addresses they had lost. Researchers from the university asked women out shopping their opinion of the neighborhood. Storekeepers were asked to participate in market research by bright young men from an advertising agency. New customers lingered and gossiped with barmen. The questioners were all detectives and there were more than two hundred of them on the street.

It was one the busiest times of day in the police canteen at Latina. The detectives might be absent, but the uniformed men, just going off duty or else coming on, still filled the place. The conversation was noisy and animated. The air was thick with the smoke of black tobacco.

Decker and Martínez had decided that they would be more useful here than out on the street. There was just a chance that someone in the uniformed branch, one of the patrolmen, had noticed something. It could be a small detail, an unusual happening, which had meant nothing, but which had been stored in a policeman's trained mind and might possibly fill the gap in the investigators' picture.

They had started at opposite ends of the room, sitting at each table and asking a few short questions. Now they were drawing closer. Three more tables each, and they would meet in the middle.

"I don't know exactly what you want, señor." The desk sergeant opposite Decker looked puzzled. "Everything that happens around here is unusual."

Despite the grim situation, Decker smiled. It was a comment that could have come from any sergeant in any police force in the world.

"Take this morning," the sergeant continued, "I was nearly belted, at my own desk, by a mugging victim. And at the same time I was supposed to be dealing with a crazy old woman who'd come to complain that a young man was killing her cats or making phone calls—or some such crap." The sergeant thought for a minute and lit another cigarette. "Poor old thing, she'd waited three hours. I wonder what the man was supposed to have done, anyway. Still, she'll be back, she always is."

Phone calls? And she had been in the police station all morning. . . Decker suppressed the mounting sense of urgency.

"Tell me more about her," he said.

"She's a night bird. Looks after dozens of stray cats. Quite a character, really, but a bit of a pain."

"She feeds them at night?"

"That's when they come out. Always on about drunks and lowlife molesting her—"

"Where?"

"Oh, that's easy. Everyone knows where Doña Carmen's cats are. The Calle Nuncio."

"Is that a pedestrian street?" Decker asked.

"Yes it is, sir. Why do you ask?"

"Don't worry about that, sergeant. Get yourself a replacement for the rest of your shift."

He beckoned to Martínez, who, seeing the captain's excitement, joined him immediately.

"Julio, we're going with the sergeant to have a talk with a lady named Doña Carmen.

They left the car at the end of the street and walked one at a time, well spaced out, to the old woman's house. The agents sized up the houses on each side of the narrow road.

"Not a bad place to hide a hostage, buried away in lower-middle-class respectability—that is, if she is here," Decker thought.

The apartment was up three flights of worn wooden stairs. The door, huge and solid, was painted dark brown. When the sergeant, now out of uniform, knocked, the peep-hole opened and they heard the sound of a key being turned.

'I had to leave the police station," Doña Carmen explained. "I just couldn't stand all that swearing and shouting." She shot the sergeant a hard look. "I hope you locked him up. His kind shouldn't be allowed on the street."

"Doña Carmen," the sergeant said, "these gentlemen want to ask you some questions about the man you saw."

"The man with his picture in the papers? What do you want to know?"

"Tell me about the phone call," Decker said.

"Well, I was feeding my cats, poor little things, I don't know what they'll do when I'm dead and gone, they're all so thin and—"

"When exactly did you see him? Decker interrupted.

"You mean last night, or the other times?"

"You've seen him more than once?" Martínez asked.

Both he and Decker were keeping cool, but threads were beginning to make a pattern.

The old lady looked at him as if he were mad.

"Well, of course I have. He lives across the street." She led the Inspector to the window. "I don't go out much in the day-time. My cats come out at night, you see. So I just sit in my chair and look out of the window. I don't miss much," she said with pride.

"Which house is it, Doña Carmen?" Martínez asked, disguising his impatience.

She pointed a bony finger.

"That one there."

It could all be a crazy old woman's ramblings, or her attempt to make herself seem important, Decker thought. The reference to the phone call could be just a coincidence.

"How long has he been living there?"

She looked vague.

"Not long."

But how long was 'not long' to someone who had seen at least eighty summers.

"Last week?" Doña Carmen said hesitantly.

Or the week before, or last month? Just how sharp was this old woman? Was she the type of person who could log every moment, every little scandal, as well as a computer? Or were these just the meanderings of a fading mind?

"Have you seen anyone else come out of the house?" he asked hopelessly.

"Oh yes, all four of them. There's his wife, at least I suppose she's his wife, but you can never tell these days, can you? Then there's the older man. He walks very stiffly, I think he must have arthritis."

"Or a bullet wound," Decker thought.

"You said you'd seen four of them coming out."

"Well, not exactly coming out," Doña Carmen admitted. "But I did see the other one go in once. Another girl—a bit tarty, she was."

Decker looked out of the window onto the street below. If the other woman had been the Princess, how good a look could Doña Carmen have got of her as she was hustled out of a car and into the building?

"What makes you think she's a tart?"

"For a start," the old woman said, in a tone which clearly indicated that she would tolerate no argument with her opinion, "she was wearing a wig. I know that because she hadn't even bothered to put in on properly. I could see her real hair underneath. And it wasn't black like the wig. She had bleached it. Trying to look like a tart, as I said. Or a foreigner."

Chapter Twenty-Three

Decker looked through the window of Doña Carmen's flat at the house opposite. The front door was solid. The downstairs windows had iron grills over them: the upstairs ones did not, but they were too small for an armed specialist to crash through as the SAS had done on the Iranian Embassy in London. The roof, he noted, was of thick tile.

Even so, entry presented no problem. The door could be blown or the roof smashed through. It would only take a few seconds, but that was longer than it would take a man holding his gun on the Princess to pull the trigger.

Decker turned and faced the room. It had become the nerve center of the operation. As well as the investigators, it now contained Colonel Valdés and two officers from the GEO.

"According to the audio expert's analysis of the tape," Decker said, "they have her in the attic and if that's where she is, we have to rely on the element of surprise, hitting them before they even know we're there."

"What about sending a man in to look around first?" Martínez asked. "Pretending to read the meter or something?"

Decker shook his head.

"They must be edgy, given the latest news. They'll be monitoring television and radio constantly. Someone knocking on the door would only make them more nervous."

Valdés was feeling better than he had since the night of the cornfield. His men had the bastards trapped. They weren't going anywhere now. If only they could get the hostage out safely. What an achievement!

"When do you intend to go in?" he asked.

The temptation, after all the searching and frustration, was to hit them immediately. But psychologically, it was better to plan every step and wait until the heat of the day had had its effect, when they were most off their guard.

"Late afternoon, I think," Decker said. "They have a definite time to shoot her. Even if we wait until seven o'clock that still gives us a five hour margin."

Guadaña, The Scythe, was dying, and he knew it. Bouts of delirium were more frequent now, and the early days, the days with Iñaki, seemed to hold more reality than the present situation. At the moment, he was lucid, but he did not know how long it would last. And even though he could think quite clearly, the shapes of Xabier and Idoia, looking on anxiously, were blurred, sometimes double images.

"I will execute the woman," Guadaña said. "Now. Help me upstairs."

"Our orders are to wait until midnight. That's what was stated in the ultimatum. A lot can happen between now and then. I still believe they might cave in."

Xabier waited, hoping that Guadaña had fully understood his point.

"There is no High Command any more. Don't you understand that?" Guadaña was aware that he was slurring his words. "This operation was Iñaki's and now Iñaki is dead. There will be no deals, no last minute surrenders." He forced himself up onto his left elbow. "They know what you look like, Xabier. The longer we delay, the more chance there is that they will find us. That is why we must carry out Iñaki's order as soon as possible."

243

But fear of the police was not the real reason for his desire for speed. This would be his last operation and completing it, by executing the woman, would be the final, crowning act of his struggle—the ultimate gesture. It would make him a legend. The name Guadaña would always be mentioned when, in the days of liberty, they remembered the war and the men who fought it and he did not think that he would last until midnight.

His temperature rose again and once more reality and imagination became fused.

"Did I do well, Iñaki? Did you see the policeman fall?" he mumbled.

Xabier turned to Idoia.

"What do we do now?"

"You heard him," Idoia replied. "He wishes to kill the woman himself, and he's the leader. He will be normal again in an hour or so. Then we will help him to do it."

Xabier followed her across the room to the door that led into the kitchen.

"Idoia," he said, almost conspiratorially, "whether Iñaki is dead, whether no one is left in command, is all immaterial. Operation orders are never broken. The prisoner is to die at midnight if there is no agreement. How can we disobey that order?"

There was scorn in her eyes and bite in her reply.

"I had you figured right at the start, with your posh accent and your so perfect English. Intellectual is written all over you. One of the theorists who think a lot and does nothing except talk."

By now, both were in front of the window and Idoia inched the drape back to scan the street outside.

"We are an autonomous unit, not responsible directly to ETA Military Command. We can act without consulting anyone if the situation demands it."

She spotted a man in blue overalls walking past. She wondered if... but there were bound to be people on the street in daylight. She recalled that in previous operations, in tight situations, everyone looked suspicious. It was a time for restraint, to stop nerves from jumping in alarm at the sound of a cough.

"In this case," she continued, "the one man who could change the operation's timetable is dead. If Guadaña chooses to execute the woman upstairs before the deadline, then so be it."

Her eyes were emotionless as she looked at Xabier. "You've never been on an operation like this, have you? On an operation where people die." She looked at the open door that led to the living room, a nod of the head indicating the man who was in that room, lying on the couch.

"This is when theories end and the reality of the struggle starts. If the Spanish manage to find us, they'll show us no mercy. And do you know why? Because they know that we don't expect it—we don't even want it! They might hate us, but they respect us, too. Because we're not afraid to die, and we always carry out our threats."

Once again, Xabier felt the surge of admiration that this woman could inspire in him. What she said was true. ETA had fought hard and made sacrifices to earn not just the loathing, but also the respect of the enemy. They must not lose it now.

"I will not have the slightest hesitation if I have to pull the trigger," Idoia added. "I don't consider I will be ending a woman's life. What I will be doing is fighting the class system, striking a blow against Spanish imperialism. Above all, I'll be winning a battle for the Basque country."

Diana thought she heard the groan of the staircase several times since Xabier had left and each time she imagined the girl, or the pale-faced man, gun in hand, ready to put an end to her ordeal.

She had tried to get a message out, but had no idea if she had succeeded. She had tried to win Xabier over to her side and had clearly failed. She attempted, by standing on the chair, to touch the skylight in the sloping roof, but she knew before she began that it was far too high.

245

She had run out of ideas, run out of hope. For a while, she paced the room, her brain welcoming the movements of her body. Such movement helped to slow the pace of her heart.

Then she knelt on the dusty floor and pressed her hands together.

"Dear Lord," she said aloud, "if you cannot save me from this, then give me the strength to face it bravely, as a good Christian should. And please let it be quick! But if there is hope, Dear Lord, then please consider... Oh God."

She could see her children as clearly as in the photograph she kept by her bed at home. She could see them on the beach playing sandcastles in the sunshine of a summer's day. She could feel the little arms around her neck, hugging her, depending on her.

And she could see her husband, strong and determined. He would take care of them and give them the love that she would no longer be there to provide.

She could imagine her funeral; the solemn cortege parading through the streets of London; the carriage drawn by black horses with her coffin on it, draped in the Union flag; the marching soldiers; the dense and silent crowds along the route. There were always crowds wherever she went... She smiled sadly at the irony of it all.

It was a terrible thing to have to face these last few hours alone, without her husband, without the children, without the family and friends. Every dying person was entitled to that. It saddened her that no one would ever know how brave she was trying to be in the face of death, not even the boys whom she would now never see growing up.

Would the terrorists let her write a final letter to her husband, just a few lines to tell him her thoughts? They were robbing her of her life; they would surely not refuse her this last request. Her head fell forward and her hands brushed through her hair to grab the back of her head. She was determined not to let them see tears when they came through the door.

Looking out of the car window, the Prince saw the King taking the steps down to the palace forecourt three at a time. Something had happened—he dreaded to ask what. He had the door open even before the car had stopped.

"They've found her!" the King said.

The Prince looked anxiously at the expression on the King's face. He could tell that his wife was not dead, but neither was she safe. *Found* her?

"What I mean is, they know where she is."

So the nightmare of uncertainty was to continue.

"*Where* is she? Is she all right?"

The King took the Prince's arm and the two, without a word to the Duke of Casla, Lady Margaret or Isabel, walked up the steps into the palace.

"They've located the safe house where she's being held."

"I have to go there," the Prince said, his voice cracking slightly.

"I know."

"You're coming with me?"

"Of course I am."

They had reached the top of the steps.

"Do they have *any* idea what state she's in?"

"No. But ETA do not usually mistreat their hostages."

"Until they kill them."

The King could only grip the Prince's arm harder.

Valdés took Decker and Martínez into Doña Carmen's tiny kitchen.

"All operatives are in place, captain," he said. "I have spoken to the Minister. He has conformed that agreement has been reached between the two governments that the decision on the nature of the assault is to be left to you—subject to my final approval."

He was sounding very formal, but he had been told to spell it out. It had been made clear that it was to be an Anglo-Spanish assault—joint blame for failure.

Fuck it! He was not a politician and neither were these two men. Now the fallout had been divided up, perhaps they could get on with the job.

"If I was in charge," he added, "I'd do it the way you suggested. Surprise them from the inside."

Decker nodded.

"I'll go in myself."

"How many men will you take with you?"

Decker had examined the plans of the house. The rooms were small, the corridors were narrow. It was all too enclosed for a full team, but it was difficult to decide just how many operatives to take in.

"I think I can only effectively use one man."

"One of the GEOs?"

Another decision—already made. He wondered whether he was letting personal preferences blur his usually clear thinking. Martínez had been good in the raid on the first safe house. They seemed to click.

"I don't think so. Throughout this operation, we've been keeping things as quiet as possible. None of your Special Operations Group knows who's being held hostage. I think we can keep it that way."

"Then. . .?"

"I'd like to take Martínez in with me." He turned to the Inspector. "You don't mind a smelly job, do you, Julio?"

The Inspector hadn't been quite sure what his role would be in the final assault. He was a police officer; he had not received the same training as Decker. If he had been left out, he would have understood—but he would have been bitterly disappointed.

He smiled at Decker.

"Nothing wrong with a bit of shit."

At 4:30, the Calle Nuncio was as quiet as on any normal warm spring afternoon. The residents who had returned for lunch were mostly having an afternoon siesta, and the traffic running past the end of the street was minimal.

The discreet bustle of armed and highly trained men had not been noticed, except by the owners of the cafe and the shop, whose premises had been commandeered. Inside these buildings, a team of GEOs with scaling equipment, stun grenades and small arms sat quietly awaiting orders.

The two house painters further down the street went about their task at a leisurely pace. A parabolic antenna, the first in the street, was being installed on the roof above Doña Carmen's flat. The drunk sprawled out in the doorway, an empty gin bottle at his side, appeared to be oblivious to everyone. The unmarked police cars at the end of the street could have been tagging any vehicles illegally parked. No one had been stopped entering or leaving the pedestrian street. But everyone had been photographed and three people had been followed until it became obvious that they were going about their legitimate tasks.

Earlier, a police helicopter had passed overhead. It was a common occurrence and most people did not even look up. But the authorities were now in possession of detailed photographs of the rooftops along the street, including the attic with the small window.

The police had details on every resident of the street. They even knew about the afternoon lover of the housewife who lived on the corner. Nothing had gone unobserved. The Calle Nuncio had within a few short hours revealed its secrets— except for what was happening in the house at the end of the street.

Chapter Twenty-Four

The tunnel was so narrow and low that after walking doubled up for a hundred meters, the five men decided it was easier to continue on their hands and knees. The thickish brown effluent slopped around their ankles, its odor filling their noses and making them retch. Even so, it was more comfortable than putting on protective masks would have been.

Decker saw small gleaming eyes in the beam of his torchlight, Martínez felt his hand brushed by the fur of a huge rat as it swam past through the rippling slime.

"Here," the sanitation engineer said authoritatively, pointing to a section of wall.

The GEO tunneling experts began exploratory taps. A small pipe ran into the main tunnel, the occasional drip of water moistening its rim.

Martínez unhooked the field telephone.

"What is the situation in the house?"

Valdés's voice came through clearly.

"Little activity, although the drapes have moved several times. Someone there is nervous."

That didn't help.

"We are beginning the tunnel now," Martínez said. "Start diversionary action."

The low whine of the drill echoed down the sewage pipe as the GEOs started to cut around the edge of a thick stone block.

Idoia went down the old basement to be alone. She could no longer bear to be close to Xabier, and it disturbed her to look at Guadaña.

She prowled back and forth, nervous and tense. This was the place where, in the old days, the servants would have spent most of their working lives, catering to every whim of their capitalist masters. It was a cool room, but not airy. She looked at the rough walls, the well from which the downtrodden maids had drawn the water for their employers' baths, the old coppers in which they had heated it, the row of three stone sinks and the rimmed wash boards where clothes were scrubbed until they were spotless. What a life the poor bastards must have had!

The circular well-cover was cast iron and split down the middle. The heavy hinges, rusted now, left a gap of perhaps five centimeters between the well wall and the cover. Idoia drew the bolts, swung back one half of the lid and looked into the gloom.

It was a deep hole, black and musty. She felt a strange urge to step over the wall. She was sure that she would float down into gentle oblivion, and then there would be more struggle, no more disappointments. Never again would she see people staring at her face.

Fool! she told herself angrily. That was not her way. She was a fighter. When she flung back the lid, the loud clang jolted her.

"Jesus, my nerves!" she thought.

Reaching down, she pushed the bolts back into place.

It was time to get back to Guadaña. She climbed the stone stairs. A sudden sound in the street made her rush to the window. Forcing herself not to fling back the drape, she pulled it only a little, and gently, as if a breeze were disturbing it. There were workmen, with picks and pneumatic drills, cutting

251

into the asphalt thirty meters down the road. A generator was humming and she could see that it bore the gas company's logo on it. Why did it have to start at this time? But they were always digging up the roads; there was nothing to panic about.

She would be glad when Guadaña had come out of his fever and they could get on and finish the operation.

The drill hammered on, causing the window panes to rattle. It was no good her telling herself that it was normal—she just didn't like the coincidences. Again with care, she edged the drape to one side and looked at the drunk. He was still there, sprawled in the store doorway, seemingly unaware of the din around him. What would Guadaña make of that? It was no good asking Xabier.

She glanced at the attic door, turned and, with one hand on the banister, mounted the stairs. She hesitated on the landing, then drew back the bolt, inserted the key and opened the door.

The Princess was lying on the bed staring at the window in the roof. Idoia stood silently as she turned to her side and they eyes met. For fully ten seconds the two women watched each other, like wild animals, each waiting for the other to look away. Then the Princess sighed, as if the whole thing were pointless, and rolled onto her back.

Idoia was pleased that it was not her who had broken off the mutual exchange of hatred. But as she went back down the stairs, she realized that the other woman had displayed no fear, and a wave of anger possessed her.

One of the observation team scanning the terrorists' safe house with binoculars, turned in his chair.

"First floor, left hand window. The movement's stopped now, but I definitely saw a head, possibly a woman's. She appeared to be looking up the street."

"The drilling's disturbed them," Valdés said.

He had known it would, but it was an operational necessity. He scanned his mental picture of the street, imagining it from the perspective of the safe house window. The bar, the store, the men working on the road. The drunk!

"Get Perez out of there," he ordered the radio operation. "Even someone pissed out of his mind would be disturbed by that noise."

The tunneler drilled a hole down the side of the first stone block. The drill produced a powerful, high-pitched whine but it was still a considerable time before the operator was satisfied.

"They built this to last," he said to Decker. "The mortar goes all the way through. Almost half a meter."

He drilled a second hole immediately below the first and then another. Decker appreciated that it was not easy under such cramped conditions, but the operation still seemed to be taking a maddeningly long time.

Finally, it was done. The tunnelers struggled and grappled and the stone reluctantly came away. It left a seventy-five centimeter hole in the sewer wall. Decker looked through it and could see only blackness, but he knew that three meters further in—if the sewer superintendent had done his calculations correctly, and if the old plans were accurate—was the well.

The tunneler began drilling around the edge of the second stone. Decker's watch showed that they had been underground for seventy-three minutes.

Xabier's resolve to see the operation through had replaced the gnawing fear of death. Like Idoia, he was avoiding all contact with his fellow Etarras. The drill outside had shaken him. What if they were out there?

He placed a chair in the passageway between the front of the house and the living room. He was certain that the front door was the logical way in if an attack was to be launched. Magazines of 9mm ammunition lay by the side of the chair and on his lap he cradled the short, stocky Uzi.

He could spray the corridors with rapid fire. Enough to keep anyone back. There would be no hand grenades from any assault squad, not with the Princess in the house. Christ, he was acting as if they really were already out there. There was no proof of that. His vigil was disturbed by Guadaña's moving restlessly on the couch. If the fever ran its normal course, he should be conscious again soon.

"Xabier, what's the time?"

"It's a quarter to. . ."

But the sick man had already drifted away.

Once they had removed the stones, they made quicker progress, but were still not fast enough for Decker's liking.

They cut through shale, earth and rubble, and each bucketful had to be passed back down the line, then pushed by a crawling man to a dumping point further up the sewer. There, it made a tiny dam, until the brown liquid had built up enough to spill over its top. The carrier crawled backwards to the hole, and was handed another container.

The journey to empty away the rubble got shorter and shorter as the piles built up.

"They must be four meters in by now," Decker thought. "They missed the well!"

What could they do then? Make another tunnel? And if that was wrong too?

The GEO man's feet appeared, then he squeezed the rest of his body out.

"I've hit dressed stone again," he said. His voice was calm and professional. For him, it was just another job. "It must be the well."

"How long will it take you to break through?" the Captain asked impatiently.

"The well stones are probably thinner than the ones in the sewer wall, but we daren't use a drill in there because of the noise. We'll have to chip away at it with chisels and if anybody's in the kitchen, they might even hear that."

"Do the best you can," Decker said.

Dear God, he hoped they had been right to come in this way.

It was another twenty minutes before Decker was at the end of the tunnel, his torch scanning the black scene. The water level was two meters below them. Dust and small bits of rubble fell onto his face as he eased his shoulders round to stare up to the well mouth with its metal cover. He estimated that he faced a climb of about fourteen meters. There were no iron rungs to help.

Martínez watched as Decker lowered himself through the hole and disappeared. He heard the scrape of boots on stone.

The King was dressed in an old linen cap, a lightweight fawn jacket and a pair of baggy trousers, with shoes that hadn't seen polish for a long time. The Prince had on a fair wig which covered his ears and flowed down to his collar. Both felt slightly ridiculous in their disguises, but after all they had done to keep the kidnapping secret, it would have been foolish to be spotted by a local who would ask himself what exactly the monarch and the heir to the British throne were doing entering a house in the Calle Nuncio.

All inessential GEO staff had been cleared from the area. Only the radio operator and the spotter, both sworn to secrecy, remained.

"Is that the place?" the Prince asked.

"Yes, sir. But don't go too near the window—stay in the shadow."

So even at this stage, he was being kept well away, he thought frustratedly. He wanted to rush across to rescue his princess himself. But it was a job for the experts. He prayed to God that they would be in time.

Valdés knew what a great deal of effort it must be costing for the Prince to stand by inactive. The colonel hoped that he would not be rewarded with a bullet-ridden corpse.

Decker made a reverse hand hold and twisted his body round, then stretched out his legs so that they were jammed tight against the side of the well. He felt the nails in his boot soles gripping. He moved one foot, then the other, and edged his back upwards.

It was fifteen minutes before he reached the top. He felt the cool surface of the metal lid pressing against his head. This was the most dangerous part of the operation. If they had heard the tapping of the tunnelers, they would be waiting for him—and he was as good as dead.

He took out his Browning, the silencer already screwed on. Then tapped lightly on the cover, and pointed his gun upwards. Nothing happened. He tapped again. He could hear no movement. He waited for a few seconds then raised one hand to lift the lid. It didn't budge.

A bolt or a lock? And where was it? He slipped his fingers into the gap at the rim of the well. His fingers could just touch the top of the cover. Not enough. Even if the bolt was on the very edge—and that was unlikely, he would never get a firm enough grip to move it. He had to get his wrist and at least some part of his forearm through the gap—and he could see that it wasn't wide enough.

He pushed with all the strength not needed to keeping him wedged in position. He could feel the rough iron tearing at his skin. He gained a centimeter, perhaps two. Then, suddenly, both the lid and his body gave a little, and his wrist slipped through.

"I said, 'What's the time?'"

"I know you did, but when I told you, you'd gone to sleep again."

Guadaña eased himself into an upright position. His face was gaunt and his skin almost gray. He hadn't shaved for three days and the grizzly stubble only served to highlight his failing condition. He dry-retched and his body almost doubled over. Xabier moved to assist him, but Guadaña waved him away and somehow, by grasping the table, he managed to pull himself to his feet.

"Has there been anything on the television. . . anything about the government giving in?"

Xabier said nothing.

"Get Idoia," Guadaña ordered. "It's time to do it."

Decker could tell from the texture that the bolt that joined the two sides of the cover was old and rusty. He took the small oil can out of his pocket, passed it through to his outside hand and lubricated the catch. A sharp metal edge sliced into one of his fingertips. He pulled on the bolt—and it gave.

The rest of his body ached almost as much as his arm. He edged around, moving first one foot, then the other, then his back, until he was on the other side of the well cover. He forced his hand through the gap, easier this time, and slid back the other bolt.

He inched the lid upwards, grabbing one side of it with his free hand. He glanced around the deserted kitchen, aware that at that moment he was totally helpless. Then he hauled himself up, sat on the edge of the well and gently lowered the lid backwards. Almost in one movement, he had the nylon rope off his back and flung one end of it down to the waiting Martínez. Immediately he felt the tug, and he braced himself, as his fellow agent began his rapid, if clumsy, ascent.

Guadaña edged around the table, then lurched across the room to the sideboard. He realized he would never make it upstairs alone, and this time, when Idoia and Xabier came to support him, he accepted their help.

Each movement sent spasms of pain shooting up his side, but he was determined to finish the job that Iñaki had given him.

The television screen flickered, the sound was just a murmur—not enough to stop Guadaña from hearing the slight noise from the kitchen.

He half-turned his head and his helpers looked inquiringly at him.

"What the fuck was that?"

257

Idoia and Xabier had heard nothing.

"There's been quite a din outside, all afternoon," Xabier said. "Gas repair. We've been checking all the time you've been asleep. I can't see anything suspicious out there."

They began the slow and torturous journey up the stairs.

Decker and Martinez used sign language as they mounted the stone steps from the kitchen. At the top, they hugged the wall and listened. All they could hear were the footsteps on the stairs.

The Inspector breathed, rather than spoke, down the minute microphone attached to his shirt.

"Entrance effect. No sign of occupants. Moving past kitchen level. Have Assault Team alert to move."

In Doña Carmen's living-room, there was absolute silence. The King and the Prince were at the back of the room, doing their best not to get in the way. Any second, the Prince feared, there would be an outbreak of firing.

The King pulled the Prince's ear to his mouth and translated the first message that had come out of the terrorist hideaway. The silence dominated everything. Even the road drill had stopped. The King could hear the Prince's breathing, and sensed the thumping of his heart.

They had reached the second floor when Guadaña ordered a halt. He had been worried ever since he thought he heard a noise in the kitchen. He raised his left hand gripping his gun to his mouth, to indicate silence.

The others looked at him, puzzled—was he delirious again? Then they all heard the distinct click of a catch and the slight creak of a hinge.

"That's the kitchen door, I know it," Idoia said.

They had found the safe house. Guadaña looked up the stairs. Even with help, he could never reach the top before the enemy arrived. So, he was to be denied completing his final—

and greatest—mission. But he would make sure, at least, that his dead leader's orders were obeyed.

"Leave me here," he said to Idoia. "I'll hold them off. Carry out the sentence now. Xabier, you go with her."

Even as he spoke, he was assessing the field of combat. The terrorist eased himself into a full-length position, his face and body partially protected by banister rails.

He felt cold, although he was sweating, and his ravaged brain pictured the deep snow on the day his rage was satiated by his first killing.

He knew they were downstairs.

At his back, he could hear the sound of Xabier and Idoia running up the stairs, almost at the attic.

The sound above them told Decker and Martínez that their presence had been detected. Speed, not silence, mattered now. They moved rapidly down the corridor, one covering, the other running, until they had reached the foot of the stairs and the entrance to the living room.

The Inspector bunched up and then charged into the deserted room, spinning round, his machine gun sweeping the area. The only movement was the flickering light from the television set. He turned and waved to Decker to move to the stairs.

The captain edged towards the main banister rail. Rapid fire erupted, the bullets splintering woodwork and plaster, low and to his left. Decker flattened himself, clear of the terrorist's angle of fire. He waited a second, then leapt forward, low, spraying covering fire up the staircase. Martínez hurled himself past Decker and lay prone on the first five stairs.

"Come on up, you bastards! *Gora ETA!*"

The roar of rage and pain came rolling down the stairwell and another burst of fire thudded into the wall. The Etarra saw the ceiling wobbling like sponge rubber and the floral pattern on the faded carpet below him rippled as if in a breeze. He closed his eyes and shook his head. He felt beads of sweat trickling down his cheeks.

259

The flowers turned white and the snow seemed deep. The veteran of a score of ambushes, shoot-outs and close-range murders knew that this was his last mission. He was dying. But he wanted to last long enough to take these men with him. He emptied another magazine, firing wildly.

As Decker made the first landing, Martínez squeezed off continuous shots. Decker crawled rapidly to the foot of the second staircase.

Springing to his feet, and almost bent double, Martínez emptied the rest of his magazine in the direction of the prone figure he could see above him. Decker raced up the stairs, throwing himself full length, and firing at the terrorist now only a few feet from him.

Diana got slowly off the bed. She had heard them pounding up the stairs. Her mind was now a blank and she shook with fear as the door crashed open.

Xabier saw the prisoner, trembling as her hand reached out to grip the top of the easy chair.

Idoia pointed her .38 at the Princess. Xabier found himself leaning his back against the door to push it closed, as if to exclude, from the rest of the world, the sound of what was about to happen.

"Sit down!" ordered the woman.

The Princess looked at her, uncomprehendingly.

Idoia stepped forward and pushed Diana down. There was no resistance. The hostage was limp and lifeless, and as her body sunk into the chair, her head almost touched her knees.

Despite the gunfire on the stairs outside, and the obvious seconds ticking by before what must be a final confrontation, Idoia found herself rolling a headscarf she had taken from her pocket into a sash. Then she slipped the sash around the Princess's eyes and hurriedly started to tie a knot at the back.

Suddenly the Princess's head jerked up and her hands tugged away the cloth. So determined was her movement, that she ripped the scarf from Idoia's hands and hurled it across the room.

"I don't need that!"

The trembling had stopped. The Princess looked up, not at the woman, but at the skylight and she glimpsed the darkening blue of the early evening.

Her eyes were wide and moist. A single tear started to form. She placed both her hands in her lap and then turned to Xabier.

"It's no good pleading for my life. I would get on my knees if I thought you would change your mind. But I can see there is murder in this woman's eyes."

She was calm now.

"Xabier, please translate into your Basque language, what I've just said."

The terrorist started and then heard the echoing cracks of fire on the stairs.

"There is no time," he said. "I'm sorry."

"Then tell her, may God forgive her, and you."

The noise outside was now deafening, as the Princess closed her eyes, her lips moving silently in prayer.

Idoia stood behind the chair and raised the pistol, until its barrel was an inch from the back of the Princess's golden hair.

A dozen bullets caught Guadaña in a line down his body. Each made the terrorist jerk frantically, as though electrocuted. Then he was still—lying face upward, mouth gaping, eyes open. The submachine gun lay inches from the fingers of his outstretched left hand. The stained bandages that covered half his naked chest and back were wet and sticky with new blood, as it oozed from the wounds that had almost perforated him.

There was complete silence. It seemed as loud as the crash of warfare that had preceeded it. Martínez, moving up, keeping close to the wall, broke the stillness.

The two agents looked swiftly around them. Martínez pointed towards the attic door at the top of the final staircase.

261

They could hear nothing. They edged, one stair at a time, towards their final objective.

A single shot rang out.

Chapter Twenty-Five

Diana heard the crack of the single shot. It reverberated around the attic, bouncing off the walls and the sloping roof like a squash ball.

"I don't feel any different," she thought. "Perhaps death's like that. I must open my eyes, but not right now. Better to get used to the *idea* of death first, then see what it looks like. Maybe when I do open them, I'll be floating in the air, looking down at my body. I'm not sure I'm ready for that yet."

She felt a pressure under her armpits, lifting her to her feet, but it was so real, so physical, that it did not seem celestial at all. And she could feel breathing on her face.

Now she did open her eyes, and found herself looking at Xabier.

"I've never killed anyone before," he said. "Now I've killed a woman."

Idoia had been knocked backwards against the wall, then her legs had crumpled and her back had slid slowly down the brickwork. It was almost as if she were just sitting on the floor, except that there was a neat red hole in her right temple. Her face was half-turned in the direction of the shot. There was no pain on her face. Death had frozen on it, instead, a look of complete surprise.

"I don't understand, Xabier," the Princess said, "but thank you, thank you."

The young terrorist did not really understand it himself. He had seen the gun, almost as if in slow motion, rise and then stop at the level of the Princess's neck. He could not look at it any longer, nor could he bear to watch the English woman. Instead, he had turned to Idoia. And what he saw on her face horrified him! It was not the look of a cold professional, or a revolutionary fighter. A muscle had twitched in Idoia's cheek, causing a ripple to run across the rough purplish skin. Her eyes seemed to burn. This was not an execution, it was the murder of one woman by another for personal reasons—for hate.

He had raised his right arm until the pistol pointed at Idoia's head, and fired.

Xabier guided her around from the sight of death and gestured toward the door. His pistol dangled in his right hand.

"Do what I say."

With his free hand on her shoulder, he pushed her firmly to the door.

"Open it," he said.

The two agents were about to hit the door when it swung open. They saw the Princess with the young terrorist behind her. They froze and then lowered their weapons. An image of Molly rising to her feet raced through the captain's mind, and was gone in a flash.

Martínez spoke into his radio microphone.

"No interference. Repeat—no interference."

He looked up at the terrorist who was standing in the doorway, almost touching the Princess's back. The gun was inches from her neck.

"You just heard what I said on the radio. There will be no interference. Put the gun down on the floor, and let the lady walk slowly toward us."

Decker made sure that Xabier could see that his submachine gun hung at his side. There could be no mistake, no misinterpretation of a sudden move. The agents stood completely still.

"Do as he says. No harm will come to you."

Xabier touched the Princess's neck with his firearm.

"Drop your guns."

Xabier's tone was harsh and commanding, but Decker detected a hint of desperation. It was the voice of a man who had seen his world collapse and was trying to find a path—a route to construct a new one. It would not take much now to make him pull the trigger.

The two agents let go of their firearms.

"Now walk down the stairs backwards. Keep one hand on the rail, the other in your trouser pocket."

"We will do exactly what you say," Decker realized that all three were speaking English—as if to keep the Princess informed. "Let's take this very coolly. We don't want trouble any more than you do."

"Shut up!"

It was the shout of a man who had nothing to lose.

Xabier pushed the Princess forward as the agents started their slow, careful retreat backwards down the stairs. They were a good three meters in front of him.

"Stop at each level and wait for me to tell you to start again. One wrong move, and I will kill her."

"I want to use the radio again," Decker said. "You will fully understand why."

"You can do. But no tricks."

"Julio, inform the assault team of the situation. Tell them there can be no action taken."

The voice of Martínez from inside the house came through clear and precise.

The King took the Prince by both arms and whispered, "She's alive."

Involuntarily, the Prince moved towards the window.

"Keep back, sir—well back!"

The order from Colonel Valdés was as tough as if he were talking to one of his own men.

"Don't let's interfere," the King said. "Just pray."

The Prince looked at him and nodded.

Hazy ideas were forming in Xabier's mind—of hugging Marta again, of freedom at last, of a return from a trip to hell.

Martínez, his eyes never leaving the terrorist's face as he edged down the stairs, suddenly lurched backwards. He pulled his hand out of his pocket, swung his body and grabbed hold of the banister. Xabier jerked his gun nervously, almost squeezing the trigger. Then he saw what had caused the Inspector to lose his balance—the body of Guadaña, lying on its back, in a pool of blood. He thought he had heard the roar of defiance—of *'Gora ETA!'* It seemed an eternity ago. It had been the final war cry of a brave and dying man.

Xabier edged the Princess to the top of the second flight of stairs. As he did so, he noticed the bloodstained footprints. Guadaña's blood, spilt in the fight for Basque freedom—now on the boot of a Madrid secret policeman. His stomach churned. Then came revulsion at his own final treachery to the Cause—to his comrades.

He felt the Princess totter, as if her knees were giving way. They had gone round the second landing and were on the final flight of steps. He would use the Princess as a shield to escape so that he could fight another day—redeem himself. And if they didn't let him, he would shoot her and complete the mission.

They had reached the ground floor. The living-room door was open—it seemed just as they left it. The television screen still flickered, but the sound seemed much louder now that everything else was silent. He couldn't think, couldn't get his plans straight, with that noise.

"Turn if off!" he ordered Martínez.

The Inspector walked slowly and carefully into the living room and switched off the set. He could take Xabier, he thought. Spin round and in the same movement take out the snub-nosed pistol from his ankle-holster. The terrorist was taller than the Princess. If only she would make a move to give him more room.

But it was too big a risk. The Etarra was unstable, but the Princess's life was not immediately threatened. He changed a glance at Decker and knew that the captain was thinking the same.

Three steps down, to the Princess's right, was the bolted front door.

"Are you taking her into the street?" Decker asked.

"Yes."

"Then what are you going to do with her?"

"I shall take her down the road. If I am followed, I will shoot her. If I am allowed to leave, I will keep her until I am clear of the area and then release her. Give the orders now, if you want her to live."

Decker nodded, and Martínez slowly moved his right hand to switch on the transmitter that hung from his neck.

For the first time since the long walk started down from the attic, the Princess spoke. Her voice broke twice from nerves before she stumbled out her thoughts.

"D...d...do as Xabier says."

The agents were surprised at the use of the terrorist's name.

"He doesn't want to kill me. Can't you see that? He shot the woman to stop her shooting me. *Please* let him get away safely."

Xabier realized that she was not just saying it to save herself. The hostage was pleading for mercy, not *from* him, but *for* him.

267

And if he got away, where was he going to run to? To the Basque country where he would have to face the people he had sold out? Oh yes, Guadaña and Idoia were dead—they could not talk about his treachery. But could he face Marta again and hear her say, 'I love you so much, Xabi?'

Here he was, cowering at the back of the Princess, holding a gun to her head, the woman he had told so much about the peace and beauty of the Basque country and of his love for a Basque girl. And he was preparing to risk her life out on the street, where she might be hit by any stray bullet.

Xabier turned the Princess round and directed her down the steps. The two agents made no move.

The Etarra reached forward and pulled back the bolt. He placed the Princess between himself and the two other men. He put his free hand around the back of her head and gently pulled her around to face him.

"Goodbye, my Princess."

He opened the front door and walked into the street. Then he started to run—in the direction of the phone box where he had said goodbye to Marta only that morning.

He made no attempt to fire his gun. Instead, he shouted, with the same defiance as his dead leader, *"Gora Euskadi!"* it seemed to echo down the deserted street.

Below him, Valdés saw the running man. It had been made plain to him that none of the terrorists was be taken alive. There could no trial which would serve as spotlight for ETA's beliefs. After they had taken so much care to conceal the Princess's kidnapping, no separatist lawyers were going to have the pleasure of grilling her in the witness box. The secret would die with the last terrorist.

There was deep personal satisfaction as he looked at one of the cowards who had murdered four officers in cold blood, and picked up the radio mike.

"Take him out, Lopez!" he ordered the best marksman.

The bullet shattered the top of Xabier's spine, hurling him forward, onto his face.

From the open green door, a woman screamed, "No, Xabier, no!"

The voice behind him and the image in his mind fused. He saw a pretty girl, her black hair streaming out in the breeze, running down a deserted beach into his arms.

Decker reached for a jacket from the hall rack.

"We have to put this over your head," he said gently.

"That's Xabier's," the Princess replied, but in so a low a whisper that neither agent heard it.

Her head covered, the two men, each gripping an arm and flanking her in a protective shield, led her out into the Calle Nuncio. As she was taken across the street, Diana kept her eyes firmly on the body of the fallen man. There were no tears but she did not stop looking at Xabier until she heard her husband running towards her.

SATURDAY

Chapter Twenty-Six

The air above the tarmac shimmered under the relentless afternoon sun, but in the departure lounge of Torrejon Airbase, the conditioning unit was keeping the temperature down to a comfortable level. Decker and Martínez, not yet quite standing to attention, watched the King's custom-built VW bus pull up in front of the building, just ahead of the back-up cars.

There had been plenty of evidence of security on the route to the base, too; police cars were parked at every intersection and green-uniformed Guardia Civil Officers were posted on bridges that crossed the main highway. If only there had been that degree of security the previous Sunday afternoon.

There were too many 'if onlys' in life, Decker thought. If only he'd realized earlier what his father was really like, if only he'd been able to find out in time where they'd taken Molly. . .

But not all of fate's little ironies were malevolent. If Xabier hadn't bought that tape, if it hadn't been possible to twist the terrorist message into a hidden meaning, then the Princess would have been dead.

There was no pattern or logic to life. You just have to accept what had happened and get back to the business of living.

The King stood by the side of the vehicle and helped the Princess to step down. Then the door of the terminal was opened and the royal party entered. The last time Decker had seen her, she had been huddled and sobbing, on the verge of mental and physical collapse. Now, with her hair newly coiffured and wearing a smart green two-piece that finished just below the knee, she was looking just like the radiant Princess whose photograph had smiled at him from the covers of so many magazines.

She had been close to death, but now she was ready to face life once more. There would still be room for pleasure, for fun, for laughter, but it would never be quite the same again.

She felt the weight of her responsibilities. Life was difficult. Xabier had shown her that, in his futile attempt to balance the duties he felt to his homeland against those he had as a human being.

No, her situation wasn't easy, but she could handle it now.

Her kind, strong husband had got her through the night, patiently stroking her hair, holding her in his arms, helping to erase the image of Xabier, the man who had stopped her execution, lying in the street.

And he would help soften the stark images that would return repeatedly until faded by memory... of brave police officers dead in bathrooms, of a woman with hate in her eyes, of the delirious rantings of a wounded man. Of a man, then very much alive, who told her of a country he adored and of a woman named Marta he loved.

She would develop her own role more, so that when she did die—and who knew when that might be—people would be able to say that she had left a contribution behind that had made the world a better place. There would be a new start when she got back to London—but now was the time for farewells.

She walked over to the two officers.

"Captain Decker, Inspector Martínez, I owe you so much that I can never express my thanks. I will never forget you."

There was warmth in her grip as she shook hands with them both.

"I want to thank you, gentlemen, from the bottom of my heart," the Prince said.

He was keeping in the background. This was his wife's farewell to very special people.

The Princess turned, and walked confidently toward the Spanish girl standing shyly by the glass door that led onto the tarmac and the waiting aircraft. The blue contact lenses were gone, she was a brown-eyed, señorita once more.

The two young women stood a foot apart, looking at each other, curious, eyes taking in the similarities.

"She isn't my double at all," the Princess thought. "If anything, she's prettier than me. How remarkable she must be to have carried the whole thing off."

Isabel bent her knees and curtsied.

"I want to. . ." the Princess began.

A look of panic crossed the Spanish girl's face. Of course, she didn't understand!

The Princess stretched forward her right hand. The girl from Madrid took it with her own. There were tears in their eyes. Then the Princess smiled, the smile became a laugh and they were in each other's arms, like two school chums meeting after a long absence.

The royal party disappeared through the exit. A plane flew noisily overhead and Decker and Martínez both winced. They had had very little sleep. After the flamenco restaurant, they had gone on to a disco which had not closed until seven in the morning.

"I need a drink, James," Martínez said. "What you English call 'a hair of the dog.'"

Apart from the three NCOs who were just giving their order, the base bar was empty.

"You dance very well—for a foreigner," Martínez said. "At

275

least that young lady from Andalucia seemed to think so."

They laughed. It hurt!

"What do you want to drink?" the Inspector asked. "A Cuba Libre?"

"Not after last night!" Decker grinned. He had enjoyed dancing with the Spanish girl and would like to see her again. Perhaps he had finally forgiven himself. "Just give me a good Scottish whisky—nice and long and over ice."

The news bulletin was on the television. The two men watched it as they sipped their drinks, remembering that the last time they had seen one was in the Calle Nuncio. The newsreader was handed a piece of paper.

"It had just been announced in London that the Queen will pay an official visit to Spain next autumn. It will be the first official visit of a British monarch to Spain. . ."

Decker, the glass of whisky raised to his mouth, looked at Martínez. Neither said a word.

WITHDRAWN

M   Brown, Alan.
B877p Princess
        923081 17.95

TEMPLE PUBLIC LIBRARY
101 North Main Street
Temple, Texas 76501